UNCORRECTED PROOF

~~Publication/Embargo: 29 August 2016~~

Text Publishing Melbourne Australia

D1339287

The Rules of Backyard C~~ricket~~

- A gripping literary crime novel about Australian masculinity, talent, fame and family

- Wide review coverage in newspapers, magazines and sports and literary media, in print and online

- Major print interviews expected

- Select radio interviews in Australia and New Zealand

- Comprehensive trade marketing campaign, including the cover of *Books+Publishing* magazine

- Huge consumer marketing campaign around Father's Day, including phone boxes in capital cities and full-page ads in *Good Weekend* and the *Monthly*

- Major online advertising and social media campaign, including extensive distribution of electronic chapter samplers

- Bookclub notes available on publication from textpublishing.com.au/book-clubs

C-format paperback $29.99 (NZ$37), ISBN 9781925355215, 234 x 153 mm, 304 pages
ebook $29.99, ISBN 9781922253798

Please note that these proofs are uncorrected and that substantial changes may be made to the text. Before quoting any material in a review, please check it against a finished copy of the book.

For all publicity inquiries, please contact: **Léa Antigny**
Text Publishing, Swann House, 22 William Street, Melbourne VIC 3000 Australia
tel: (+61 3) 8610 4512 **fax:** (+61 3) 9629 8621 **email:** lea.antigny@textpublishing.com.au

To place an order, please contact United Book Distributors
orders@unitedbookdistributors.com.au **AU:** 1 800 338 836 **NZ:** +64 9 442 7410

Jock Serong was formerly a lawyer and is now a feature writer and the editor of *Great Ocean Quarterly*. He is the author of *Quota*, winner of the Ned Kelly Award for First Fiction, 2015.

FICTION FROM TEXT PUBLISHING

The Rules of Backyard Cricket

Jock Serong

UNCORRECTED PROOF

Publication/Embargo: 29 August 2016

Text Publishing Melbourne Australia

textpublishing.com.au

The Text Publishing Company
Swann House
22 William Street
Melbourne Victoria 3000
Australia

First published in 2016 by The Text Publishing Company

Typeset in Minister by J & M Typesetting
Page design by Jess Horrocks
Cover design by WH Chong

Printed in Australia by Griffin Press, an Accredited ISO AS/NZS 14001:2004 Environmental Management System printer.

Print ISBN: 9781925355215
Ebook ISBN: 9781922253798

THE RULES OF BACKYARD CRICKET

The Boot

The broken white lines recede into the blackness behind us as we hurtle forward.

Do you remember this?

I knew it in childhood; this feeling of the irretrievable past slipping away behind the car. These things, gone and unrecoverable.

Cars on the other side of the divided highway are fading embers that spear into the dark. We *thurrump* over the cats' eyes, changing lanes. I look out every time I feel this cue, the markers and the slight shifting of weight, wanting to communicate with those sleepy, indifferent drivers. They have their own reveries. Night-time lives suspended between origin and destination, just like mine. I want to talk to them; I know they wouldn't want to talk to me.

Maybe I had an inkling of this as a tired child in the back seat. Maybe I recognised that something was ebbing away into the night. Back then there were antidotes to the melancholy: the promise of a warm bed; a wide, expanding future. The sadness now is uncontained. It sweeps over me in waves. It wants to drown me.

I've always slept with the lights on, fending off an indefinable sorrow in the night. Even when I lit it up, with stimulants and willing companions, it watched me scornfully, knowing it had me at bay. *That melancholy?* it said. *It's just a taste of the vast, immeasurable silence that awaits.* A speck on a pebble in a galaxy that's dust in a supercluster.

I can't see much. Just the narrow tunnel of vision directly behind the car. I've managed to get my hands up in front of my face and bring my fingers together, unruly mob that they are. I'm wedged towards the rear corner, driver's side, so close I can smell the hot plastics of the tail-light. I've felt my way to the back of the bulb, squeezed and twisted until it came free. And as it fell it revealed the light, the view, the road.

I've had my eye up against that tiny opening for—well, for how long? I don't know. They took my watch, along with so much else.

The hands are reluctant dance partners but they can't move away from each other. Like it or not, they will have to waltz. The cable ties are drawn taut around both wrists, cutting into the flesh. Well out of reach of any finger. The feet, from whom I've heard nothing lately, must be in a similar predicament; more cable ties around the ankles, drawn so tight that the malleoluses are pressing into each other. A bizarre and exotic pain that surely wasn't contemplated by my tormentors, a happy accident of sadism: two small hammers, banging it out. You're wondering how I knew that word, the Greek one about the hammers? Physios. I've spent a lifetime listening to physios.

My breath is hissing in and out of my nose, my mouth tightly taped.

I've been thinking for some time about bringing Squibbly into play. I'm not, in general, given to nicknaming my own body parts but I've made an exception for the thumb of my left hand: the kernel of my genius and also my Achilles heel. Mangled, knobbly and dead. Squibbly won't mind being pressed into service because it's all the same to him. And although it seems futile, equally, it seems unsporting not to try.

So now I'm jamming him into the hole at the back of the tail-light and pulling as hard as I can. It takes a moment or two, and I have to suspend my whole weight from the bound hands to make it happen, but Squibbly finally gets enough purchase to break open the light fitting. There's a loud *snap*, and I'm looking out through a bigger hole at the wide open theatre of night.

The car slows. They've eased back to listen.

I wait in perfect silence, and presently the pace picks up.

The other fingers register stickiness, and I know that I've slashed up Squibbly in the process, but neither of us minds. He is, as always, a dumb and obedient martyr to the cause.

There was a kid once, I read somewhere, abducted and stuffed in a car boot. Just like me, though probably innocent of anything. She had the good sense to bite off a crescent of fingernail then unscrew the tail-light globe and drop it in, so that if ever the authorities searched the car later on—whether in pursuit of her murderers or upon her rescue—the DNA would tie the crime to the vehicle. Such a detached response to impending death. I'm not sure why I'm drawn more to the genius of the idea than the central question of whether the child was rescued.

So I'm more or less resigned to this.

It's a moral counterweight to the things I've done. It seems a shame and more than a little vulgar. But there would have been undignified aspects to cancer or heart disease too. No one's giving me sponge baths or feeding me puree through a tube.

They'll torch the car, I suppose. These people have a strong sense of genre. It'd be inappropriate not to torch the car.

The trip from Geelong to the western suburbs of Melbourne is about fifty minutes, and half of that must have elapsed by now. I've assumed we're headed east, towards Melbourne, though they didn't say. Anyway, the road would be quieter, driving west. I've been lying on my left side, which is the way they threw me in. My left arm, trapped under me, is numb. My left leg is too, although there's an unnatural buzzing coming from my right knee, like the humming of a powerful stereo before the music starts.

It's nothing like the movies, being shot.

There's no great explosion of agony. I didn't hop about grimacing and going *Ugh! Ergh!* or swipe fretfully at the air or hiss curses through clenched teeth. There's something more pressing about taking a round through the kneecap. A feeling of *wrongness*.

My right knee has a hole in it. Not cavernous, but large enough to admit, say, a finger. One of them, not the one who fired the gun, actually stuck his finger in there at one point. Under that hole there's a slurry of shattered bone floating around like the shaved ice in a half-drunk caipirinha. There's another, bigger hole out the back, strings of tendon and ligament hanging from it. I know because I saw them. It's not bleeding much. I can only assume the shot missed the major plumbing.

It buzzes for some strange reason, reverberating up through my thigh and into my hip. If they pull me out of here before the *coup de grâce*—and it's quite likely they won't bother—there's going to be a white-hot moment when that leg hangs straight again and all the smashed bits slice and grind against one another. In respect of that development, I'm electing not to get ahead of myself.

Apart from that, it doesn't matter much whether they get me out of the car. I'm lying on a shovel. Down near my feet I know there are two large paper sacks of quicklime, and it's more than a little confronting to be snuggled up against the means both of interring your corpse and dissolving it.

The shovel can be read either way. Or is it a spade? I've never been clear on the difference. Again, a fan of the genre would have them lighting black-market cigarettes and training handguns on me while I dig my own grave. But efficiency would suggest a short volley of fire, straight into the boot, and then firing up the car. I can't dig in this state. It'd be comical. Who wants to sit around all night getting lung cancer and waiting for a cripple to entomb himself?

I've contemplated this once or twice. My death, I mean. And I always thought when the hour came there'd be clarity. Perception, through the limestone-filtered water of total mental acuity, of the pebbles on the bottom, the tiny invertebrates scuttling in between.

A poignant end. A sorbet after the greasy business of living.

But no. To my sad surprise, whether you're crawling home from Christmas with the aunts, or waiting to be shot dead and incinerated by gangsters, the Geelong Road turns out to be just as boring.

The Backyard

The first and only choice: do I accept this as my fate or do I keep fighting it?

The air, filtered through the tape over my mouth, tastes faintly of exhaust. Slow suffocation by carbon monoxide might be as good as I can hope for. Either way, I have a feeling I'll be in here for a while.

So while we're waiting I'll take you through it. The sequence of events, some predestined and some entirely of my own creation, that put me in the boot.

You're seated on a plastic-strip beach chair in a suburban Melbourne backyard. Fernley Road, Altona. It's 1976. February, late on a Tuesday afternoon.

Two small boys, shoulder-lit by the late sun of daylight saving, are playing cricket.

The smaller one, batting, is me.

Darren. Daz. Dags. Scrawny, short, cheeky grin and a thick clump of mustard-brown hair. I'm in school uniform, the small grey squares of a grade two. I'm red-cheeked with defiance but grinning. Standing my ground because I'm being accused of cheating. My reflex in such situations, then and now, is to deny everything then laugh it off. Dimples deep, teeth out. Lean on the bat. Point at the bowler's crease, tell him to get back to work. Later, I'd see Viv do that and I'd swear he stole that move from me.

My accuser, casting thunderstorms my way with ball in hand, is my older brother Wally.

Grade four, older by nineteen months. About four inches taller at this stage, and undoubtedly stronger. If it comes to blows I will lose. Wally is my idol, and yet my inverse in all respects other than our shared obsession with cricket. He is a purist and a respecter of rules, a methodical, ambitious bore with an insistent need to take every-thing—and I mean *everything*—literally. You'll get the hang of him as we proceed, so I won't start piling up adjectives just now.

Although…wait. *Insufferable*—in case I forget later.

But I still worship the guy. I know it doesn't make sense.

I no longer remember where this ritual came from: the bat, the tennis ball, the twelve metres of shorn grass. There's a line somewhere in any childhood. Before the line, all knowledge and habit is contrib-uted by adults. How to eat with a fork, wash your face, wipe your bum. On the other side of the line, the magpie child starts to gather and collect from everywhere. How to swear. How to kiss a girl. Where you go when you die.

Backyard cricket must have been absorbed on the parental side of that line. We've been doing it ever since I can remember, and I can remember back to about three. But who taught us the rules? Who showed us how to mow the strip, to play a cover drive, to bowl a yorker? Who explained the dozens of tactical options, the physical vocabulary? It must have been Dad, but I don't have the memory. It saddens me that I don't.

Ground Zero is the stumps, represented by the severed foot of an apricot tree. In life it had sprawled out to about twenty feet of blossoms, leaves and fruit, open enough at its centre that we'd made a platform in there. Too basic and rickety to call it a treehouse, but serviceable enough for various kinds of warfare and for hiding when any shit had gone down.

The tree bore so much fruit that a large proportion of it—even beyond the harvest taken by us and the birds—just disintegrated on the lawn. For years after the tree was gone it would deliver painful reminders of its existence in the hard stones left by the rotted-down fruit under our bare feet. Its fate was a common one for a stonefruit tree: it started to rot and split down the middle, oozing shiny globes of sap. The plywood platform that had sheltered pirates and cowboys and bank robbers began to lean on a crazy angle, and with every gale we'd find new branches fallen on the grass.

But the fruit kept coming in staggering quantities, so it seems no one had the heart to deal with the problem—and of course, that no one can only have been Mum. It wasn't as though Wally and I were ever going to take to the thing with pruning saws. I'm pretty confident we never affected any kind of chivalry for Mum. Anyway, we liked the old tree, especially when it thrashed drunkenly in the wind and we could hear its tortured wooden squeals from our beds.

But eventually the platform became too dangerous, and Mum appeared one day with the chainsaw. We'd been kicking the football, and suddenly she was there at the side gate with this forestry-grade monster she'd borrowed from a neighbour. A huge, ravenous-looking thing: teeth on a chain bolted to a motor.

I can still see her, paused at the gate with one hip slightly a-kilter, projecting an inner awareness of how cool she suddenly appeared. She had her massive imitation Dior sunglasses on, probably in lieu of protective goggles, and her hair pushed back behind a paisley bandana.

Wally dropped the footy. There could be only one purpose for her appearance and, although it was going to cost us our lair, it was going to be good.

It took her a couple of goes to get the saw started. Then it coughed and caught, there was a squirt of blue smoke and she held it up with a satisfied look round her mouth. She gave it a rev, then another as she eased it into the bark. Sawdust swirled around her and settled in her hair. She worked the blade horizontally into the trunk, weaving the saw in and out, squinting behind the Diors; I can still see the veins running down her biceps. There were two loud *cracks* as the timber gave way, and the entire weight of the tree settled onto the bar of the chainsaw, choking the chain and killing the motor. She stood back for a moment, indecisive, with a hand on her hip.

Then she did the best thing I ever saw her do.

She jumped up from where she stood, hooked her hands on a low-hanging limb and hung there like a gibbon, yanking at it. She swung through the air a couple of times, kicking freely with her bare feet—the girl we'd never known her to be—and the tree reacted with a few more fibrous pops. Then down it came, apricots thudding and rolling all over the place, Mum lost completely under the canopy of leaves. We could hear her under there, shrieking with laughter, cracking twigs in her efforts to climb out.

The foot of the tree was cut off square except for a jagged horn of timber on one edge, where it had stretched and snapped. The chainsaw had fallen out by this stage and Mum took it up again, working the cord and the choke until it spluttered into life once more. With a sweep of the snarling arm the splinter was gone. We raked and scooped and brushed for an hour or more, the brittle afternoon sun of autumn picking up the gold among the leaf litter.

By the time we cleared the whole mess away, a squared-off stump stood in the middle of the lawn, roughly equidistant from the three paling fences. Wally disappeared into the garden shed and emerged with a tape measure. She'd cut exactly at bail height, twenty-eight inches by nine. We watched her saunter off, twigs in her hair, the chainsaw resting on that same cocked hip. Accident or design? As with most things Mum did, the line was blurred and she wasn't saying. But forever after the stump was our stumps.

And in the current memory, the stump is an arm's length behind me as I stare down my brother. The bat in my hands is an SP, as used in Tests by England captain Tony Greig. He's tall, implacable, patient. All the things I'm not. The dog at our feet is Sam, a grossly obese staffy. The lawn's kept down by an ancient handmower that's always been there. Razor sharp blades made to look innocuous by rust. It didn't come from anywhere and it'll never go anywhere.

Those deep shades of autumn are last year now, when we were smaller. Here in high summer, where my memories crowd more, sunlight is a scatter of bleaches and reflections. At backward point there's a banksia. At extra cover, a holly bush where Sam likes to shit. At mid-off, a bare patch where nothing, not even grass, grows. It's lightning fast if you send a drive through there. Off drive I mean. I assume you're keeping up. I'm a lefty.

Mid-on's the vegie patch, never grows anything but tomatoes this time of year, stinging nettles along the back. Dirty bare feet in there come out red-welted. Midwicket is the shortest boundary, formed by the Apostouloses' fence. Directly behind those palings, separated by a spindly pittosporum, is their kitchen. If you really middle a pull shot— wrap the handle around your ribs and smack that ball sweet off the end of the blade—it makes the finest sound hitting the timbers out there. I can only imagine how it sounds at the Apostas' kitchen sink.

Fine leg is into the corner, towards the crappy asbestos outhouse that contains the second dunny and the laundry. Something about the plumbing in there; there's a smell even when no one's been.

Keeper and slips are automatic: the big sheet of trellis that Mum put up to grow climbing roses. Snick it onto the trellis on the full and you're gone. Hit the dog and it makes a hollow thud.

Sam's a random element in all this, wandering around sniffing the air. Occasionally he lies on his back and does that thing fat dogs do when they wriggle around just scratching the bejesus out of their backs. You can't shoo him away. You have to get on with it no matter where Sam is located, and you can't hit him. Hit him and you're gone. If Sam decides he wants to stop and eat a bee off a clover flower right in the middle of the pitch, you play around him. In future years, under greater pressures, I sometimes wonder if Wally and I learned to stare through distraction because we had to play around a fat dog.

So you've got Sam acting as a sort of close-in fieldsman at large. But then you also have inanimate fieldsmen you can place yourself when you're bowling: the metal rubbish bin, the little tripod barbecue, the two swans made out of painted tyres. When I'm on the attack I like to have all of them crowded round the bat so close that it's actually hard to bowl through them.

In this memory there's insect repellent in the air. Mum's been out with the blue can. She never says anything when she's focused like this: just presses her mouth into a firm line and does the necessary. Economy of movement. We've both frozen in position and scrunched our eyes shut. The can hisses; her bangles tinkle as she sprays the stinging fumes, greasy on the skin.

The ball in Wally's hand is a Slazenger tennis ball we pinched from the proddie church tennis club, because in those days tennis balls could only be purchased new as a set of four in a vacuum-sealed can, unattainably expensive.

We figured out we could sit in the primary school playground just over the far end of the tennis court and wait for the pennant ladies to sky one. The ladies knew we were waiting there and we knew they

11

knew, but they were never going to catch us, not with two Malvern Stars leaning against the cyclone wire and at least a twenty-second head start.

While waiting for this particular ball, I'd got us a deck of Extra Milds: the shiny gold pack, the cellophane with the little tear strip. 'And a box of matches and a packet of Juicy Fruit, thanks. For Mum.' Eyeballing the guy as the guy eyeballed me and we both reflected for a moment on the nature of truth. So the brother and I sat there in the shade, enveloped in a bitter blue cloud, arguing over who was doing the drawback. We were both coughing—me because I was doing the drawback, and him because it was some kind of weird habit of his.

The yellow stain in the middle of the filter is called a pig root, I explained to him. It's not cool. People will think you don't know what you're doing. You're eight, he came back. You actually *don't* know what you're doing. Throughout his adult life, Wally will say 'actually' when he's getting all shrill and emphatic. Besides, he went on, pig rooting is what dogs do. Pretty sure it's what pigs do, I said, and he punched me in the arm with one knuckle out for extra bruise. I squawked and spluttered smoke.

The ladies watched disapprovingly, but by and by their lack of interest in other women's kids took over and they resumed their gentle lobbed exchanges.

Our vigil continued: every ball they produced from under their knicker elastic was a pending addition to the stocks at Fernley Road. Like I said, they knew it; we knew it.

Thwock. Thwock. Birds chippering somewhere up high. A lawn-mower droning away. Planes in an empty sky. And if you listened closely, the crackle of the smouldering tobacco as we pulled it to a red hot glow. *Thwock, thwock-thwock…Poong!*…that's a mis-hit, and over it comes. Gaffers in mouths, squinting, we reel it in and hit the road. At ten, Wally can bounce a tennis ball along the road while he rides, although he's carefully ditched the cigarette for fear of being reported by neighbours.

Morally, to him, the theft of the balls was excused by sporting necessity: a matter of subsistence. He could rationalise it that way, and liberating the odd Slazenger from the ladies was a whole lot different than, for example, badging their cars. Which was something I did without regret.

And right there you have an essential distinction between the Keefe brothers. I would do these things for the sheer joy of it. Busting free, sending my blood roaring in the knowledge I'd flouted the rules and disappointed expectations. The problem for me is that the more times you do it and the more you get caught, the lower the expectations become. Correspondingly, the lesser the thrill.

I'm surprised at you, the teachers would say. But they weren't.

The previous term I'd been caught watching the girls doing handstands in the area of the yard reserved exclusively for the girls to do handstands (which I think owed more to the Brothers' voyeurism than to any desire to afford the girls privacy while they inverted themselves). For this I was caned, which in retrospect must've been a double payoff for the Brothers.

I'd cheated on tests (detention), burned centipedes with a magnifying glass (caning), thrown a bolt-bomb on the road near the bus stop (caning) and fed a paper clip into a powerpoint (electrocution *and* caning). Most recently, I'd clean-bowled a grade-four during recess and, when he refused to vacate the crease, I'd spontaneously waved my dick at him. The timing was poor: Brother Callum was standing directly behind me as I did it, confirming that if you chant the Litany of the Saints often enough, the Holy Ghost will grant you invisibility.

Brother Callum (Calumn?) was an Irishman of the ancient kind with a temper that seemed to channel centuries of rage. His chief responsibility was teaching us obscure prayers in a viscous Donegal brogue that left us guessing dangerously when we repeated the lines back to him. The metre ruler awaited any transgression. Only the Mother Church could conceive of a torment so exquisitely weird as ordering eight-year-olds to recite forgotten chants back to an armed sadist who couldn't pronounce them in the first place.

So you can picture my horror when I saw the batsman's eyes looking back at me—past me and my pecker—over my shoulder to Brother Callum. I was still turning and simultaneously restuffing my shorts when he pounced, crushing me in a headlock that shut off the sun and silenced all sound. The next bit I have trouble describing, such was the intensity of the pain, but those watching told me later that Callum drove two or three punches into the top of my skull, his big pewter rosary ring leaving lumps on my head that I could still find with my fingertips at fifteen.

He was grunting something, yelling something as he did this, but between the oxygen deprivation and the tortured dialect, I was never going to hear what it was. Eventually he dropped me and I slumped to the asphalt, dazed and bleeding.

The school must have rung Mum. She was down there within the hour, barely long enough for the nurse to clean up the wounds. I was made to wait for her on the steps of the school, and as her car pulled up I felt a rush of shame and anger and also tears and I can still see her coming towards me, her face a shifting landscape of fury and love and insight. She'd read the whole thing by the time she reached me, wrapped me in a hug that smelled of her, one that I never wanted to leave.

She ran gentle fingers though my hair, felt the cuts and took me by the hand. Her face was white, her lips clenched. Fury had won but it wasn't directed at me. She flung open the glass doors and rained hell on everyone in sight.

•

Brother Callum. Jesus, he must be long gone. He clearly *has* haunted me till the day I die, though.

Anyway, we're back home, sun's still shining.

I wanted to tell you about showing the ball: a particular ritual that must be observed by the bowler before any recommencement of play.

First let me say that upon our return from the proddie tennis courts I would of course be bowling because I am the younger, and the role of the younger is to feed deliveries to the imperious elder.

But to the ritual.

First you have to declare who you are. You don't just lob the ball down using your own action and personality, you have to *be* someone. Lillee, Holding, Bob Willis...Doesn't matter who it is, but you have to nominate and then you have to impersonate their run-up and action, follow-through, the lot. The great benefit of this arrangement is that you can select a bowler who fits with the conditions and your mood: the gentle guile of Derek Underwood if it's hot and you can't be stuffed; the silent menace of Andy Roberts if you're carrying a grievance. Failure to adopt a persona when bowling attracts no particular penalty, but it's poor form.

The most formal bit is showing the ball.

We picked up somewhere, maybe on late-night coverage of Wimbledon, the moment when a tennis player taking new balls must hold them aloft briefly for their opponent to see. In tennis, it's common sense: the new ball will look different and bounce differently, and therefore it would be unsporting to make the change unannounced. Equally in the backyard, where there's an even greater variance between one ball and the next, to launch a fresh pill without some declaration would violate an unspoken code of decency. You've probably already discerned that decency, like the February grass, was thin on the ground in the Keefe backyard. But this was bipartisan. Ball etiquette was fundamental.

Balls turn grey when left for months in the sun. Tennis balls can be split by impacts, or by the dog's exploratory jaws—and a split ball will bounce either higher or lower depending how it lands. Balls can be taped—all over to make them heavier and more painful on impact, or half-taped to simulate the swing of a real leather cricket ball. In times of high conflict the ball might not be a ball at all—it could be a piece of fruit or a small rock. So we placed a simple constraint on our own deviousness: show the ball to the batsman prior to play, or any wicket taken thereafter would be declared null and void.

Of course, this created the opportunity for even greater conflict. A cunning batsman, having noted the bowler's failure to show the ball, would swing with cavalier disregard, aiming at windows, trying to bullseye the metal bin, the swans or even the dog, in confident assumption of immunity. Once dismissed, the batsman would lean smugly on the bat and shake his head. Voices would be raised, equipment thrown. Unless Mum intervened, it would end in a red-faced tangle with fingers in eyes and gappy milk teeth sunk into soft flesh: an itchy, grunting wrestle that never produced a clear winner.

But there was one strategy that got around the apparent full disclosure of showing the ball.

We were among the first in the neighbourhood to own a microwave oven. It was a Philips CuisinArt. To this day I don't know what inspired the old girl to make such an esoteric purchase. We weren't remotely affluent, and this gadget was the province of rich people.

However, that was no concern of ours. Overnight, a technology had entered our lives that could bring slabs of congealed pie back to life so we could consume them at tongue-blistering speed. You could dry wet sneakers in it, melt a brother's GI Joe—or doctor a tennis ball.

It's relatively simple, I suppose. The ball goes on the turntable and the air inside expands: *ergo*, if you overdo it, the ball explodes. If you get it just right, however, you wind up with a ball that will bounce to incredible heights, making it virtually unplayable off a good length. But like the moral payoff in a Greek tragedy, once the magical powers are spent, your ball is flat, listless and liable to be smacked all over the place. Ten minutes of preternatural spring and the ability to hit your opponent's body repeatedly without effort. After which, if you haven't managed to get him out, revenge will be a slow and painful business. Such is the counterweight to any exalted state of being, as I would find out much later on.

And it would be me, time after time, who would misjudge the axis between glory and humiliation, revelling in my temporary ascendancy rather than effecting the dismissal. And on more than one occasion, when I *had* turned my mind to the central issue, scattering his stumps or luring him into the false shot that would bring the inanimate fieldsmen into play, he'd casually lean back on his bat and laugh at me. In my impetuous rush to get from kitchen to pitch with a newly cooked ball, I'd failed to make the necessary disclosure before delivering.

•

The neighbours comment euphemistically to Mum that her boys are 'very spirited' or 'remarkably competitive'. It's impossible for us to see that we're forming an obsessive antagonism, an entanglement placental in its depth.

I know Wally deeper than biology. His frame, his posture, his voice and movements. That dry, chipping cough of his, the one he issues all the time, whether he's sick or well. The way his eyes dart and I know he's switched mentally from derision to anger; and equally, when and why he'll laugh uncontrollably; when his strength will give out in a fight, where he'll try to hit first.

I know his ribs—hell, I've aimed at them enough. I know how the sun burns him in late spring: a glow over his shoulders, blisters bursting and flaking on his nose.

I can recruit him from a conversation with adults, from his homework or from his perch on the toilet. I can claim him from in front of the TV or when he's half-asleep. One look, a nod towards the back door and he's out there, because he wants to beat me as much as I want to beat him.

From the day—lost now in the Kodachrome blur—when we take up backyard cricket, we are an independent republic of rage and obsession. Our rules, our records, our very own physics. Eye-to-eye and hand-to-hand combat. By the time we emerge into the world beyond the paling fences, it surprises us to learn that anyone considers this a team sport.

Mum

The bulb idea has come to nothing.

It burst easily enough when I squeezed it, but into fragments so tiny and delicate that none of them were any use. And the effort of popping the globe drove quite lot of the shards into poor old Squibbly.

I gave it a go, fumbled around for a while for the biggest pieces of the bulb that I could find. But it was like trying to scoop up thick guacamole with a thin chip: every time I sliced, the fragment broke into a smaller fragment.

Squibbly is bleeding rather a lot, and I'm tired. There's so much to explain, but my blood's like cold oil. I'm suspended in space here, between wakefulness and sleep, maybe even consciousness and death, and I fear the gag will suffocate me if I doze off.

A world apart from the world in here. The dark side of a frozen planet.

•

Mum is the centre of our solar system, the single deity in whom all powers are vested.

Looking back, she's not yet thirty, although to our eyes she's more than halfway to being an Old Person. Dad's just a void into which we tip our speculation. He might have done this, or that. His presence is lost in the haze of our pre-school years; tall, scruffy, and downcast. When I look for him in the dark I see the hollows round his eyes, his moustache, the pilling where his stubble has worn away the neck band of his jumper.

Mum came from a fabled place called the Eastern Suburbs, a faraway land on the other side of the city. We hear the names on the news sometimes, and I argue with Wally about which suburbs are *Eastern*. We can work out some of them from the footy: Hawthorn, Richmond, St Kilda, South Melbourne. The others count as western suburbs. It's much later that I realise Collingwood, on our side of a divided universe, is actually north of Melbourne, not west.

It was Mum's fate to fall in love with a footballer.

Dad was someone's friend's brother, or someone's brother's friend. In the oral history of our family Mum was Mum—defined by her own presence. Dad, however, was defined by his connection to Mum. A guy who knew someone who knew Mum. Apparently he was a savant in footy boots—all the intellectual spark of wet cardboard, but freak-ishly light-footed; wired with a spooky intuition for where the ball was and where it needed to go. But these skills are, by definition, not trans-ferable and it seems Dad struggled on any surface that wasn't grass.

A year in with Mum and she'd alienated her family, dropped out of school and gone to live with him in Footscray, busy gestating Brother Wally. They eloped to Glenelg. Civil ceremony. No family, a handful of friends.

Footy didn't work out for Dad—he did an ankle. The club paid for a reco but he'd lost his trademark ability to bank laterally out of trouble at speed. And the elopement had its consequences. Wally and I never knew our paternal grandparents because Dad was gone so early in our lives. We never knew our maternals either: they'd turned their backs on Mum.

It meant too that our childish fascination with our own genetics could only take us one layer deep. We had Mum's hair, thick and somewhere between blonde and brown. We had her light scatter of freckles. But where her bones were fine and sharp, ours were thuggishly stout. Did we have Dad's ankles? Was it a design fault that had caused his downfall anyway, or just a divot in the earth somewhere?

Their first home was a Commission rental in Footscray's backstreets. The house is still there, in the ironically named Gallant Street. Dad took a full-time job in a warehouse, shuffling through his day and into his evening. Home at night, grinding his molars at the squawking of baby Wal, he'd chug his way through the beers until he fell asleep in his armchair. I see Mum perched in the chair beside him, breastfeeding Wally and watching her young husband descend. Not violent; not raucous or randy. Just sinking slowly like a man half-asleep in a parachute.

This is what I feel, what I glean from interrogating Mum. I can't know enough of him to care about him as a person, but I care a great deal about the idea of a father. A dad. So I collect the little clues she leaves. I go through private drawers sometimes, searching for his identity. I build him painstakingly from these twigs and straws, but the shape he takes always feels hollow.

I imagine she wondered how long he'd last, whether he'd end it with some horrendous flourish. Gas himself in the car, perhaps—the most suburban of exits.

Wally and I pass the house sometimes on our bikes, both trying to look at it without the other seeing. The Gallant Street house: behind its nature strip, a modest brick veneer off a government plan. It would've had a big backyard, we figure, after riding around the corner to assess the depth of the blocks.

It's impossible for me to know whether my parents still talked in those days, whether Dad had retreated into glum silence. Whether they fought, even. Whether despite all this there were moments of bliss. At some stage he must have come up with the dopey idea that renting wasn't enough, and that in order to sail his little ketch of family out of the fog he'd have to buy a house. Would Mum have passively agreed? She was more forceful than that, but maybe passivity was her mode before she became a single parent.

I picture an agent with massive sideburns reassuring them of their own great potential. Showing them the houses they could afford; explaining their shortcomings. Driving past the ones out of their reach, dismissing those too in a voice just above a stage whisper, as being for management-level couples. Go-getters. And Dad, taking the bait, asking him to stop the car.

So Mum put her name next to his on a mortgage that was spectacularly beyond their means. *How else do you get anywhere?* I imagine him saying.

But what if it was Mum who said it? What if it was Mum who loaded them both up?

They moved into Fernley Road in March 1969, and the repayments immediately started to bite. How do I know that? Because in my regular fingering through their belongings, I found a file with all the bank's correspondence: the stern warnings, the official threats, the beginnings of recovery action as they missed one repayment after another. Dad emerged from his midlife cave for long enough to find himself a new job at the munitions plant in Footscray.

Heavily pregnant with me, Mum somehow started working in pubs: the Commercial in Yarraville, the Mona Castle in Seddon, the Prince Albert in Williamstown. She took buses between shifts while

Dad had the family Zephyr parked in the lot at the factory. None of it made sense. Yet they clung to the house.

I'm intrigued by this other side of Mum's life, the pub side. Wally isn't. He consciously avoids it, as though it diminishes her to think of her in subservience to strange men. Occasionally she works a day shift that coincides with me being off school sick, and she takes me along and perches me like an exotic bird on a stool. The illness is treated with an endless stream of chips and post-mix lemonade. The framed pictures, the illicit adult smells of cigarette smoke and old beer. The races on a radio somewhere. Old men with flat-football faces, straining to listen, betting slips clutched in spotty hands.

The thermometer governs all of my phony fevers. Mum jams it in my mouth then rushes away to berate Wally about homework and make his lunch. Alone in the bunk, I'm holding it under the reading lamp. The searing-hot globe has burned me more than once and, if I don't get it right, it will shoot the mercury up to indicate a life-threatening fever. I need it to say sick but not malarial. When Mum's footsteps return, I whip the warm glass tube back under my tongue and look sorrowful. We'll get through this together, Mum. I know I'm brave. Take me to work with you.

Seeing the world from what I presume to be its centre, I fail to notice that Mum's happy to go along with the charade. Maybe it's comforting for her to take a talisman of her home to whatever bar she's working. Remind the world of men that she's someone's mother.

She's an uncommon bartender, even from my small and simple perspective. I have no other bartenders to compare her to, I know. But she's not buxom and flirty, not mean and defeated. Something else: dry, caustic, wise. She runs a very tight bar. There's no muscle to back her up—she's often said since that the pubs she worked were running on autopilot, owned by absentee investors. Mostly, she seems to find pubs where the regulars are old and frail. But from time to time, never seen by me, the balance must break down and their wilder instincts take over.

The façade of control is strengthened by her ability to absorb sporting trivia. It's obvious to me now that this is a mark of an intelligent woman consigned to a menial job, but she absorbs the commentary drone of the front bar TV and somehow filters it from the jabber of the Lens, Larrys and Georges in front of her. From countless hours of telecast she builds a warehouse of knowledge. Our friends' mothers look at her distastefully when she explains the slope of the grass at Lord's or lays out the numbers that attest to Greg Chappell's mid-career slump. The mothers of the 1970s weren't supposed to know these things.

Mum's pub years, and my role in them, are reduced in memory to brick walls in the sun, tattered live music posters peeling away. Graffiti, cold tiles and reflections in glass, voices as monotone noise.

Somewhere deep in these years, I first catch a glimpse of the future for me and Wally. It was available on telly at home I'm sure, but I know for a fact I see it on the big black-and-white Rank Arena behind the bar at the Commercial.

The future is Jeff Thomson. It's him and Lillee bowling at the Poms that I see, so it must be the summer of '74–'75.

The long, long run in.

And then somehow, the tipping of the right side of his body way back, slinging the ball into an unerring trajectory that ends at the terrified batsman. When they show it in slow motion his limbs contort to impossible angles. His eyes roll back in their sockets like a great white bringing death by dismemberment. The ball only becomes visible to the batsman at the last possible instant: Thommo's spring-loaded body has obscured it almost until it's released from his hand.

His yorkers shoot straight home into the base of the stumps. Bouncers spit viciously from the turf. And in the wreckage of the moment—batsmen on the ground, stumps all over the place, Thommo grins like the sales reps I've seen at Mum's bars. This cricket thing's a lark innit? says Thommo's grin. I just do it to hang out with my mates.

Menace and charm. A potent mix.

I can now see, very distantly, a sketch of a man I could be. Laughing at my foes. Capable, casual, contemptuous.

The first time I see this vision I'm desperate to tell Wally, to share with him the prospect of what we could become. He scoffs: says he already knows about Thommo. And his scorn doesn't matter. Larrikin Man has become my template.

Just as Thommo arrives in my subconscious, the role model in the foreground departs.

Dad simply doesn't come home from work one Friday night. There's been a pattern of absences, brushed off as roster changes at the factory. Then a Friday night absence becomes permanent. No tears, no scenes, no recriminations. He was there, and now he isn't.

Wally's the first to articulate what we all know. There's a fathers versus sons cricket game the next week at school. He stands there in the kitchen, scuffed school shoes on the lino, and hands the note to Mum. She reads it in silence, puts it down and looks at him.

'You wanna play?' is all he says.

Mum makes a creditable sixteen that day, swiping consistently through mid-on. It's where Wally and I have been making the bulk of our runs in the backyard, and I know she's seen it. Bent double in the vegie patch pulling weeds, she's been struck on the arse by this very shot. Instead of rising to her full height and cursing us, she responded by turning slowly under her sunhat and telling the striker—me, I think—to play it along the ground.

She also takes an outfield catch that day, running flat out to her left in Dunlop Volleys and a tracksuit as though it's the most natural thing in the world. She doesn't celebrate or carry on when she snares it. Just looks at some indeterminate point on the grass in front of her as her sprint dwindles to a walk. People at their barbecues around the boundary are cheering and tooting car horns. *You know he shot through,* they'd be muttering. *So sad for the little ones.*

Mum's work means we're at home unattended for long stretches of time. She tries to get the day shifts, but even then she'll be at work until seven, and we're home from school at three-thirty. This suits us fine—we know where to find enough food, and once it's eaten we'll wring out the remaining daylight into cricket or footy—in the winter months pushing as far into the gathering darkness as we can.

The evenings are long and quiet, and she fills them by reading.

Early days, this takes place on the couch: Dr Seuss, *Harry the Dirty Dog.* Her reading evolves over the early months after Dad's departure, as she hears her own words commanding the air in a bewildered house. She's tentative at first, droning like we drone at school, but it's her inexperience with us as an audience, not her ability, that's holding her back. Sunburnt or cold, sticky with food, we drive our heads into each of her armpits and let the words wash over us. Sendak and C. J. Dennis, Enid Blyton, then Roald Dahl. She's doing voices, the pitch rising and falling as the narrative swells and recedes, and calling an abrupt halt to the night's reading just before a crucial event so we'll anticipate the denouement all day.

But even if I've nodded off and been shifted to bed, I click the reading light on and the bulb burns yellow into the night. It's my lighthouse, my beacon.

He might come home.

•

One spring evening comes an event that stands, like Dad's disappearance, as a marker of history's forward momentum.

It's the week after the '76 grand final, the one they called

Crimmo's Cup. We're in the backyard. Mum's at work, and we're in a state of limbo because the Big Footy's over and now it should be cricket. The garden's bursting into a smash-up riot of flowers—you can smell it everywhere, that honey reek, hear the swarms of insects, the birds darting among them for the easy feed. The place is alive.

Wally's fiddling with the bat, rolling a new grip onto it, pushing the rubber down over the coils of string wrapped around the handle. As he works, he's coughing away, those little ones he always seems to do when he's concentrating, when all of a sudden he sort of stops and chokes. He's just—one minute he's bent over the task, and the next he's looking at me like he can't comprehend what's going on. He's pointing at his throat, so that at first I think he's choking on something, but I know he hasn't eaten for hours. I wonder if he's swallowed a bee, I wonder if he's been poisoned, I wonder a dozen stupid and unhelpful things as he changes colour to a stricken white and begins to collapse, waving vaguely in the direction of his head as he lies on one side on the grass, legs kicking feebly while a hideous blank wall of panic rises in my gut, brick by brick cancelling any chance of clear thought.

He's still breathing but shallow and fast, the breath of a small frightened animal. I'm standing above him, bending over him, hopping around and saying stuff about God and what's wrong and somebody help and just saying them quietly and pleadingly and the dog's turned up and he's licking Wally's face but not like he thinks it's a game, not at all, and he's started whimpering and he's squatted back on his haunches in a tense weird way while he licks and snuffles and Wally's lips have gone blue and his eyes are locked on me like I've got an answer and I don't have an answer and now I'm screaming and screaming and screaming.

Right now I'm in a car boot with my hands and feet bound and a hole in my knee and all sorts of cracked and broken bones and I can feel the terror of that moment clear through all of it and the forty-odd years between. The white-hot searing horror of watching my brother dying on the ground in front of me.

The moment ends; it has to end somehow. It ends with old lady Apostoulos tearing across the yard at full speed and taking hold of Wally, without a word to me, without a question to him. She bundles him face-down across the shelf of her bosom and takes off with me in pursuit of her floral pinafore. As she runs down the drive, out, round the corner, past her own gate and further down the street, his arms and legs draping from her bouncing hips, I'm crying harder and sobbing *what's wrong with him?* She hauls in a breath and whispers, 'Asthma. He having asthma attack,' and for some reason this infuriates me and I cry in response that Wally doesn't *have* asthma.

'Does now,' she puffs.

Her big calves and ankles, pounding at the concrete like heavy machinery made flesh.

I stub my toe viciously on a raised footpath block as I run beside her but I can't cry any harder.

She thumps up the garden path of a house about four down the road, a place I've never been.

Bangs on the door, bangs again.

Yells at the top of her lungs, *Vera! Vera! Vera…turn off fucking television, come out!* She shuffles Wally's weight in her arms as she waits. A sleepy-looking woman in a dressing gown answers the door. Thick glasses, Jiffy slippers. Her eyes widen as she sees Mrs Aposta's load.

'Boy have asthma attack. Need machine.'

Vera throws the flywire screen open with a clang and we charge in, Wally's limp head smacking on the doorjamb as he passes through. In a front room he's dumped on the bed. On the bedside table, under a lamp, is a strange device, brown and beige with a power cord plugged into the wall and a white plastic tube running out of the front end.

Vera flicks a switch on the box and the machine hums into life.

She uncoils the plastic tube and finds a clear facemask on one end, which she places over Wally's mouth and nose. For a long, agonising moment, nothing at all happens. Then his chest rises, falls. His fingers uncurl.

She holds the facemask in position while Mrs Aposta goes to a telephone on the other bedside table and calls an ambulance. She's made to repeat herself, over and over. Now I can see that a Greek woman in late-seventies Altona would have suffered this indignity many times a day. Once she's satisfied with the call, she hangs up and dials another number, says my mother's name hesitatingly and, realising she's got her on the first try, explains what's happened.

'No, Missus Keefe, he fine. He resting. I call ambulance to make sure. I meet you there, yes. Yes. Good. Yes.'

She hangs up, looks at me solemnly and says, 'You be good boy, run home and get he pyjamas and toot-brush. Put in bag and run back here, yeah? Quick, before ambulance come...'

I take one last look at him before I leave, the steady swell and fall of his chest, the colour coming back to his face. He raises a thumb, feebly.

When the ambulance has come and the men have done their thing and they've carted Wally off to hospital, Mum and I follow in our car. Mum's thrown her hair back into a half-arsed bun and packed a bag. I see Wally's Bradman book go in, from the desk next to the bunks. He loves that book.

In the hospital he's sitting up in bed, looking perfectly fine. It's Mum who looks like she needs a doctor.

She unpacks his things, helps him into the pyjamas while he wriggles with embarrassment, and then climbs onto the bed as I get up on the other side of him. This terrifying day, like all of our days, must end with a book.

Mum, in her halo of old pub tobacco. I'm picking the dried blood

29

from the stubbed toe. I'm picking my nose. Mum drones through a few pages before falling asleep mid-sentence.

I look at Wally and he's asleep too. It's just me and two valves on the wall with hard blank signs that say OXYGEN and SUCTION.

For the next week I refuse to be separated from him for any reason.

Club

It's pointless, this. Clinging to memories. Rewinding them, replaying them. But it's compulsive: I feel them rushing forward to be counted, the people and occurrences whose very existence depends on me recalling them.

The dark, the prickling carpet. The small clanks and knocks of loose things in the compartments. I'm a child again, I'm myself again, the whole self without all the punctures and bruises. The self I was before everything became so tawdry.

I'm thinking about love, because this place is a vacuum where love does not exist. It can be summoned into recollection, turned over in the hands and examined, but it cannot exist.

It's the night before our first game for All Saints Parish CC. Mum's lined it up—we've heard her on the phone to the club secretary.

They're really very good...

No, both of them...

He's a lefthander. Yes, it's very young but I can assure you, that won't be a problem.

Tough as nails, our mum. Wally's a sure thing at ten, but the old girl has to tell them I'm nine, and even then she has to beg. Their lowest level is under-twelves, kids who tower over me. We've done the two net sessions ahead of the opening round, and neither of us is even slightly troubled by the bowling. There's a transition to be negotiated, from taped tennis balls to hard plastic balls and the protective equipment that goes with them. In my hunger I can only see this change in a positive light: when I hit the plastic missiles, they rocket away from me twice as hard.

What gets it over the line with me being underage is, the coach knows I can hit. He finds out the hard way—chatting to a parent when I smack a straight drive into his shins, eliciting a full-volume *fuck!* and a lot of irate hopping. He won't be forgetting me.

In the bunkroom, we're each engaged in the rituals of pre-match preparation. Noises from the top bunk, twangs from the little springs that form a roof over me. Wally's doing his stretches.

'You're not gonna pull a hammy,' I tell him.

There's no response, other than grunts.

'You're ten, idiot. No one even does stretches in the under-fourteens.'

The grunting from above stops momentarily.

'So what are you doing?' he says.

'Nothin. Just relaxing.'

Which is mostly true. I've got the bat in my bed, but that's routine. I'm staring at the McDonald's team poster on the wall: the Benson and Hedges World Series Cup, a three-cornered stoush between Australia (moustaches), the West Indies (beards) and England (I don't even care). They sit and stand in their bleacher rows in the burgers-and-cigs promotional shot, front row (keepers, spinners and batsmen) with fists neatly clamped on their knees, back rows (the quicks) with hands behind backs, exactly the way we're drilled in school photos.

Wally's gone quiet. He's got his bat in the bed too, I know. It's a Gray-Nicolls, the plain one with the red stripe down the back before they started making one-scoops (like Clive Lloyd, the Big Cat, used) and double-scoops (Hookesy). I've been enduring weeks of Wally's knocking-in rituals; the patient tapping of the bat's face with a rubber mallet the sports store lent him. The pinpricking of the timber so the linseed oil seeps in better. I can smell the linseed now. If he gets it on the linen Mum's going to explode.

'What are you doing up there?'

'Lying straight.'

'Why?'

'So I don't get any cricks.'

I feel a stab of panic. Should I be doing this?

'What's a crick?'

'It's when you lie crooked, like when you sleep with your head on one side and you wake up and your neck's all stiff.'

'That's the dumbest thing ever. I'm not going to do that.'

'Fine. Didn't ask you to.'

Despite this, I spend a few minutes getting myself in a position in bed from which I can watch the poster but ensure no part of my body is disarranged in any potentially crippling way.

I'm still looking at the poster. To my eight-year-old eyes, these cricketers are Men. *Men.* Tough, resourceful, but other-worldly.

I wonder if Dad plays cricket. I forgot to ask him.

Tomorrow I will take on whatever Our Lady Help of Christians Laverton can throw at me. I will hook and pull and cut and drive, and lean nonchalantly on my bat handle as my shots hurtle past faraway boundary cones. Tomorrow, hair will appear on my forearms. Sharp catches will no longer sting. My voice will drop and I will use it sparingly and without emotion. Unless, of course, I am appealing for a leg before.

Tomorrow, I will join their ranks.

Wally clicks his light off. I leave mine on.

If he comes back, I'll ask him.

•

It dawns bright and hot, as I'm sure all those days did. Statistically of course there must have been cloudy ones, rainy ones—probably more then than now—but memory's discarded them. There's a thing about dawn on such days. It smells clean and promising, the dew on warming grass, the house silent and close.

We're sharing a bag of gear; two bats but one pair of pads. I get gloves because I'm a lefty, and the communal kit at All Saints will have right handers' gloves. Mum will have gone without something to make this happen, but I'm not wired to consider it.

She's whited our sneakers the night before, left the coloured stripe at the heel unpainted as she knows we like it, and she zincs our noses before we leave. Lastly, she solemnly presents us with our new caps, shaking our hands and patting our shoulders. Sponsors and dignitaries will perform the same ritual in coming years, and it won't compare. I can still see her now, just lingering a moment as we try to get to our bikes. She's watching us, feeling something.

We ride down to the oval, elated, swerving great loops as the sun begins its arc. Wally's tucked the right leg of his whites into the sock so the chain won't grab the hem, and I've loudly mocked him. This of course disallows me from doing the same, and by the time we get to the LA Reid Memorial Oval, my right hem is all chewed up and streaked with black.

None of the kids in our side or theirs goes to our school, but they're all older and they've been taught to shake hands.

Someone tosses a coin, we bat, and Wally's opening. I'm batting number six: I'm the smallest kid in the team, and it's made clear that I should count myself lucky I'm not number eleven. I sit on a concrete step outside the grotty-looking clubrooms and plonk my head in my hands, supported on two knees. I can feel tears stinging my eyes.

The greedy eyes of a seagull bore into mine. It watches me, cawing at half volume. Do you realise I'm making my debut here, you stupid bird? Mum will come down shortly with a polystyrene cooler of red cordial and her big sunglasses on, before she nicks off to work at the pub. And I'll be sitting on this concrete step watching Wally bat with some idiot.

I study Wal closely as he strides out across the mown grass, the patches of yellow daisies. The other kid's a bit shorter and quite fat. He's got a helmet, first one I've ever seen, with a big sci-fi-looking perspex faceguard. He's talking to Wally. I know my older brother well enough to know he's not listening. The fielders wander around trying to decipher their positions.

A plane drones faintly across the sky.

They're settling in their spots as the other kid takes guard. He asks for two centres and then tries to scratch the mark with his shoe which is, of course, impossible on concrete. The keeper points out the stick of chalk behind middle stump, so now he has to take off a glove and painstakingly draw a line on the pitch. It's supposed to represent the line the ump gave him between the middle stump behind him and the one at the other end, but it looks to me as though he's forgotten about that during the charade with the scratching and the chalk. This is confirmed moments later when the opening ball of the match— the first, glittering red new ball I've ever seen firsthand—takes out his off stump as he theatrically shoulders arms. The impact makes a woody *doonk* and the bails spin through the air like shrapnel from an explosion.

I watch him trudging back towards us, trailing the toe of his bat. The bees circle out of his way.

Past the opposition's jubilant huddle I see Wally leaning on his bat, entirely unmoved.

The umps are standing together at mid-off, deep in conversation as the next batsman frantically buckles his pads on, caught short by the sudden wicket. I didn't mention, did I—the umps are the two coaches. Ours is Mr O'Flaherty, a strange little man.

Strange.

He doesn't run, but sort of skips. His smile is birdlike. He watches everything intently. He watches us. At first I think it's his attention to technique, but he's not watching our shot selection. He's watching *us*. At the second net session, Wally mistimed a hook shot then gave me a look of horror as O'Farty darted into his net and took up a position behind his back, arms wrapped over Wally's shoulders and sharing his grip on the bat. His peculiar little belly was pressed into Wally's shoulder blades, and there they remained, like the mating bears in the *National Geographic*, while he called for several more balls to be sent down.

Here's O'Farty in the bright sunshine of Saturday morning, standing swaybacked like a cartoon character, hands on hips and lips pursed in sour disapproval. He pushes his comb-over down on his scalp as the breeze lifts a single strand. *Cricket is a game for gentlemen*, he told us on Thursday night. *At All Saints, we are all the best of chums…say it!*

Sullen silence.

Say it!

A mumbled repetition of his words floated back as we sat cross-legged on the grass.

And nothing should get between a gentleman and his chums.

O'Farty heads back to his position behind the bowler's stumps as the next batsman reaches the pitch. The kid bowling has paced out a giant run-up. He's been watching too much Lillee. In he charges, and new kid gets a nick through slips. *Nobody can take a slips catch in junior cricket*, Mum reckons. *So have a fling when it's outside off. If you nick it, you're safe as houses.* How right she is. The ball streaks down to third man. New kid crosses through for a single and Wally's got the strike. He puts his bat on the chalk line, confirms he's a mile off middle, and sorts it out with the ump. Then he settles down over his bat and waits for Laverton's opener to huff his way through that marathon run-up.

He pitches it in the dust beside the concrete and Wally watches it roll through to the keeper with a look of disdain. He wanders down the pitch and flicks a clod of dry dirt off the surface with his bat. It looks cool: I make a mental note to copy him.

Fourth ball is on his pads. Wally remains perfectly still, apart from his arms and bat, which swing a whipping half-circle around his body. The crack of perfect contact resounds around the agapanthus beds on the boundary. The ball bounces once on the field and comes straight to me where I sit outside the change rooms. People are cheering. Wally hasn't moved. I take a quick look at the ball in my hand, gleaming a mysterious blood red in its coat of varnish. The centre of the sphere is embossed like a gravestone with gold lettering:

KOOKABURRA—VCA APPROVED—5½ OZ.

I am in love.

I toss it back to the fieldsman and watch Wally smash it to the boundary twice more before Lillee ends his over and retreats to fine leg. Wally hasn't looked up, hasn't acknowledged anyone in the world.

The kid bowling from the other end isn't really up to it. His face is a tangle of reluctance. One look at him and I know what his schoolbag would smell like.

He waddles in and bowls off the wrong foot, rolling his head with his arm as though they're connected by one giant tendon. He looks like he's learning freestyle. The results are much like last over: the kid batting with Wally gets dollar signs in his eyes as the swimmer lobs one high in the air. Down the pitch he charges, and misses it in a whoosh of flailing bat. The keeper has time to snatch at the ball twice before he finally gloves it, and he still makes the stumping. He whoops and runs around the stumps towards the bowler to celebrate. His shirt's out and flapping in the sun. Mum told us never to let our shirts hang out.

Second drop charges straight out there and moments later he's back, having run himself out at the bowler's end. At least it puts Wally on strike, and he doesn't waste the opportunity—waiting for the swimmer's looping deliveries to bounce, then swatting them tennis-style from overhead. The violence of his swings amazes me.

Now it's me wrapping my legs in the club's pads, velcroing my wrists into my batting gloves. For a while I stare down the back of my bat towards the grass, my nose resting on the tops of the gloves. I can smell the timber and rubber of the bat handle. The clamour of another wicket comes to me, and I'm up and walking out there.

I'm aglow. The world feels still and quiet. Wally is the most dependable presence in my world, even if he's dependably annoying. And he's out here in the middle: where I want to be.

Now I'm looking down at that chalk line. Now I can see my feet placed either side of the crease, and looking up I see the circle of fielders closing around me. They're all looking at me, trying in their childish ways to sledge me.

Hey, who brought the club mascot.

Don't hurt him, Doggy.

This one's yours too, Doggy.

It doesn't matter at all. I can see the bowler at the far end of his Dennis Lillee run, shuffling the ball from side to side. He flicks his fringe, waits.

Mr O'Farty is explaining to me that the bowler will be bowling

38

right arm round the wicket, something I didn't realise they do in real cricket. I can still see the faraway ball in his hand and I just want the thing. I want him to bowl it.

He runs in and steps up into his delivery stride, the whole world silent but for those skipping footsteps and his breath, and he flings it and I can't believe it's a nude half-volley outside off stump, after all those taped balls and microwaved balls and assaults with sticks and wrestles on the ground and here I am in real cricket and I plonk a foot forward down the pitch and drop onto the other knee and give it everything and I get it a split second off the bounce and squarely in the middle of the bat and I can't even feel the contact I've hit it so sweetly. I've wrapped the bat in its follow-through over my right shoulder and the ball is somewhere out past cover with a kid half-heartedly strolling after it but it's gone, it's gone, clattering into someone's timber fence.

At the end of the over I wander down the pitch to Wally, who is standing there mid-track like he's brought my lunch to the grade two room.

'Did you see that?' I squeak.

'Don't stuff it up,' he says. 'We've got all day, and the bowlers are shit.'

'You told on me last time I said shit.'

Wally ignores me and points his bat vaguely back at the other end. 'This guy's just lobbing it. Real slow, doesn't spin. But it bounces pretty high.'

And he's right. The ball is rapidly getting chewed up by the concrete, and it now looks all shaggy and pink. The first couple bounce over my shoulder and the keeper, pale and pudgy, has to leap up and glove them over his head. I'm not going to let him bounce another one of these farcical deliveries past me, and when he does it again, I swipe at the thing somewhere near my ears and succeed only in getting a thick edge on it.

For a second I have no idea where it's gone, but then I'm conscious of a second noise. A sort of tempered *crack*.

I look back to see that my nick has shot straight into the keeper's eye, and there's already blood running down his cheek from a split in his eyebrow. He's squealing, looking at me in outraged self-pity like I meant it. He shakes his keeping gloves off and puts his hands to his face. The blood leaks through his fingers and onto the white cuffs of his long-sleeve shirt. The colours, under the bleaching sun, are so beautiful I find myself transfixed for a moment.

And now there's another noise—Wally's thundering down the pitch yelling at me to run. The ball's ricocheted off the keeper's face and out to point, where the fielding side seem momentarily to have forgotten it.

I take off as directed by Wally. The last thing I see as I leave the crease is three perfect drops of blood on the grey-white concrete.

•

By lunchtime, Wally and I have retired on thirty, then come back in again after the other wickets have fallen, finishing on eighty-two not out and fifty-nine not out respectively. Towards the end, Wally has started farming the strike to prevent me catching up with him. I'm tempted to run him out.

Someone's mum has provided lunch. Jam sandwiches, squashed and warm. Cheese sticks. Apples and bananas. We are the toast of the All Saints under-twelves, and for the first time in my life, older kids want to talk to me, want to ask me what I think. This is unprecedented of course, as Wally would no sooner seek my opinion than volunteer that it was him who put the Lego man in the gas heater. As I bask in the warm glow of celebrity, O'Farty approaches.

Wally moves imperceptibly closer to me.

'Now lads,' he begins. 'Very proud of you. So proud.'

His face squishes into a sort of joyful cat's bum squint, like he's bitten a lemon and somehow loved it.

'But.'

Now he's spat the lemon.

'I was saddened by your display of poor sportsmanship out there.'

I'm immediately baffled. No one had even got close to getting us out. No one had had anything to appeal for.

'Darren, you struck that poor boy on the face. He's gone off to the hospital for stitches. But you didn't even look back at him, you just took off running. And you, Wally, you were possibly worse because you're older and you called him through. You should know better.'

The Brothers Keefe are dumbstruck. Wally finds his voice first.

'But there was two in it. 'Snot my fault they weren't looking.'

'No amount of runs or wickets should ever replace common decency, you two.'

He has his hands on our shoulders. I'm developing doubts about his version of common decency by now. The hands move to our hair, ruffle it. I've got my face down in confusion, and I observe that he has an odd-shaped, pouchy groin.

'Next time, your priority should be to ensure that he's all right. Now put in a big effort in the field and play like men, not boys. Eh?'

My face is hot with embarrassment. Other kids are staring at us, trying to eavesdrop as they chew like Herefords on the spongy white bread.

We watch him skip off, with his strangely light-footed gait, into the pale green sea of the field.

'That man,' declares Wally, 'is an idiot.'

●

Home that night, cheese and crackers after enduring a bath with Wally. All Saints have won the game by, I've lost count, by a lot. Winners are grinners, Mum chirps as she gets out the special glass platter that crackers always go on.

It's pine stools at the kitchen bench, the last of the day's sun making golden squares on the wall.

We get a Tab Cola to share while she flips the lid off a bottle of beer with a little *fft* and pours it into a special glass with a gold rim. I know from my pub days that she never drinks at work, not even a knockoff when she's done. The drinkers would assume she's a teetotaller. Never at work and never, until now, something she does with us. I take this as further evidence that something massive has shifted today. A door has opened into a new realm.

She slides open the second drawer, under the bench next to her stool. Out comes the ashtray, one of her tiny personal totems. Fine china with sparrows on it. A flat rim with the four little dips where the cigger lies.

She wants to know about footwork, running between wickets. Wally answers all the questions with his phony man-voice on. Until, mouth deliberately half-full of biscuit, I ask Mum about the keeper, about O'Farty's lecture.

She blows her smoke high towards the kitchen fluoro, aiming at the silhouettes of dead insects.

'Did you do it deliberately?' she asks, after a thoughtful pull at her beer.

'No. It was an edge.'

'It was,' concurs Wally. 'It was a crap shot and he had no control over it.'

'Don't say crap,' says Mum. She pushes the biscuit crumbs into a little pile on the laminex with the side of one finger. 'Was there two in it?'

'Yeah, I called it,' says Wally. 'Kid was on the ground, no one was even watching it.'

By now I'm sensing no one's much interested in the moral issue. Mum's cricket purism obscures all else. 'You know if the ball goes to point, sometimes that's the striker's call, not the non-striker's...'

'Yeah, but he was just standin' there like a stunned mullet.'

'Was the kid all right? The keeper?'

'Yeah,' scoffs Wally. 'He came back when we were fielding. Had a black eye, couple of stitches. He was kinda bragging about it and telling everyone he nearly got the catch.'

Another gulp from the glass.

'The coach gave you a telling-off about running?'

'Yeah,' we chorus simultaneously.

'We'd better find you another team I think.'

And so our competitive debut teaches me two things: one, the Keefe brothers are so far in front of our peers at the game that we're wasting our time among them, and two, if you want to feel sorry for people, you're going to get left behind.

I smash another Salada into my mouth and turn on the TV. Nestled in the couch, I can feel a tightness in my calves from the running, the warm sting of sunburn across my neck. Kids in other houses would be talking about the Keefe brothers right now, about how the eight-year-old hits the ball like a dad. How they were far too good for anyone.

Later that night, lying in the bunks in the darkness, Wally tells me he will one day captain Australia. I laugh at him, like always. But privately, after I hear his breathing turn to snores, I wonder if anything might be possible.

The Firsts

I'm running my fingernails lightly over the underside of the boot lid. Just tracing a line.

Who would tear their finger-ends to stumps trying to claw their way out of a box? And why won't I?

The exhaust smell's getting stronger, making me sicker. Lifting the clumped hands towards the roof of my crypt, I can feel the contours of the metal, the lining material.

It's Poe. Mum used to read us Poe. Scared the pants off me—I'd wind up in Wally's bed whimpering. Poe wrote stories about people being buried alive, and this, in metal and carpet, is the modern equivalent. Entombed in a moving vehicle on a freeway. Buried alive at ninety-five.

It's the summer at the end of form two. We've got jobs, both of us, with the greengrocer in Barkly Street who is somehow connected—I don't recall how—to the Italian lady around the corner whose nebuliser saved Wally.

On Saturday mornings we get in there around six and help unload the truck that's come from the markets around the corner. Within weeks we've learned where to stack everything in the displays, where to toss the leftover stuff and what to put in a box for Mum. Wally decides this is the perfect opportunity to enact a training diet, and uses his first couple of pays to buy a blender for the fruit.

We shuffle between the chill air of the refrigerated truck and the storeroom behind the shop, heaving the shallow waxed boxes. The men work around us, swear at us from time to time, but there's an underlying affection to it all. Their bellowing is as much a part of the place as the slippery floor and the intoxicating smell of fruit.

We're out by ten with a box of fruit each on our bike carriers. Once we're in the door at home, there's an hour available to us to eat, to change and get on the bikes to wherever the day's game is taking place. Mum cuts sandwiches or makes a foam cooler of drink if she's not getting ready to work a shift. She talks tactics as the big knife works through a watermelon and the chunks are lined up on the clingwrap.

These are the easy Saturdays, uncomplicated and pure. There are girls to watch, sly eyes and giggling, nothing more. Neighbourhood girls, girls from school. Unspoken, our shared strategy is to look the other way and try for heroism of a kind we can't yet identify. We're cricketers. It's terribly serious.

Around the time school breaks up for summer, we get a letter from the association asking us to take part in the Eastern Suburbs versus Western Suburbs Schoolboys Carnival.

I can still see the envelope, the official typeface with our names on it. The envelope's wet and limp from lying in a pool of leaked rainwater in our letterbox—December's been unseasonably cold and wet.

Mum's chopping carrots with the radio tuned to 3DB.

She takes the knife and slips it carefully through the top of the envelope, removes the letter and reads it aloud, a satisfied smile at the corners of her mouth. This qualifies as representative cricket, Mum says. Mum thinks like Wally does where ambition is concerned: we're serving a long apprenticeship for the rarest of careers: her boys will be professional cricketers, and it's her mission to ensure this occurs.

We've been playing for the St John's First XI, among grown men with moustaches and mullets, for a couple of years by now. Mum took action immediately after our debut with All Saints, marching us into a junior training session at the bigger club, one under each arm, demanding to know who was in charge.

As we climb through the ranks the challenge never seems to grow: the bowling is quicker in the higher grades, but our reflexes are easily keeping pace. The muttering from the close-in fieldsmen is more explicit, more sexually directed, but we're so confident that their insults are wasted.

By a special resolution of the club's match committee, it's agreed that we can play for the seniors at twelve and fourteen provided we wear helmets at all times when batting. We're the youngest brothers ever to receive First XI caps.

•

Those caps, symbolising our elevation into a grown-up world, somehow become the centre of a childish squabble. We manage to turn everything into a battle between us, but this one leaves a scar.

I've wandered out to the backyard at Fernley Road one morning, drawn by the sound of the handmower, the whirring and zinging of blades. Wally's making a brisk pace up and down our pitch, shaving maybe half an inch off the grass, leaning to one side to check that he's drawing a straight line down the edge of the pitch. The tiny bristles of new growth stand proud after last night's watering and fertiliser pellets. He's in his school uniform, using up the last half-hour before he jumps on his bike to head off to class.

With his First XI cap on.

The chocolate brown with the gold hoops, the gold and blue crest front and centre. The idiot.

'Don't have to wear that, you know,' I tell him.

'What?'

'The cap. Don't have to wear it. You're just mowing the pitch. No one can see you.'

'Fuck off,' he shrugs. 'Wear it if I want.'

'It's a quarter to eight. It's Tuesday morning. You're not playing cricket till Saturday. *Duh.*'

'Why's it bother you?' He shoots me a shit-eating grin. It annoys me more than it should.

'You're such a fucking idiot.' I step forward from near the back door, make a lunge for the cap. He rears back.

'Whoa, little guy...'

He knows that fires me up.

'Fuckwit.'

This time I make contact, manage to pluck the cap by the edge of its peak. I flick it away Frisbee-style before Wally can react. We both watch it arc through the air. It gets more lift than I'd intended, and sails over the fence into the Apostouloses'.

His face turns to thunder. 'Go and get it.'

'Make me.'

This is pathetic, but I'm committed now. He advances menacingly, still wheeling the mower. 'Fucking go and get it.'

'Or what? Gonna tell Mum?'

He revs the mower at me, lifting it slightly off the ground at the end of his swing. The blades spin, spraying me lightly with cuttings, which land on my cold bare feet.

'Don't be stupid Wally.' I'm looking sideways, looking for an exit, but he's got me against the fence.

'Looking for Mum to save you, *little guy*?'

His face is lit by fury. He pushes forward again with the mower. Jerks it at me, watching my feet.

I dive to my left but the grass is deep there, and still damp with the overnight dew. My right foot slips out as I jump, and it shoots forward.

There's a loud *poong*, like you hear when you hit a stick with the mower. But it's not a stick, it's the outside of my foot, my toes. It's flesh, soft and pink, and there's enough of it stuffed into the blades that it jams them up, and for a frozen instant we both stare at the helix of sharpened metal, the foot caught hopelessly within and the pearls of fat under the sliced flesh, butter-yellow in the seconds before the capillaries fill and gush blood.

Some of it's shock and some of it's pain but I'm screaming and he's instantly sorrowful and concerned, winding the blades backwards, trying to extricate the foot. He's only making it worse, the top of the foot bending further and exposing more flesh, the red gash growing and spilling more blood down over the steel and onto the grass, where it's forming a sticky pool. Now he's looking up, looking at me, at my presumably ashen face. He's winding the wheels again, back and forth, back and forth. Then he's running into the house to find Mum.

I'm on my back all this time, propped on both elbows, hopelessly caught. Aside from the pain and the rage, I can feel a gnawing sense I asked for this. But who the hell escalates a petty squabble that radically?

Wally Keefe does.

Cannot back down. Cannot lose.

He's contrite afterwards, after the casualty doc's put fourteen stitches in the foot and given me a tetanus shot in the arse, and after Mum's delivered Wally a frightening shout-down. Odd kind of contrition, though. It's not the phony kind that kids often display when they've been put up to it by adults: *go and say sorry to your brother.* This is genuine, but weirdly disconnected.

'I'm sorry Darren,' he says, standing gravely by my bed. 'That was a serious error of judgment. It will never happen again.'

Assuming you'd reasonably expect that it *will* never happen again—does anybody get deliberately rammed by a handmower twice in a childhood?—'error of judgment' is a profoundly cold assessment. In his blind rage, he nearly severed three of my toes.

•

He also costs me a month of cricket. Once that month of bored abstinence is over, the season passes in predictable rhythm.

Each week the opposition captain questions why St John's are fielding two children in their firsts. A short exchange usually follows, which finishes with the other skipper shrugging and walking off. We walk out to bat, weathering a burst of ridicule from the slips and the two or three blokes they've dropped in close to try and terrify us.

Wally bats higher, and by the time I come in he's normally cleared out the close fielders through a combination of dangerous hitting and an icy stare that unsettles grown men when they see it on the face of a fourteen-year-old. The field is shuffled back to a safer range, then it goes back even further as the skipper sends everyone out to defend the boundaries. We no longer even call our runs, relying on instinct and a meeting of eyes. Confusion results for the fielding side—no one knows we're running until we've already run.

In the evenings we analyse over drinks with Mum, or sometimes she'll take up a deckchair in the backyard, beer in hand, watching us knock a few around while the mozzies descend. The taped ball feels light after a real cricket ball delivered at pace.

•

So on a Tuesday in February we get the day off school for the representative match.

The game is scheduled for Punt Road Oval: neutral ground, and nearly as good as playing on the MCG. We get the train there because Mum's got to work as usual. Wally wants to travel in his whites. I flatly refuse and wear a tracksuit. Eventually he relents.

It's hot—December dried out into an endless arid northerly off the Mallee, bringing streams of floating dandelion seeds from far away. It's so hot that Brunton Avenue is sticky as we cross with Sunnyboys from the kiosk at Richmond Station. The stifled roar of the city fills the gaps between the traffic sounds. As I cross, watching for traffic and also watching Wally's shoulders ahead of me, I feel a random pang for a father. Why this happens halfway across Brunton Avenue in the sun I cannot say. Would I call him Dad? What did I call him back then?

Dad, Dad.

Wally's shoulders in his Crystal Cylinders shirt. Wally will be a dad. He understands responsibility.

On the north side of the road the roots of the giant liquidambars have pushed the footpath up into ridges. As we enter the ground I realise this will be the first time we've played to a grandstand. There's no one in it, but that's immaterial. Out in the middle, there is complex equipment: motorised sprinklers, mowers, heavy rollers. There's sight-screens at both ends and a scoreboard. Again, they haven't opened it up for our little show, but *there's a scoreboard*.

The outfield's billiard green: no bare patches, no flowers. The things that are painted white—the sightscreen, the pickets around the boundary—are so white it hurts. The hoses and the boundary line are white. The entire playing surface is perfectly flat and level. And in the middle of the ground, across that wide carpet of perfect grass, the holy of holies.

A turf wicket.

We've both spotted it the instant we cross the concrete bleachers, and we don't exchange a word as we climb over the boundary fence and walk to the middle. It's slightly scuffed, having been used the previous weekend for a district game, but they've rolled it, watered it, repainted the creases. The stumps stand sentinel at each end in perfect symmetry.

On my hands and knees, I press four fingertips into the surface. It's hard and waxy, almost as unyielding as concrete. It smells wonderfully of cut grass. I look at Wally, who's also pressing the surface, but from a stooped position.

He looks back and smiles at me in an unguarded way, a generous way.

'This is gonna be so good,' he says.

•

In the shade of the grandstand, a couple of association officials stand around, studying clipboards. Two uniformed umpires—another first in our cricketing lives—are perched on the benches. They've got crests on their shirt pockets, and they're good and fat, as cricket umps should always be. Take it from me, you don't trust the skinny ones.

An official wanders up. Balding, no discernible chin. Long nose, topped with a schoolmaster's thick glasses. This is 1983, remember— the plastic frames are so big they reach halfway down his cheeks.

'The Keefe brothers, no doubt,' he smiles. 'We've heard so much.'

He extends a hand to each of us.

'Now,' looking from Wally to me and back again, 'You'd be Wally. Congratulations son, you're skippering Western Suburbs.'

Wally smiles modestly. This honour is the most natural thing that could've befallen him.

The association boffins have all sorts of ideas about the batting order, who they want bowling and in what sequence. Wally takes it all in, nodding and pointing at the clipboard now and then. He laughs politely at their witticisms. This is the beginning of Wally's career-long habit of easy sycophancy with officialdom. As I watch, I'm torn between the desire to interrupt and offer my thoughts, to be a part of this earnest exchange, and the stronger urge to stick a wet finger in Wally's ear.

Wally wins the toss and elects to bat. Ten minutes later he's out there opening our innings, and I'm lounging in one of the plastic chairs regaling the boys with a few tales about how they do things in the Eastern Suburbs. Up to this point, I've never been there.

The pattern of things is much like always. No one can get through Wally's defences. Not an edge, not a swipe, not a chancy lofted shot. He exudes permanence, even as wickets fall around him. He defends a lot: stretching into technically perfect shapes that look like fencing. He is very still, stiller than I've ever seen him. He is, for the first time, imposing.

Rifling through my bag to get padded up, I can tell that Mum's been in it. The pads have been strapped neatly around the bat, and inside each of them is a rolled-up bathtowel. A Granny Smith in the bottom of the bag. Spare socks.

It's eleven. She'll be mopping out the bar at the Mona Castle, rolling in the new kegs.

Twenty minutes later I'm standing in the middle with Wally, who's unbeaten on forty. I'm not going to ask him how the bowlers are, because I can see. The wicket's clearly not treacherous.

'You right?' he asks vaguely, and I nod and wander to the striker's end.

They take a while setting the field. Their skipper has a smug look which to me says either he's already played a lot of representative cricket or he's accustomed to running things. He's clean-looking, new shoes. He stands only metres away, arranging everything as though

I'm not there. He even talks about me as he does so.

'No, come straighter. He won't hit wide through there.'

Then he gestures to the guy standing at deep backward square. He's tall, and I recognise him as one of the opening bowlers. Skipper winds him right in until they're standing side by side.

'Come in to short leg, mate. Right under him, please.'

And so this big lummox squats down almost within reaching distance of my bat, watching me. And as soon as his skipper's moved back to slips, he starts on me. As I scratch out my guard:

'Fucking peasant.'

I tap my bat gently on the turf as the bowler reaches the end of his walk back and turns to run in.

'Dad on fucking welfare, mate?'

The bowler's almost all the way in towards me and I wait until he's just about to leap into the air, then pull away and raise my bat. The bowler staggers to a belligerent halt. I point my bat at Short Leg in accusation.

'Good one, cockhead,' I mutter softly.

He swings immediately towards the square leg ump. 'I'm sorry ump, but there's some very ugly abuse being directed at me by the batsman,' he says, mouth full of private-school plums.

'Fucking sook,' I add. He's a foot taller than me.

'What'd you say?'

He's advancing on me as Wally comes down the wicket to defuse. The two umps meet us mid-pitch. One of them's got his hands out in a conciliatory way like he's soothing dangerous animals. Short Leg gives me a death stare as everyone gets back into position and the bowler runs in again.

This time the bowler's high in his delivery stride.

'Commission-flat maggot.'

His timing's very good. I've pressed forward and missed outside off as the ball bends elegantly way from the edge of my bat. I turn and look him over without responding.

'Fucked your mum,' he adds, staring straight back. 'She fuckin loved it.'

I curl and uncurl one hand on the bat handle, imagine crushing the bridge of his nose with it so his breathing crackles through little chips of bone and the blood makes bubbles as the air comes out.

Curl, uncurl.

But somewhere within me, a switch is tripped. Not the one you'd expect, perhaps, from his inclusion of Mum in the banter. It isn't tipping me towards white-hot fury, but into a state of perfect composure. A sudden understanding.

I'm not hosing out a urinal so you can lose your temper and blow your big chance. That's what she'd say.

The bowler runs in again. Pitches perfectly straight at good pace on middle stump. Ordinarily, and two balls into an innings, I'd carefully defend such a ball. Not this time. I drop onto one knee and sweep across my front pad, making clean contact and whipping it square.

There's never any time to react at short leg. The best you can hope for is to flinch before the shot's made, as you see the bat coming round. This fool hasn't even moved and the sound of ball hitting bone just below his knee is nearly as sweet as the shot itself.

He drops like a shot dog.

It feels just like All Saints v Laverton. Wally calls me through, and we run two as Short Leg clutches his knee, a concerned mob gathering around him. I make sure I saunter, nice and relaxed, back to the crease and then turn to face him. You don't want to overplay it when you've dealt an ace in such a situation, so I just watch him patiently as the skipper calls for a helmet and box and someone else takes his spot. He grimaces all Hollywood and limps off the ground.

For another hour, the empty grandstand echoes sweetly with

each connection of ball and bat. Their attack's diminished with the opening bowler off the ground, and I can show off all I want. Wally chides me for indulging in what he calls 'ball-watching'—my habit of remaining in a pose after a perfectly executed shot, showing no interest at all in running. And he's right: I'm savouring every minute of it. In the distance I can see drivers marooned on Punt Road, windows down, arms hung defeatedly over door sills. They gaze longingly across the ground at us as though we're splashing in a pool. This is an oasis.

By lunch, Wally's fifty-two and I'm not far behind him.

•

The dining room is long and spacious. Everything's laid on, and they have staff whose only job is to feed hungry people in whites.

I scoff as much deep-fried food as I can. Wally's loading up on fruit, the very thing we can already get for free. I scan the walls as I eat. Honour boards, black-and-white photographs, serious men. A kind of gravity I've never previously associated with the game. People who lived and played cricket and went to war and then died. I can't equate all that commemoration with the joyful act of smacking a cricket ball.

Wally has his fruit scraps neatly arranged on the side of his plate.

'Let's get back into 'em, eh?' he smiles.

We walk out of the dressing room and down the steps to the ground. I want to savour this moment. I've seen footage of Bradman and Ponsford walking together just like Wally and me, padded up and casually trailing our bats.

But as the dining room door closes behind us, it's clear that something's changed.

It's hot, unbearably hot, and as we emerge from the shade of the grandstand the air tastes different. It even smells hot, somewhere between smoke and baking concrete. But something else feels wrong, and it takes a moment or two to work it out.

The light's changed.

It's heavier. No longer blinding and reflective, it's taken on a malevolent hue, a tint towards brown or orange that's loaded with menace. Wally's pressing forward through the gate and onto the out-field, swinging his bat now. He hasn't even noticed. *Task driven*, a commentator will say years later.

There are no birds. Before lunch, there were seagulls all over deep midwicket, settled on the grass, rising reluctantly for a struck ball. Now they're gone. So too are the mynas and sparrows in the street.

Within a few deliveries, Wally's gone too. Uncharacteristically wafting at a wide one, he nicks it through to the keeper and never looks back as he leaves. No doubt he's satisfied that his half-century brought him the right kind of attention.

The next batsman wanders out, looking, as I did, at the sky. Instead of heading for the striker's end he ambles up to me, a big grin splitting his features under the cap. He thrusts a hand forward in greeting.

'Mate! Craig Wearne!'

I don't know how I didn't encounter this bear over lunch.

His handshake is overpowering. I look down at his grip and see the oversize bulge of his forearm protruding from the shirt. His face is all puppydog giddy. Never have I seen a human being so desperate to be loved. Remembering after a moment that I'm no longer batting with Wally, I allow myself a smile.

He waddles off down the pitch, saying g'day to each fieldsman he passes. None of them returns his greeting. As he walks, I'm conscious of how he fills his clothes, even his sneakers. He's not fat, in the simple meaning of the term, but there's so *much* of him.

When he reaches the crease he doesn't take guard or look at where the fieldsmen are placed. He thumps his bat happily into the turf and looks up to see where the bowler is. As the ball streaks towards him he plonks a foot down the wicket and misses by at least the width of the bat. He's laughing at his own impetuousness, so he doesn't hear the fieldsmen sledging him. Next ball he plays a very self-assured glide through gully, and it runs away slowly as a fieldsman pursues it.

I call him through, charging down the pitch at him before I realise he hasn't moved. We're nearly standing next to each other.

'Craig! Go!' I scream. The fieldsman's gaining on the ball.

He looks at me calmly.

'It'll get there. Relax.' He still hasn't moved. The fieldsman lunges and slides. The ball finally tumbles into the gutter under the advertising boards.

'See?' His face isn't boastful. He's just happy things worked out.

The next over, I finally reach fifty and he runs down the wicket and hugs me. We've known each other for eight minutes.

'We'll remember this,' he says, suddenly dead serious. 'You and me. This is special.'

I don't know where to look.

It's getting steadily darker, and now the umpires are looking skyward. It's hard to tell what's going on because the sun's moved behind the grandstand and the MCG next door. The sky's tint has become an orange glow like an eclipse. The umps confer briefly then ask me if I want to go off. I don't. Craig, who hasn't been asked, makes it clear that he too wants to keep batting.

As the bowler wanders back to his mark, a stiff breeze picks up, swirling papers and leaves across the ground. It's cold, cold air, instantly chilling the sweat on my back, and for a moment it's a relief to feel the layer of hot air stripped off my skin. Then I'm cold like the heat never existed. I'm screwing my gloved hands against the rubber grip of the handle, trying to regain my concentration, when I realise that all the fieldsmen, and the umpires too, are looking up.

There's a wall collapsing across the sky.

A plume, a cloud, an avalanche: none of these things. It looks like smoke but it's a deep, rich brown colour. Although it floats across the sky like cumulus, it looks unbearably heavy. By unfortunate coincidence, we've been doing Pompeii in Ancient History, so I assume we're all about to be petrified under ash. I'll be found by archaeologists in cricket pads, smothered under the considerable bulk of Craig Wearne.

People are running for the grandstand. I look at Craig, who looks back at me, momentarily unsettled. Then we both run after them.

·

Outside the world drowns in haze. The stumps are still out there, lonely sentinels. But the far boundary is gone. Punt Road is not only invisible from here but silent too, like someone stopped a printing press. We sit around in the dining room under the stern gaze of the old bearded gents. One of the officials comes over.

'They're saying on the radio it's a dust storm. Topsoil blowing down from the Mallee. Take a couple of hours to clear, but they reckon no one should be outside till it's gone. So we're abandoning the match.'

Amid the chatter and complaints, he eyeballs me.

'Well batted, son. Terrific.' He's looking over his glasses at me, like he really means it.

I find Wally in the dressing room, carefully repacking his gear.

'Would've been nice to win it,' I venture.

'We've made our point.'

I feel a surge of irritation at this. 'Don't you want to bury those snobs?'

He thinks for a moment before responding.

'Not really. It's rep cricket. It's there for people to get a look at us, and they got a look at us.'

Why doesn't he feel these things? He's placing a rolled-up towel into each pad as Mum did for me. Which reminds me, my pads are on the floor where I left them.

Walking down the same flight of stairs I'd earlier used to go for a dart, I look at Wally with his bag slung over one shoulder, me with mine, and for a moment I could imagine autograph hunters awaiting us at the foot of the stairs. Passing through the gateway at carpark level, the light has brightened a little, though there's still a heavy haze that shrouds the canopy of the big trees.

There's a huddled group waiting for us, but they aren't autograph hunters.

The skipper of Eastern Suburbs, now dressed in brand-name track gear. Hundred-dollar gym shoes. He's gelled his hair and he's leaning casually on the bonnet of a car. Beside him, their keeper. Beside him, the sledger from short leg.

As soon as we emerge from the gateway, the keeper scuttles round us and seals off the exit. I hear Wally sigh in a way that says *this is going to hurt*. He puts his bag down, and I know he's not thinking right now about the thrashing that's imminent nor harbouring any concern for his kid brother's safety, but weighing the prospect of getting through this without having his gear smashed up before his eyes.

We've stopped walking. The skipper and the short leg have got up off the car bonnet and are advancing on us.

'You fucking dirty bogan cunts.' That's the skipper, charmer of private-school mothers. 'Did you try to backchat my friend here?'

He's looking at me. 'Fuck, seriously, you're a weed. What were you thinking?'

Short Leg hasn't spoken. Suddenly he leaps forward and swings a punch at Wally, who's slightly closer. He staggers as he pulls up from the swing and extends a leg to try to kick Wally, who does the obvious and grabs the leg. They both tangle themselves faster than fishing line, but Short Leg's got the better of it and he's landing a few on Wally's head as he clings on grimly. There's clothes tearing and scuffing sounds from dragging footwear. I'm cursing Wal's insistence on fighting fair—there's ample opportunity to grab his balls or bite him, but oh no, not Brother Wally. And I shouldn't be watching this because it means I'm not watching the skipper.

Next thing, I'm lying on the gravel, face up with a clanging sound in my right ear where he's hit me. I can't work out how it took me down so easily, and how the world is swinging and tilting. It makes no sense, and then I see him coming again and I know why. He's got a cricket bat. *Wally's* cricket bat, raised above his right shoulder and coming down.

I roll left and it smashes into the ground, but that only delays the inevitable, because he's got it golf-style beside my head now and he nine-irons me hard in the ear.

This one hurts. I squeeze my eyes tightly shut as he starts getting into my ribs with those expensive boots; again and again, grunting slightly with the effort each time. I watch him wind up the backswing for another kick when he's struck from the side with enormous force by a flying human who isn't any of us. From inside my private cloud of pain and disorientation I struggle to recognise the bulky stranger.

My new best mate, Craig Wearne.

The skipper's winded by the impact, lying on his side a few metres from me, gasping like a goldfish. And Craig has left my field of vision. He comes past again seconds later with Short Leg under his arm in a headlock. He's just trotting, calm and unhurried. His left fist is holding a ball of Short Leg's hair, and Short Leg is half-running and half-letting himself be dragged.

I find myself feeling quite sorry for Short Leg.

Craig's taking him to the same car on which he and the skipper were leaning. He lifts his captive out of the headlock and for a moment holds his head with both hands at arms' length. Then he crashes the head down onto the bonnet, face first, so hard that the metal flexes in a loud *whoonk*.

Short Leg's resistance, such as it was, has ceased but Craig takes the head up again and brings it down again. This time he lets go, and Short Leg slides bloodily down the slope of the metalwork and slumps against the grille. The skipper's seen all this and is crawling to nowhere in particular, away from me and the blood on the car.

These are just impressions, dabs of paint. My head's spinning. Craig overtakes the skipper in a few bright steps and takes hold of him under both armpits, ramming him forwards and directly into the grille, just beside Short Leg. The sound is snapping plastic this time, and the meaty slap of the skipper's palms on the asphalt.

With the two of them bunched there as though the car had hit them, the happy man-child ambles back towards me. For a second I don't know what to expect—is he going to beat us all to a pulp? But his eyes fall slightly to my right. He picks up the fallen bat and weighs it with a lazy swipe through the air.

Then he turns towards Short Leg and the skipper, who still haven't moved.

I can't look. I have a rough idea how it's going to sound, but I can't look. As I bury my head I hear Wally's voice, faint and far away.

'Don't.'

Wally's got up and is shuffling towards Craig with a hand extended.

'Don't hit 'em. Thanks for, for…Don't hit 'em.'

The transformation in Craig is immediate: whatever animal trance had occupied him is gone, and he carefully helps Wally to sit down again, gathers the scattered gear and replaces it in the bag. The two Eastern Suburbs players find their feet, edging away. The keeper's nowhere to be seen.

I watch our saviour squat down before Wally, take him in both hands and look into his eyes.

'You good?' he asks. 'Okay?'

Wally nods faintly.

'Remember this, mate,' he gives Wally a little shake. 'Remember this. I'm your friend now. Anybody fucks with you, they're fucking with me.'

Grade Cricket

They're waiting at the lights. Indicator going *click-click, click-click*, brief orange flashes like snapshots of my situation. Sheet lightning in the darkness.

One shin bloodied.

The torn threads of the jeans leg standing to attention where the hole is.

A pair of ordinary brown shoes mobbed together under the cable ties.

The carpeted backs of the seats.

Could I rotate myself into a position to start kicking at the tail-light? Would it achieve anything, other than persuading them to stop the car and finish me off quickly?

In the middle of a string of hot days, January 1986, it's my turn to get up early and water and mow the pitch. I don't know how I got roped into this, why it has to be done at dawn. Wally's got some theory about water burning the grass if you do it in the middle of the day—I don't see why it can't be left until the cool change comes through and waters everything. So I'm up, stumping around in thongs making breakfast. TV's on in the living room to get the team for the one-dayer in the evening.

Desiccated white bread toast and a smear of marmalade because I can't find the cereal. Toast's got me thirsty so I look for the milk, and there's the cereal. Mum's put it in the fridge again.

There's a female voice coming from the TV; the news, Florida. *Special bulletin*, she says. And then I hear the distinctive monotone of mission control.

Obviously a major malfunction.

They run it again and again, the urgent repetition of the footage blurring live images into recorded vision. I wander into the living room and see the curlicue of smoke in the sky, the Medusa's head. On the ground, people weeping, hugging. Americans, all of them born to witness. Five-minute monologues straight to camera, even as they weep.

I'm chewing the toast mechanically.

The eastern light creeps past the edges of the blinds and into the house. Outside, traffic is starting to move, thinned by summer's lethargy. They're running official shots of the crew, focusing on one woman over and over again—Payload Specialist Christa McAuliffe, a civilian mother of two, blown to smithereens on live television.

Mum's in the shower as I pass the bathroom door. She hums sometimes when she forgets herself. Large water goes *crack* on the tiles. Small water sounds like rain.

Out the back I run the handmower over the pitch. The stubble of dried grass spins out from the blades, whirls in the air for an instant, landing soft on my feet as I pass. They'd formed an arc, the astronauts. A beautiful parabola in the sky projecting them at impossible speed heavenward. And something failed. Did they fail? Or the machinery, the fine orchestra of milled steel and glass and cables and fluids, was it that? Altitude and cataclysm. I've never considered their relationship before, certainly never heard of Icarus.

But as the wheel of the mower rolls over and flings the chopped grass at my shins, landing once again on the scar Wally gave me, I have a sense of consequence.

•

Later that same day Wally's at the wheel of Mum's dinged-up hatch-back with his P-plates up and Mum issuing directions from the passenger seat. She takes us through the bottom half of the city and down past Albert Park Lake and the Junction Oval, between perfect rows of palm trees.

The sun's out over the Junction, and a groundsman's pushing a heavy roller over the centre wicket. Wally's got his window down and he's sniffing the air like a happy mutt. Grass cuttings.

Along Fitzroy Street and round past the Esplanade Hotel, where ten years later I will put my tongue in a bouncer's ear and he will repay me with two broken ribs. Into Elwood, the streets named after poets—Byron, Shelley, Keats. Mum's slowing as she checks street signs. She gets us lost twice, even though the map is on her knees and she's rotating it every time Wally turns a corner.

Eventually we wander down a bluestone laneway to a small tin shed with a peeling timber door. A hand-painted sign above the door reads: *Hope Sweeney, Bootmaker*.

The small man who ushers us in reminds me of Burgess Meredith in *Rocky*: the pugnacious creasing of the jowls, the big knotty hands. Hell, he's even got a cardigan on. He greets Mum like she's his daugh-ter. The walls are covered in old shots of cricketers—Wes Hall, Ray Lindwall, Lindsay Hassett, even Dennis Keith Lillee. This man we've never heard of, who's currently dunking a teabag for our very own mum, is obviously Someone Important.

At first I think he might be one of Mum's barflies, but he's too vigorous for that. He's got a bulbous nose, but as far as I know all old codgers have bulbous noses.

He takes an A4 notebook from a pile on the bench, places it on the floor, says to Wally, 'Find a clean page, son.'

His voice is pure backyard Strine. Not the Brooklyn patois I was half listening for.

Wally starts leafing through the pages. Around us are piles of rolled-up fabric and materials, spools of thread, sewing machines, hammers and abstract cut-out shapes. The tumble of these things is just short of chaotic, a busy man's light-handed organisation.

Wally doesn't appear to have noticed his surroundings at all. He's still flipping the pages of the notebook, each of which has a traced pencil outline of a foot on it. Inside each foot, in sharp, spiky cursive, is written the name of the foot's owner, and his special requirements. *Charlie Griffith, calfskin, removable stops. Bruce Laird, ankle boot, rubber lining.*

And then a page with only two-thirds of a foot on it, a giant foot. *Joel Garner, long stops for wet grass. Kangaroo hide.* The top third of the foot, toes included, turns up on the following page. Wally's stopped breathing.

He finds a clean page and Sweeney hands him a pencil. Wally carefully draws around his foot and hands the pad and pencil back when he's done. His foot is only worth about three-quarters of a page, a short story among the great novels he's just passed. Sweeney looks at the outline over his heavy half-glasses.

'Is the other one the same?'

Wally, the literalist, can't see the joke. 'Y-yes sir.'

'Now, stand on the outline and press your weight down for me.'

Wally does as he's told. Sweeney makes some cryptic marks with a stubby pencil of his own, the gristly fingers clenched.

'Lift up on the ball of your foot'.

More hieroglyphs on the notebook.

'Good. Now you.'

He hands the pad and pencil to me. Mum's watching, pleased as punch, from a small cane chair near the door. A blade of dusty sunlight falls on her shoulders, and I can see stray hairs lifting away from her ponytail. She's beautiful.

I place my foot on the pad and watch while Sweeney makes his scratchings.

'Hey, Hope,' I say. 'You can just give me what Border takes. He's my man.'

Sweeney gradually straightens and peers into my eyes for a long time, seeing something in there he doesn't like at all. I find myself looking from him to Mum and back again.

'Fine, okay.' I mumble. He's grimacing.

'None of this is instantaneous, son. Doesn't just *happen*, you know. People put lifetimes into these things. Making boots. Batting...' He points at Mum. 'Raising children. Stuff that's worthwhile doesn't just...turn up.'

'I know.' I'm not sure why he's decided to pick on me.

He's scowling at me now, the canyons of his face all snaking south. 'I don't think you do.'

Wally's got his back to me, looking up at the photos. I know he didn't miss a word.

Half an hour later, old Sweeney's guiding us out the door. Mum gets a hug, Wally gets a firm handshake, eye to eye. The handshake offered to me is short and cursory. Our boots will be ready in a month. As we drive away I know this tough little man has read me clearly.

Rather than taking this as an indication that perceptive people can see my faults, I take it as a warning to avoid perceptive people at all costs.

•

In the winter of 1986, I know that school and I are about to part ways.

I'm halfway through year eleven. Wally's finished year twelve, is studying some shopkeeper's accounting course at TAFE while he works for Brewer's Sports and Leisure, two blocks from home.

Though I ridicule him about the job, which requires him to dress like a VFL trainer every day, we both know it's a splendid lurk—he gets to handle bats all day long, swishing them for customers, sometimes just shadow-batting under the fluoros. The times I go to visit him, he picks up a brand-new four-piece ball while we talk, flicks it from hand to hand. He's developing a sideline in leg spin: each flick of the ball involves a complex rolling of the wrist which I've tried (in secret) but never mastered. He shows me things around the shop—new gloves, helmets, training shoes. He gets to handle cash, even order stock.

But the highlight of any visit to the shop is when Bobby Brewer's out and we can slip into the indoor net.

The net is there so people can try out the gear—kick footballs or swing racquets, maybe face a cricket ball or two. But mostly it lies empty. I'll be at home, sometimes faking an illness or not even bothering, and the phone will ring. I race down there and Wally puts Hunters and Collectors' *Human Frailty* on the tape deck behind the counter. We slip into the net, resuming our endless hurl and crack as though it's the backyard.

The Brewer's job is a holding pattern for Wally, nothing more. So is the accounting diploma. In everything he does, he's waiting for fate to come and knock. Not in a passive way, but in the absolute assurance that his time will come; he merely needs to be available to answer the call.

But that's him: I was telling you about school.

History is dull but tolerable. Taught by a small, sad man in a vee-neck jumper with thick glasses and a moustache that says *I've given up*.

English I understand from my years pressed into the crook of Mum's arm. Melville, Verne, Conrad and Steinbeck. I know stories. What my classmates call my bullshitting—even while they laugh along with it—is just storytelling.

I have a tale in my head that's me and Wally and our future and it fits neatly with the contempt I feel for the sat-down life. Every time I relax into the tale, I'm adding chapters—the adulation, the beautiful girls. Centuries in Adelaide and Sydney and walking off the ground to rapturous applause in the golden light of a dying scorcher. Baggy greens on both our heads, lots of trips on planes. The public bar talk of us breaking records, of who'll get there first. And in my head, it's always me.

Hungrier, faster. More fearless. *The Keefe brothers, they're a phenomenon. But that young Darren, he's just got the edge.*

These are the things I dream about as school starts to slip away from me. The abrasive flats of Sunshine Tech reflect the winter light back at me, day after day.

Trigonometry brings on the first wave of despair. The zombie groans of sine, cosine and tangent would have chased me out earlier, if not for the intervention of the wonderful Emma Maric: a girl who wears jeans perfectly, who's got the accessorising swagger to sling her father's hunting belt round them, the little leather bullet loops vacant as though she's just emptied a magazine into a rhino.

Emma Maric understands trig as I never will but has the decency to despise it as I do. Or at least the tactical nous to fake it. When I tell Mum Emma's coming over to help me with my maths, she looks at me with pity. *Really?* she says, having looked Emma up and down.

The effectiveness of these tutorials depends on your point of view. We make progress on trigonometry if Wally and Mum are in the house. But if they aren't, or if they're preoccupied, we chance it on the bottom bunk, rolling and grunting and mashing our faces together until a desperate glance at her watch or mine forces us to disengage.

After these sessions we sweep through the dark streets on my ten-speed, Emma dinking on the rack above the rear wheel with her hands on my ribs. Sometimes we pass a quiet joint back and forth and sing to each other, the hedges and fences flying past, startled cat here, possum there. The ten-speed's got a bell on the handlebars—one of Mum's weird insistences—and sometimes I just let it rip, over and over, as we careen down the footpath.

Thinking of them now, they're all winter nights. Cold air on the face, knuckles burning. One night there's a hard rubbish collection on the nature strips, and we loop from house to house, sifting through their piles until we find a wood-grain television. We swap seats and I perch on the rack with the TV in my arms as we wobble all the way to her house. In ten minutes we've got it working perfectly, and in twenty minutes we've forgotten it's there, twisted in her doona and groping happily with our clothes on the floor.

And just down the hall from her room, the front door opens.

By the time the latch has finished clattering and her rhino-shooting old man has called *helloo*, I'm in the wardrobe and she's dressed. I can hear her greeting the folks, feigning boredom while I've got dry-cleaners plastic pressed against my screaming teenage balls. She boils the kettle for them. Asks them sweetly about their night out. Christ, they're talking about school.

At some stage she's said goodnight and closed the door softly behind herself. I don't recall it because I've fallen asleep in there among the coats. But she's with me all of a sudden, her soft mouth and the gentle skittering sounds of the hangers.

Our movements are small and charged now, perfect stealth, and I'm inside her, a secret place inside a secret place, her fingertips tracing electricity on my shoulders, and the world is ours alone for those golden fleeting minutes.

I suppose it ends with Emma in the way that teenage things usually do. One of us just forgets we owe anything to the other and moves on. At that age you understand that everything is alluring and everything passes. The colours are brighter, the music hurts like it's real. No one stays together long.

So Emma gets me through maths until my own selfishness or maybe hers undoes our arrangement, costing me a mid-year fail in year eleven and sealing the deal. I'm not repeating year eleven. I'm not going to be one of those nineteen-year-olds who finishes school with a driver's licence and a fiancée, for God's sake.

All this time, our new mate Craigo hovers in the wings. He has a way of placing himself side-stage in our lives, just there, just in the background. Emma's departure inches him into the frame without me even noticing it's happening.

We're standing in a nightclub queue, each of us clutching the birth extract certificates we've made out of blue ink and craft glue.

Mum doesn't know we're here. She knows Craig, but never inquires about his life. It's a surprising intuition of hers: Craig seems born of nowhere and no one. His garrulous nature subtly pushes any discussion of his origins into the background. So Mum thinks I'm staying with a kid from school I nominated, a reliable one. I don't know what Craig told his parents, whether they'd care, or even whether they exist.

We're both wearing Doc Martens and op-shop trench coats. I can hear The Cure thudding out from deep within the building. There are girls in the queue dressed like women, heavy makeup to put a few years on their eyes. Craig's disappointed Wally hasn't come, but it never feels like I'm second-class company.

I don't want the conversation to come around to school, but somehow it does.

'It's a waste of time,' he's saying. 'Keating left school at twelve and he's the fucking treasurer.'

Like a moron, I correct him. 'I'm pretty sure Keating was fourteen.'

'Well you're sixteen. What the fuck's holding you up?'

Craig's been working for the bookies at Flemington since he left school at the end of last year. He's a lackey of some kind, talks in turf dialect, laced with old-bloke terminology. *We had a thing in the fifth, got a rails run.* He even affects the trackside nasal twang, like he's holding a pair of binoculars under the brim of a trilby. He's verifiably a teenage kid with fistfuls of cash, bursting with impatience for adulthood, generous and secretive in equal measure. For my sixteenth birthday he buys me a top-shelf Gray-Nicolls bat. I check with Wally—he confirms with horror that it would be worth three hundred dollars, but it certainly didn't come through his position at Brewer's.

Craigo shrugs it off when I ask, and I begin to wonder. Has he bought me a bat, or has he *got* me a bat? The difference is slight, but carries a tiny edge of moral uncertainty.

Those moments of doubt are only fleeting. Being the objects of Craig's fixation makes us proud and confirms us in our belief that we're something special. It's the Big Guy who sets us on the paths of our own typecasting. Wally as responsible, grave: a leader. Me as a force of nature: a talented freak with no mooring.

It's tough getting the leaving-school idea past Mum.

She has a belief—I'm not too self-absorbed to see it—that me being in school is a form of insurance against a fate like hers. But where self-absorption takes over is in my unshakeable belief that I'll do better. I know that a buffer of education might have saved my undoubtedly clever mum from having to pour beer for rheumy old bastards. But I don't accept the third plank of the syllogism. I'm convinced it won't happen to me.

So she puts it back on me.

'If you're going to join the adult world,' she says, 'you can live like an adult.'

And living like an adult means moving out.

It might be some kind of bluff, like she'll spook me into staying a few more years. Or maybe she just knows in her heart that the small and perfect sanctuary she built for us against the world is outgrown now.

I discuss this earnestly with my fat turf-accountant mate. He assures me it's a piece of cake, the living out of home business, and he will find us a place. Somewhere a little closer to the great dormant dreamscape of the Eastern Suburbs.

We're deep into spring by the time he turns up with a rented trailer to collect my single bed and milk crates full of LPs. He's recently acquired a newish Commodore with a spoiler and mags, and the interior feels just like the nightclubs he likes. He's building a habitat around himself. This impression falls away a little, however, when we reach the destination—Cubitt Street, Richmond. It's a forgotten industrial laneway running north from the garment factories of the riverbank to the cluster of railway tracks that run out to the suburbs. Trams rumble in the distance. Aside from our place, a small timber cottage with its door on the street, there's a cluster of dark terraces across the road, screened and fortified with shards of broken glass in the cement and huge sheets of steel over the entrances.

I point it out as we draw up outside our future abode.

'Dennis's joint,' says Craigo. 'Don't think we'll drop in for a beer.'

As he backs the trailer, tongue-poking with concentration, I realise that our place has a little fortification of its own—a roller door to one side of the house, concealing a short driveway and a garage. It's not the sort of place you'd leave a car on the street.

In the first few weeks Mum visits often, bringing roast chooks and taking away my washing in baskets. It stings me occasionally when

I see her struggling to let go. Wally's transition into adulthood is more staged, more structured and painless. Mine is a rending of the fabric—I just left—and it's simple maths. The population of the Fernley Road house has dropped by a third.

But as the days go by she turns up at Cubitt Street less and less often. She doesn't like the place. Never says so, but you can sense it. She's seen a thousand losers and petty crooks, and she's looking at Dennis's joint out of the corners of her eyes when she comes and goes. Never sees *him*, thank God. He's a sight—short, fat, covered in blurry blue-green ink and heavyweight gold chains. Yellow eyes, carnivorous grin. Craigo disconcerts Mum sometimes, but Dennis is like Craigo dipped in hell.

Gurgling motorbikes turn up across the road deep in the night. There are fights, squealing tyres, even occasional gunshots. When they have parties over there, they manage to do it without a trace of festivity: it's grim and lewd, like dogs fucking. Each time the police visit, someone turns up on the fortifications afterwards with a welding rig to improve the barriers. Craigo reckons they've got an escape tunnel out the back onto the tracks.

I'm coming to a new understanding of the Big Guy through living with him.

There are aspects of his daily routine that are surprisingly spartan: he will eat only muesli for breakfast, hoofing it down between gulps of black coffee. His room is impeccably clean. He reads newspapers obsessively, reassembling their various component sections afterwards and stacking them by the kitchen door. Every week on a Friday afternoon he walks down to the old Italian nonna's place and gives her the stack. She thinks he's a good boy. The newspapers go on her tomato patch or something. He returns with jars of pomodoro, sometimes dried fruit.

He's tuned the kitchen radio to some classical station. If he can chance upon some opera while he's tooling around with the nonna's sauce, then that's about the happiest he ever gets. Given that Pacino's *Scarface* is running on almost constant loop on the VCR, I should be more alert to the nascent gangster fantasy: the opera, the charade of being a *good boy* for a nonna. Easy in retrospect, isn't it?

But the thing with Craigo, the thing that keeps you coming back, is that he's a giver. He gives me the Commodore because he's upgrading to a Skyline. Low-slung, darkened windows, and an air intake hump in the hood. The Big Guy has to pour himself in there, but once inside, it's his cave. The interior smells of his aftershave, and there's an array of membership and special parking stickers along the edge of the windscreen.

The Big Guy's found a job at a place called Corporate Vehicle Solutions, a hire-purchase joint for fleets. I can't imagine anything more boring. The racing caper I could relate to: hell, he was probably trading coded handshakes with some heavy characters, which is Craig's idea of fast times. But the car leasing crew is a bunch of fried-food-eating, bomber-jacket-wearing good-time guys sitting round in a badly fitted-out shopfront in Keilor, working the phones. Within a few short years, the advent of the internet will fill the days of such journeymen with online casinos and endless porn. But in the late eighties, it's hard to imagine what they do with their day once they've made their handful of useful phone calls.

The race-track inflection disappears from Craigo's speech within days of him taking up his new role, in its place something more unctuous. He's happier than ever, which in turn makes him even more tactile. And he still holds Wally in a kind of awe. On his rare visits to our place, Wally shares his views about the national side, about business and politics. The Big Guy laps it up, but Wally never stays long, never overindulges.

Although Craig knows lots of girls, none of them could be

formally termed a girlfriend. So I remain the chief object of his outsize affection. Sometimes he attacks me with a bearhug for no reason at all.

When September rolls around I shuffle between Richmond and Altona. Training for the district squad is Tuesday and Thursday afternoons, with optional extra fitness work on Wednesdays. Wally, you may have guessed, is a regular at the Wednesdays. I'm sporadic.

Mum comes to every day of every game, sometimes even to training. The pubs tend to roster the young kids on weekends to save on penalty rates, so her work rarely gets in the way. She likes to stand alone in the empty bleachers on the far side of the ground, marking the scorebook I bought her for her birthday; her sunhat on, head bowed over her work.

My club career with Altona follows an inevitable progression. Brought in from local cricket at sixteen with a fair bit of advance publicity, I'm like an allergen to the older blokes.

First practice session, they wait for me to start putting the pads on and then move themselves into my net: hard-faced men, much older, not looking to enjoy their Saturdays but eyeing a career. They mark out a longer run-up, charging in with renewed energy and aiming relentlessly for my head. The lazier ones don't have the backbone to bowl bouncer after bouncer, so they lob it flat and full, eye-height. They don't understand, any of them, that I was raised on cheap shots. Time after time, I hoik their deliveries into the net, over the net, even through the net. Now and then I catch a top edge and the ball rockets over the top and out into the carpark. When this happens, I like to lean on the bat and smirk as they trudge off to retrieve it. Once in a while they land a blow, and there's always a half-hearted apology or the suggestion that the ball might've slipped out of the hand.

But again, they don't know the history. In private, surrounded by the house and three paling fences of our backyard, Wally would follow up a stinging blow with a spray of invective.

I've worn black eyes for years. These dilettantes don't know the first thing about mental disintegration.

Which leads me to an odd thing about Wally. He's come to Altona with every bit as much advance publicity as I have, yet nothing changes when he turns up to bat. No one gets fired up. They bowl the usual assortment to him, nod politely when he scoops up their ball in his gloved hand and flicks it back to them.

He is denatured by batting.

As he waits, he's a helmeted statue, silent and implacable. I've never seen him brush a fly in that state. They could wander over his face, even up his nostrils and he wouldn't know. It seems like languor if you don't know what to look for. But it's the invisible building of energy and focus to a point of detonation, a form of biomechanical perfection only revealed in slow motion. Deadened eyes that don't squint or blink. Hands that follow the shortest path to the tiny point in time and space where contact will occur. Not an application of bodily force, but a harnessing of other forces.

When he misses a shot, as he rarely does, he raises a hand to stop the next bowler from running in, then swishes through phantom repetitions of the motion until he feels he's found the error and corrected it. Nobody minds him doing this. There is a complete absence of spite in his interactions, though he seethes with competitive intensity. Observers interpret his failure to fire up under provocation at the crease as evidence of phenomenal self-discipline, but that's inadequate. He *cannot* react: sledging him is as pointless as conversing with someone in headphones.

That's how he operates in public. In the backyard, he's vengeful, savage and petulant.

In September, we hear about the tied test in Madras: Dean Jones's double century in forty-degree heat, forty-five-degree heat—the numbers keep growing. I've heard they had to give him a transfusion from a coconut. Wally's contorted with scorn.

'Do they even *have* coconuts in Madras? And why would you get a transfusion from one if they did?'

'Dunno,' I reply lamely, 'heaps of people are sayin it.'

He slaps his thigh in derision. 'It's called an urban myth, dickhead.'

This is during one of our net sessions at Brewer's Sports. I look around and ensure there's no one else in the shop, then I charge straight at him and throw him to the ground. He's still laughing while I try to get a hand free to hit the smug bastard.

Three minutes later, a lady with two small boys has entered the shop and Wally's standing behind the counter smiling politely with his hair all over the place and one ear bright red from being crushed in my fist only seconds before. I'm standing slightly off to stage right, breathing hard and rearranging my shirt.

The woman looks askance at us, but leaves a tennis racquet for restringing.

One night at Altona, as dusk softens the colours of evening training, we're called over from the nets to the empty seats, where a girl not much older than us is waiting. We're introduced by a club official: Amy Harris is from the local paper, a cadet journalist sent to do a story on the school-age prodigies playing first-grade for Altona.

Her brown hair's pulled back into a tight ponytail. No makeup. She's tall and athletic-looking, dressed for work, not display. I like her immediately. She snorts when Wally tries to impress her by quoting from C. L. R. James: 'What do they know of cricket who only cricket know?'

'I dunno,' she counters. 'What *do* they know?'

Wally's crestfallen, and I'm left with an opening to field the next few questions. She's done her research, even knows somehow about Mum and Dad. Her questions to me are all angled at my character; Wally's are all about his cricket. It takes me a while to latch onto this, but like an idiot I play extravagantly into her hands.

'See, I don't think there's much public interest in purists,' I say. 'Cricket's getting shorter and faster, and people don't want to see the ball gliding along the ground. They want action. Drama. That's what we bring. Bradman is dead.'

Wally's looking at me with unconcealed horror. He tries to take the conversation back. 'Everyone brings their own approach of course,' he says stiffly.

But she ignores him. Instead, she's spurring me on. 'Do you have the potential to play for Victoria?'

'No doubt at all.'

'For the country?'

'Pretty likely.'

'And you, Wally? What are your ambitions?'

'I'd rather let my batting do the talking.'

She snorts again. 'That's a cliché, isn't it?'

'It's the truth.'

She's writing in a spiral-bound notebook as we talk. The plastic biro hovers momentarily. She chews the other end of it lightly as she forms the next question.

'Do you two get along?'

'Of course we do,' snaps Wally angrily, just as I'm saying, over the top of him, 'Mostly.'

Faint smile.

'I'm going to make a note in my diary to talk to you two at the end of the season, and again this time next year. Would that be okay?'

I find myself agreeing enthusiastically. Wally's more circumspect. The photographer, who's waited just beyond her left shoulder, now pushes forward to get his shots. I look straight down the barrel, aping the boorish invincibility of Botham. Wally looks away over the ground, towards the scurrying players in the soft light.

The next day, the image appears across half a page, strangely beautiful. Wally's face is all shadows and dreams, his decision to look away cloaking him in remoteness. I'm captured by his image for so long, wondering if I really know him at all, that it takes me a while to see myself. No mysticism there: I look dumb and aggressive. And the story appears under a headline I should have seen coming.

Bradman is Dead.

State

More lane markers thirrupping under the tyres.

Consciousness ebbing, the past playing out in living colour as the blackness in the boot consumes me. The world I left behind. Lost in time; discarded by a series of choices. The things I can't retrieve.

My fingers have chanced upon another shard of the tail-light. I can't tell if it's from the lens or the plastic backing—cornea or retina. It's triangular, a matchstick in length. I can tumble it from finger to finger, though I can't fully grip it because of the pressure of the cable ties. If I stretch my hands downwards, I can make the tip of the shard reach the cable ties and rub them lightly.

But I'm not sure that should be my priority. The tape over my mouth is driving me insane. It's irrelevant to releasing my bonds, though, and there's only so much effort I can apply. I don't know where to start.

●

If there's a corner that you turn at some point, mine was New Year's Eve 1989.

I mean, that's not strictly true because you turn corners all the time. Life is comically pointless and composed almost entirely of corners, like a go-kart track.

On the last night of 1989, when the Berlin Wall's been disintegrating for months, attacked by frosty-looking Germans in dark anoraks, David Hasselhoff is inexplicably there. Exploiting it as his personal contribution to the downfall of the Soviet bloc.

I'm on a mustard-coloured corduroy couch with Craig when Hasselhoff appears on the telly in the world's most bizarre jacket—imagine the Fonz's black leather motorcycle jacket, but with pulsating waves of tiny light globes all over it—and he's standing on the Wall ('Christ, the Wall!' screams Craigo. 'People get shot for lesser jackets!') singing a vaguely freedom-themed big-hair anthem, like the song itself could break concrete. Maybe it could, the way he sings.

Craig and I have been on the bongs for a couple of hours by this stage and it's more than we can take. The pipe *du jour* is a china dragon with a snarly mouth and flared wings. You pull on the top of his head, and the cone goes in a little mount in the region of what would presumably be a dragon's lumbar spine. Craig's roaring with laughter, his belly wobbling up and down as his hand fumbles around for some kind of handbrake on the hilarity and he snorts as he struggles to get air in. A thrashing foot takes out the bag of Twisties, the china dragon and four or five stubbies on the coffee table.

And still the Hoff is yowling. The crowds below him are rapturous at first but as the same dirge-like verses loop over and over they visibly tire of him. Someone lobs a firecracker at him, and he ducks it mid-chorus.

Craig has sensed the mood of impatience in Berlin: he leans forward and kills the telly, turns to me with the last vestiges of a chuckle dying round his cheeks. 'I gotta go get something.'

There's a jangling sound as he scoops up his car keys.

'Can't it wait? It's, what, two a.m.'

Since we've rented the Richmond place together, we've had a loosely synchronised life. He works for the leasing company by day, while I train and annoy Wally at the shop. Then he disappears at night and I sometimes tag along to clubs and bars, but more often I leave him to his other life, whatever it is. Every so often it comes down to these Nights of the China Dragon and VB in front of the box. The ritual is a particular favourite of his. So the idea of him wanting to run errands at this hour is a little perplexing.

'Coming?'

'Where?'

'Just gotta get something. What's this, the Spanish Indecision?'

I'm too stoned to argue and quietly intrigued about what Leasing Boy might be up to.

'Relax, you fat fuck. Bring the Twisties.'

•

We're going to Doveton, apparently. In the dark interior of Craig's Skyline, we're locked in one of those long silences that car travel and cannabis can produce. Every few minutes an idiotic smile spreads over my face.

Later we're deep among tilt-slab factory walls, the wrappers of two burgers at our feet. Craig's counting off numbers and names along a concrete apron. *WM Ready Panel Works*, *Permafilm Industrial Coatings*, *Aquarium Supplies Ltd*. He brakes gently outside U-Store Self Storage and jumps out, sorting through his keys before a huge roller door.

'Whose place is this?' I ask.

'Just some guys from FLS.'

'They do a lot of business pre-dawn?'

Craig finds the key and hauls the door up, ignoring me. Down a narrow corridor, we come to a smaller roller-door. Inside, a miniature city of office equipment: copiers, printers, faxes, computer terminals. There's a lot of polystyrene packaging and stacked cardboard.

Against one wall is a piece of machinery I don't recognise. It's not electronic.

'What's that?'

Craigo's already on one end of it, lifting from the floor. 'Grab the other end, will you?'

We haul the thing out of the storage bay and into the back of the Skyline. On the way home, he tells me it's a pill press.

Yeah, I know.

Well, I do now. At the time, I truthfully didn't have the slightest notion of what that meant or why someone would want one.

'Remember the pills we had at Pulse, the night you'd made that ton against Northcote? Well that's MDMA. The kids are calling it ecstasy. You make it in a garage for nothing and sell it for fifteen bucks a pill. Almost pure profit. Cut it with ketamine, it's even cheaper.'

'What's ketamine?'

'You don't wanna go into that. Put it this way, it's to do with horses.'

'So,' I probe, feeling the giggles wear off, 'the thing in the back?'

'I'm going into business with some guys,' he says.

I feel a tug of sadness at these words.

I get it, I get it—he's already been in business for some time. I've looked the other way because I prefer my version of Craigo, the affable fat man, mister dependable. Buying and selling for mates, moving a few things. Harmless, gormless. These 'guys' feel like an infidelity to me. Fair enough, he's been drifting away from Wally for years. But that's more Wally's fault. I've been staunch.

I'm sullen on the way home, sluggish and silent.

The pill press shifts with a clunk as we swing onto Punt Road; a blind corner, as it happens. We're deep into the turn, committed, when we both see the lights. A dozen cops with witches hats and a queue of cars.

Breath-testing station.

I look at Craigo, who's looking at the road, assessing options. He appears shrewder and harder than I've ever known him. He rolls conservatively into the queue and we wait in silence, until a young officer approaches his window with the breatho in his hand.

'Had any alcoholic drinks tonight sir?'

'I have,' smiles Craigo. 'Had a couple an hour or two ago.'

'One continuous breath until I say stop, thanks.'

Craig blows. The cop holds the device and he's looking. Looking in the back. The device buzzes, but the cop's not looking at it. He's still looking in the back. Craigo's got a hand on the transmission. The cop returns his attention to the breatho.

'Do you have far to go?'

He's a junior conny, this bloke, trying to muster a senior voice. The queue ahead's inching forward.

'No, no, couple of hundred metres. Why?'

The car in front is clear to go but it hasn't left.

'You're just under. What's your address? I...er...' He shoots one more look in the back. 'You better give me a look at your licence, mate.'

The car's cleared the breatho station and it's just us now. Us, with a dozen cars queued behind and I'm pressed into the seat as Craigo punches the accelerator. In a second, we've cleared out and left the roadblock in a cloud of smoke. My heart's hammering.

Out the back window, past that fucking press, there's cops running all over the place. Car doors opening and closing. Suddenly I'm in Craig's lap because he's thrown the car left and raced up a side street. Cult on the stereo, very fucking loud. 'She Sells Sanctuary'. I crash into the passenger window as he swings right down an alleyway.

'Will you do up your fucking belt?' he yells. 'You'll get us both in trouble.'

I can hear sirens now but there's no sign of lights. They're well behind, and Craigo's still snaking through the narrow lanes of Richmond, bottoming the Skyline out in the bluestone dips at the crossroads.

The streets again become familiar to me and he slows, crawling to a stop in our drive. In seconds he's out and the roller door's closed, the car completely concealed. I wonder now at what a goose I've been—is this why he chose the place?

We jump out and he's straight round the back, hauling the pill press out. As we heave the thing onto the front step, I can't help myself.

'Craigo you dumb fuck, you've gotta go back. They're gonna have your plates.'

He looks at me, looks back at the car.

'No, mate. They're gonna have that guy's plates.'

I look back at the Skyline, at the rego it didn't have yesterday. Stolen.

•

It's a restless night, as I'm sure you'll appreciate.

I leave Craigo banging and crashing in his room and try to catch a couple of hours before dawn. I'm normally okay doing this. In fact, I've scored big runs doing this. But this time I'm just chasing sleep and I wake up foggy and depressed. Craigo tells me it's the hydroponic dope. Skunk, he says, nasty herbover. I'll get us some good bush stuff.

In the middle of this exchange the phone rings: Wally, saying a letter turned up at Mum's yesterday, and it's a VCA envelope.

Over at Mum's place, I see the familiar Nissan parked in the drive. Louise, Wally's girlfriend of six months, perhaps even more morally constipated than he is. Louise is studying community development at the Footscray Institute. Wants to be an aid worker in Tibet. I trust they're having sex—Christ I hope for his sake they're having sex—but she won't move in with him because she thinks it wouldn't be *special* then. I've never heard her say this, of course—what I've heard is Wally reporting it in this smarmy tone like he's explaining it to an eight-year-old. I don't even know where to begin with my exasperation: getting lectured on sexual ethics by a man with almost zero miles on the clock, or just her general appropriation of my brother. Her taking liberties with my family.

Parking in our driveway, for instance. First a bunch of 'guys' take up occupation inside my best friend's soul like some alien life form, and now Wally has become Occupied Territory.

He greets me at the door, big grin on his face. We sit around the kitchen bench; me, Mum, Wally, and Louise, who is wearing some sort of ethical hemp. Wally's got his arm around her as I rip into the VCA envelope. He seems proud.

I read through the letter. It's only short, and when I'm done I read it again to let the good bits sink in.

I'm in the state squad.

I'm twenty, I'm the leading run-scorer in Victorian district cricket and I'm in the state squad. I can go to their office in Jolimont, collect my uniform and sign a contract this week. Blue cap. Tours, sponsored gear. They're going to pay me to play cricket.

I study Mum intently, searching for any sign of what this means for her. Her eyes are happy, above the sad crease that always runs from her cheeks to the sides of her mouth. At forty-one, she's spent more of her years looking after us than she has living a life of her own. She likes Louise, trusts her; she knows Wally's found a kindred spirit.

At the moment Louise is fiddling with her purse on the kitchen bench with her long, clean fingers; Mum jumps up and starts fussing

JOCK SERONG

with the kettle. I watch her flip the switch and boil it twice before she gets round to the teabags. As she makes tea I'm looking at the little routines of her kitchen, the neat pile of papers, the other pile with the clippings she's cut about Wally and me.

Lists.

She's always writing lists: she even writes down things that are routine and recurring. *Put bins out. Spray whites before wash.* Her lovely handwriting, nearly as familiar to me as her voice.

Tucked in a little magazine rack on the end of the bench against the wall, I can see the spiral binding of the scorebook we gave her for this year's birthday. I'm flicking through it, I'll admit, to find the days I outscored him. And I'm slowing down as I'm flicking because something's wrong. In the end I'm staring at a solitary page. In fear of being caught, I shove the book back into the rack.

Wally's locked his eyes on me and he tilts his head towards the back door.

There's a bat and a bucket of balls in the laundry. He bats first as he's always done. The grass is perfectly mowed, the edges cut straight, and the bald patches where bowler and batsman stand have had a chance to recover since we played last.

'Lawn looks good,' I say. 'Mum hired someone?'

I let go a short one, aiming for his ribs. He rocks onto the back foot and smashes it into the Apostouloses' fence. The bang on the palings won't raise any reaction these days: old man Aposta died last winter, keeled over near his front gate, and Mrs Aposta doesn't cook anymore. Mum reckons she's just withering away, picking at meals on wheels.

'Mum can't afford it, you fuckwit. I did it.'

I go long, aiming a full ball at his toes, but missing the length by enough inches that it reaches him as a half-volley and he straight drives past me. His backlift is high today, his follow-through extravagant.

88

He's stinging inside, batting out his aggression.

'You can't be far off, mate. Half the squad's up for national selection.'

He doesn't appear to hear me. Misses an easy one outside off with an angry swoosh of the bat.

I try again. 'I thought you'd be happy for me.'

'I am,' he says bitterly.

He swings the bat though phantom arcs as I hold the ball. Yes, I was fortunate, but I deserved it. The fact that he also deserved it is none of my doing. I'm a lucky guy. Just am.

'Bowl the fucking ball,' he says. Every muscle in his body is tensed. But I hang onto the ball.

'Something's wrong with Mum.'

He straightens up, exasperated. 'What? She's fine.'

'Have you looked at her? She's lost weight.'

'So what? Prob'ly menopause.'

'Is that even a symptom of menopause?'

'Oh excuse me, *doctor.*'

'You know that scorebook we gave her?'

'Yeah.'

'Ever looked inside it?'

He shrugs a little. 'Nah. Why?'

'It's all fucked up.'

'What do you mean?'

'Full of nonsense numbers. Stuff that doesn't add up. Big gaps between things, like she's...'

'So fucking what? She probably doesn't know how to score.'

'Wally, she knows more about cricket than you and I do. She knows how to score.'

He's silent for a moment, but the look on his face makes his contempt very clear.

'There's one page in there, this is only eight weeks ago, that's just hundreds and hundreds of threes. They're all just threes. And she forgets stuff all the time.'

He scoffs at this. 'Like you don't,' he mutters. 'Bowl the fucking ball.'

So I drop one short. Dig it right in and watch it rear up towards his head. For a split second it takes him by surprise, but then he's onto it, swinging through a hook shot that carries it far over the back fence. There's a loud crash as it knocks over something in the neighbours' yard. We don't even know those neighbours, he's hit it so far.

'Go and get it,' I say.

'Fuck you,' he responds, and then, almost as an afterthought, he throws the bat on the ground and charges at me, catching me off-guard around the middle.

We both collapse in a grunting heap, but with his momentum he's managed to get astride my back. He grabs hold of my head and drives my face deep into the lawn, a manoeuvre I recall from our early child-hood. I can smell soil down there. The answer is to push even further forward until you can get your knees up under your chest, then buck him off forwards like a rodeo horse. I try this, but he's moved his grip so he's got both my ears. The pain is excruciating, especially once my move takes effect and he does topple forward. Now his entire weight is being supported by my ears. I'm roaring, God knows what I'm saying, but he's totally silent, intent on inflicting as much pain as possible.

He's down on one shoulder with his arse high in the air from where he spilled forward, so I take the obvious opportunity and fish around the front of his Young Liberal chinos until I find his balls. Then I grind them good and proper, and sure enough, he releases his grip. For a moment or two we both roll around on the grass moaning, and then I'm conscious that the women are standing above us. Hands on hips, heads shaking in dismay.

'What the hell was that about?' Mum demands. She doesn't look remotely frail now.

Wally's up first, dragging a sleeve across his nose. 'Nothin.' He takes out his puffer, administers a few squirts. I watch with a stab of long-forgotten terror.

'You two are pathetic,' says Mum. 'Twenty and twenty-two! Do I have to send you both to your rooms? And you—' she points at me, dammit. 'If you're going to play for the state, could you try to avoid these scenes in front of large crowds? Dear me.'

•

I celebrate the state selection with a bender.

Wally comes out early and puts in a decent effort at the pub. He and Craig are like long-lost friends, arm in arm, singing songs and slopping beer on each other. Craig, as always, wants the benefit of Wally's wisdom, has to be prised off him when Wally starts making *gotta go home* faces.

The rest of the night's a blur to me now, unexceptional. Except there's this girl.

Carly.

Craig introduces me to her, though she seems to know who I am. There's some leather. Leather top maybe? Heavy black eyeshadow contrasted against white, white skin, like a sexually charged panda. Her arms round my neck, her tongue in my mouth on the dance floor, and I'm instantly aware of the clacking of metal against my teeth. She withdraws, flashes me a wild grin and pokes out the tongue, coloured lights reflecting off the ball-bearing stud in the centre of it.

Carly is a naughty girl. Naughty in the cab on the way home, and uncontainable once the bedroom door slams behind her.

But when she wakes, late and harshly lit by unforgiving morning sun, she wants to talk. I've got no aversion to learning a little about the person who's wandered into my life overnight, but she's maudlin and more interested in talking than checking in on whether I'm listening.

She tells me she's twenty-two, a teenage runaway, lived on the streets for a little bit and then got into stripping. The place where she worked in King Street was run by bikies. Small timers aspiring to Comanchero affiliation. The manager kept a close eye on her. Huge man, scars, tatts, filthy beard. Stank, she says. Pretty quickly, what began as professional protectiveness turned into ownership. Her body was his. Her social life was his. Her very thoughts were his. The sex was punishing. He bought her things, gave her a place to sleep and endless cash, but at the cost of her freedom. He watched her day and night, on occasions raining violence on other males unlucky enough to show an interest. He bought her an abortion and—she clutches them proudly—'these tits'.

At this stage, I'm lying propped on one elbow, smiling pleasantly but beginning to think *how the hell did your world and mine collide?*

He hit her sometimes, threatened her.

Jesus, I think, *I need this girl to get out of here*, and I do not want to get tangled up with whoever this guy is.

She leans closer, takes my chin so she can peer into my head. 'Do you know what it feels like to be somebody's possession, Darren?'

So anyway, she goes on, she's free now. He got tangled up in some shit or other, took a baseball bat to a rival. Pulverised him. Fractures that needed plates and screws. Brain injuries leading to months of rehab. Left him a wreck, she'd heard. Incontinent, dependent. But the upside is the cops picked up her beloved boyfriend when he was getting his own injuries seen to, and now he's doing seven with a five.

There's a bell ringing somewhere in the back of my mind. A nagging indicator of something wrong, something bad. I can't place it.

Then I can. 'What's this guy's name?'

She smiles, knowing she's got her finger on the button that says TERROR. 'Brett Freer.'

I'm thinking frantically now.

'They call him something else. The Dog...?'

She sees my panic, takes her time.

'The Pitbull.'

'Fuck. Brett "The Pitbull" Freer?'

She nods.

'Oh Jesus, could you not have told me this before you stuck your tongue in my mouth?'

She pats my chest. 'You seemed pretty willing.'

She steps from the bed, pulls her legs through her jeans. 'And he's locked up,' she says defensively. 'So stop carrying on.'

She watches me as she works her hair free of the leather jacket.

'You got a toothbrush I can use?'

·

I get a call from Amy Harris within days of the state selection.

She's a sports reporter now for a metro daily in Sydney. Flying down to do other stuff, she says, and wants to talk about my news. Two voices in my head; always two voices. Tell her to get fucked, apropos of *Bradman is Dead*. Or blow my trumpet like always. Hey, look at me: state squad, just like I said.

I meet her over a rear table at the Richmond Club on Swan Street, the nearest thing we have to a local in our blasted post-industrial neighbourhood. She's there before me, eyes down, fiddling with a tape recorder. She's dyed her hair blonde; more than blonde, a hard corporate platinum that startles me at first. It sweeps precisely across one corner of her forehead, curving away from her ear and resting exactly at her collar. I can only see the top half of her above the table, formally composed like a newsreader, and she's a study in poise and intent, a glass of water by her wrist. Where the white shirt parts over her breastbone there's a delicate silver chain lying on her skin, a bright crucifix at the end of its curve. I swoop in, aiming to plant a kiss on her cheek but she deftly withdraws and offers me a hand.

I'm trying to process these things when she starts the tape recorder, takes me through the selection news.

We talk team balance, the coming season, my ambitions and thoughts on the coaching staff. Then she asks me if I was surprised to get the jump on Wally.

'I'm not surprised,' I tell her. 'The whole thing's inevitable, you know? If it'd been Wally first, then me, I don't think it would've upset me. We're two halves of a whole. He'll get there soon enough.'

'Was he angry?'

I can't help laughing. Not by his standards he wasn't. He could've sunk a knee into my windpipe like he did the time I smashed his bat on the apricot stump.

'No, he was fine. He's very patient. I'm telling you, it's just a matter of time.'

She's watching me like a bug in a jar. 'Your mate Craig. He takes a keen interest in your career?'

Now *this* I didn't see coming. 'Craig?'

'Craig Wearne. Your housemate. Works in, um...' she rubs a finger on a bead of moisture left by the glass. 'Vehicle leasing.' Her eyes follow the finger on the table, lashes lowered.

'This is sports reporting?'

'I also do police stories,' she looks up sharply from the finger. 'Courts.'

'Craig's a good friend,' I stagger.

'Wally doesn't hang out with him.'

A statement, not a question. Contrasting.

'Not much. No.'

'Mm.' She clicks off the tape recorder.

I know I'm supposed to be attuned here. Supposed to know that the media aren't there in my interests. But this intrusive stranger defies judgment.

'I'm not someone who turns off the recorder, Darren. But you seem a nice guy. So I'm going to say this to you once: I've got a keen interest in Craig Wearne, and so have a number of other people. *You*, Darren, you are someone who should not have a keen interest in Craig Wearne.'

I'm floored. 'What are you talking about?'

'You heard of Pitbull Freer?'

A hot jolt of alarm spreads through me. I don't know if she can detect it, but she's watching me closely.

'Everyone has. He was on the front page of the paper.'

'Yep, and he's about to be again. The Court of Appeal just granted him leave to appeal his conviction. He could be out in two weeks. How does that make you feel?'

I laugh, but she knows how the news makes me feel. How the hell does she know?

'I'm fine thanks.'

She shrugs. 'And I don't have to tell you anything more. Like I said, this is further than I'd normally go.' She runs a finger over the tape recorder, presses 'record' again. Flicks her hair back.

'So, how's your fitness going into the season?'

Gestation

I've lost count of the number of times I've dropped the little shard of plastic.

I chose to work on the cable ties rather than the gag, only because I couldn't think of any way to rip the tape off without my hands free.

The trick to working the shard is like that thing you see Vegas card sharks doing with a gambling chip, rolling it from knuckle to knuckle until it lodges between Squibbly and forefinger like a plectrum. I'm sure it would be a lot easier if I wasn't slumped on top of my hands, and if Squibbly had any feedback to offer, but of course he doesn't. Again and again, the shard rolls across the tangled knuckles, only to tumble out halfway across. And each time that happens, I spend an eternity feeling around on the prickly synthetic carpet of the boot's floor, trying to locate it again.

It's keeping my mind off things, this little game. But I have to assume the people in the front aren't going to let me play all night.

•

It all comes to pass exactly as we expected: Wally gets picked by late February, and for the duration of that summer it's me in at four and him at number five for the state side.

The previous summer was a lean time for the side. There was a coaching blow-up, a players' walkout, a home-ground redevelopment necessitating temporary training facilities, and a dozen other minor shitfights that collectively sapped morale and plunged the side to the bottom of the table.

But we arrive after the deluge, Wally and I. New coach, new blood, an air of determination. The side becomes a formidable unit. And it happens within weeks—there's no process of forging, of grafting towards something. It's just *wham*, success. And just as suddenly we're recognisable, in a way members of a losing team can't be.

Once the initial glow of state selection wears off, the real world asserts itself. For me, this means school visits, clinics. I don't know how many kids' arms I have to hold up straight over these seasons. *Make a windmill, Joshua.* The money's good, or good enough to keep up the rent on the Richmond house, clubs on the weekends, a new set of wheels through the Big Guy.

For Wally, his natural tendency towards the monastic intensifies.

He's now a graduate in sports science with a diploma in business administration and a master's degree in sanctimonious bullshit. Nutrition has become his chosen battleground: he demands that the squad staff have everyone pinch-tested for fat.

He's gone vegetarian, does yoga, runs long-distance. He and Louise have put a deposit on a house and then installed tenants in it because, God help me, 'it's tax-effective'. She's running the Melbourne office of a global charity, and is one of the only people I know who has a mobile phone. Needless to say, Craigo is another.

But the differences between Wally and me don't amount to much in the statistics. And cricket is above all else a dance of numbers. At one in our willingness to crush our opponents, it's only at the end of a day's play that our lives diverge: his to puritanism, mine to the piss.

Four weeks before the final match of the season, I'm asked to turn up to a radio show promotional thing. It's mid-week, Valentine's Day in fact, and I'm suspended in space between a hangover and a training session, unenthused. Team polo shirt, runners, the official Victorian team slacks. Neat, short hair with woolly undergrowth sprouting down the neck. Back then, it was the day-off uniform. Appropriate, prestigious. Now, you see a photo and you laugh.

I wander up to reception at the radio station and they buzz through to the publicity department for someone called Honey. This'll be good, I think. Honey from Publicity.

But when the door swings open and Honey from Publicity enters, she's not at all what I expect. Short, dark, lit up by a smile that seems real. She takes a strand of hair between her fingers and sweeps it behind an ear as she shakes my hand. Just for an instant I forget my name.

The phone rings again behind the reception desk, and after a brief exchange, the receptionist looks up at me and pushes the phone receiver in my direction.

'It's for you,' she says. 'Your mother.'

When I take the phone and hear her voice it's clear that something's up. Something's different. She's worried, maybe, but elated, too. Tense. She runs through a few pleasantries while I wonder what she's up to. Yes, Mum, I'm doing a radio interview. Yes, I remembered it's Valentine's Day. No, I don't have anyone to take out tonight. It *is* a lovely day outside, Mum, yes. Eventually I have to pull her up, while giving Honey, who's standing at a polite distance, an apologetic look.

'So…I'm about to go on air, Mum.'

'Oh.' Long pause. 'Well, look. It's about your brother, Darren. He's gone and got Louise pregnant.'

A delicious feeling sweeps over me. Mister Organised. Mister Controlled. Miss Career-Focused. *Hilarious.*

'Oh Mum, that's just lovely,' I say, barely containing my misconceived delight.

'It's not,' she says sharply. 'And don't be a smart-arse. I'm surprised it wasn't you, frankly.'

Her voice changes to a more plaintive tone. 'They're just bloody kids. Christ, what was he thinking?'

'Ah, they can get rid of it. Can't be that hard.'

'We won't be talking like that,' she says fiercely. 'We will *not* be talking like that.'

I mumble my way through a confused sort of apology, and end the call by promising to give him a ring.

As I hand the receiver back to the receptionist, I'm conscious that I had no reason at all to sneer. It *could* have been me and any one of a number of girls. Of course it wasn't my place to suggest a termination. Sometimes I'm amazed by my ability to open my mouth and just hear my own unedited thoughts fall out.

'Sorry about that,' I mumble to the waiting Honey. 'My brother's pregnant.'

'Really?' she replies, wide-eyed with amusement.

She leads me into the studio, leaves and returns with a glass of water. They sit me at a console, put the cans on my head and the panel lights up. A pallid announcer with a Winfield baritone does his pre-fab hocum then introduces me. *Victoria's new star batsman*, he says. *Big hitting bad-boy*, he says.

Wally and Louise are having a baby.

A long glass wall lines one side of the studio, over the announcer's shoulder. Through it I can see the couches of the green room, a couple of large speakers no doubt transmitting our studio. A separate door to the green room opens soundlessly, and from where I sit I can see Honey enter. She plonks down casually on the arm of a couch and watches us, gives me a tiny smile. Her hand rises from her lap and wiggles a little wave. A feeling more complicated than lust is rising within me.

The announcer's going through the motions. Favourite ground (no one likes to hear a Victorian say it, but it's the 'Gabba), scariest fast bowler (Fed Collins), is it true you and your brother fight like cat and dog? (no, complete nonsense), and then the opening I've been looking for.

'Okay Darren, seeing as it's Valentine's Day, who's your dream date?'

I look directly at the window. 'That's easy. It's Honey from your publicity department.'

I can see her mock-shrieking, burying her head in her hands. The DJ loves it; looks over his shoulder and throws an unrequited high five towards her. Later, she gives me her home phone number, written in neat black pen on the back of a RAD FM business card. She tells me this is the most embarrassing day of her life, and that I owe her dinner.

And though I desperately want to repay that debt, I carry the card around for days before I can summon the courage to call her.

•

So it falls to me to explain how things change over the next two years of my life. How I hit a still point, where the better side of me is given air and water and light.

Honey Nicholson plays an ingenious hand early on.

She holds me in suspense, willing captive to the belief that she's preoccupied, barely finding time for me. She fails to ring for days, then calls and apologises, or turns up late at night, sweeping away my feigned sulking with her soft hands and her mouth. She's smart enough to stay away from cricket, keeping our interactions on her own terms and within reach of her many strengths.

I blow up from time to time—please don't go thinking this is an epiphany. A few all-nighters; half a dozen vehicular mishaps. There are those close to me who find the prospect of a stable, dependable Darren Keefe alarming, and they set about doing all they can to upend me. Spiked drinks and other attempts to start little prank wars, astonishing sexual invitations, emotional manipulations.

In October, Craig convinces me to head out with a crew of the state cricketers to celebrate the birth of little Hannah Keefe, the tiny pink niece-blob I've been cradling at the hospital during the afternoon. The warm blankets on my forearms, the miniature squeaks of her breath, the new light that radiates from Louise: all of it is rewiring me in subtle ways I can't place.

She has paperskin hands, Hannah Keefe, and they clutch my little finger. Her half-seeing eyes are trained towards warmth.

God. I'm an uncle. I'm anuncle. I'm a nuncle.

You're not the same these days, the boys slur that night. I laugh and throw beer on someone. There's a fight with security, staccato conversations with cricketers of the suburban park kind who demand to talk, who skitter and twitch unpredictably behind their speed-fouled eyes. They might be fine. They might also strike from behind for no other reason than to see if they can take down Victoria's number-three batsman. They evaporate along the way and there's a walk through a park somewhere in St Kilda, I think alone, then another nightclub.

Searing jabs of sound and thuddery bass I can't distinguish from my heartbeat. Blades of light cutting into my eyes, people swaying like marine growth, no sign of the walls, where are the walls. A kebab, Hindi music with a cab driver, coins spilling everywhere from my discarded jeans, face-first collision with an empty bed. I've thrown up somewhere, I can taste it, but I don't know where.

The spinning sensation, the tinnitus. The bedside lamp, burning hot and constant until dawn, keeping the dark at bay. I'm afloat on an anaesthetic river of tequila, lit from inside. Like a paper lantern drifting downstream.

Honey's smart enough to stay away from nights like this.

Honey's got a career, principles. She warms more and more towards Louise, talks to her in female asides that, far from disconcerting me, sound like unimpeachable intimacy. She minds the baby, and does it with ease. The baby is a little sun, the centre of our universe. We talk about her when we're alone. We wonder if that's normal.

Honey darts out when summoned by Louise for comfort, for the howling, clenching nights of mastitis. Often neither Wally nor I am around, called away interstate by the game. But Honey doesn't see her role with Louise merely as an extension of her relationship with me. She's from a big family and feels no burden in these duties. Takes no credit for them either.

•

At work, Wally is outstripping me in everything but flamboyance. His attitude to practice, his obliging way with the media. His ease with the authorities. He mounts performances on the field with monotonous consistency, until his results make an undeniable case for test selection. Everyone is talking about his *temperament*, like he's a show dog. Wally Keefe will roll over. Wally Keefe will not snarl or bite. Behold his glossy coat: Wally Keefe could be a future national captain.

One columnist says he'd pay to watch Darren Keefe because something amazing might happen, but he'd bet the house on Wally Keefe, because the necessary *will* happen. Journalists love the potential clichés we suggest: Cain and Abel, Jekyll and Hyde, Noel and Liam. They know intuitively that we represent something latent on every suburban lawn where a newspaper lands. We are the inseparable siblings every parent worries for: good boy, bad boy. Total connection and fratricidal rage.

The selectors are in no doubt. In the December of his second state season, just weeks ahead of the Boxing Day test, Wally is selected for the national side. There is no ugly backyard stand-off between us over the promotion, although my numbers are narrowly better than his. He's on a plane to a training camp within hours of the call from the chairman.

He's in. I'm not.

•

We're at Mum's for Mother's Day. Wally's about to go on tour to England to defend the Ashes. They've swept him into their world, and there's no higher sporting assignment for an Australian.

Which is why I consider my position to be one of rare privilege. Because I have a hard, shiny taped ball in my hand, and Australia's number-four batsman a very short twelve metres away, down a pitch I mowed. I know every inch of its surface. I've strained a net across two garden stakes behind the stumps so we don't have to go retrieving missed balls.

Mum's inside with Louise and Honey, playing with the baby. They'll be fine for an hour or more.

Australia's number four. He has his own personal physiotherapist and frequent flyer points, but I've got the ball.

He faces up with his usual poise, his weight seemingly on neither foot but on both, his chin slightly raised so his jaw is parallel to the ground. His front elbow high, bottom hand loose.

There's a weedy patch in the grass short of a length, just outside off. I dart the ball hard into it and the bounce rears up like a whipping snake, bends past his outside edge high up, around shoulder height. He fends at it; retreats at the last possible instant. It hangs for a second in the net where it hits, then falls to the ground. He scoops and returns.

He's in a good shirt, sleeves rolled up. Bare forearms, bare hands. Bare fingers. I'd love to hit those fingers.

He's smiling unaccountably. I've just beaten him outside off and he's smiling.

So I flip the ball over and bend it the other way. Lulled into a false assumption, he fends outside off again, and this one curves back in sharply and finds his ribs, hard enough to elicit a little *oof* that he wouldn't want me to hear.

He smiles again. 'Nice one. Didn't see that coming.'

It must've stung like a bastard. So why…?

'You all right?'

'Yeah, never better. You want a bat?'

No, I don't want a bat. I want to see you bent double in excruciating pain.

'Nah, you're right. Stay there.'

I straighten the next one up and he picks it correctly. Defends strongly. Next one's a careless half-volley. He steps forward and strokes it elegantly into the vegie patch. I can hear broad-bean stalks snapping in there as the ball rips through them. I'm fishing around in the pea straw with one hand to find the ball when he calls from behind me.

'Hey, I've asked Louise to marry me.'

He was talking to my arse. I spin around.

'I said I've asked Louise to marry me.'

No room for a show of emotion here. Keep it cool.

'Oh yeah. What'd she say?'

He laughs like I'm an idiot.

'Yeah. We're doing it. Fifteen June—it's the Saturday night before we fly out for the tour. You free?'

THE RULES OF BACKYARD CRICKET

Of course I'm free. It's that or two-dollar shots at Chasers with Craigo.

'Um, probably. I'll have to check.'

'Great.'

From that moment forward, I start rehearsing my speech.

About how we've always been inseparable. About how I wasn't sure if there was room in our relationship for this outsider, but that she won us over with her charm. I'll skite about how I still think she throws like a girl. I'll remind the room that Wally's a very ambitious guy, and that she may have to prepare herself for the role of Cricket's First Lady. Then I'll pull it right back. Seriously, I'll say, I'm proud of my brother, my proxy father, his advice not always welcome but invariably right. And I'll say I love him and I wish them both every success in life. And the girls in the room will go *aww*, and I'll smile bashfully before I sweep out my arm and invite him to the microphone. Hug him and slap his back in the virile way that defuses the awkwardness of man-hugs.

A week later, Wally and Louise come over to Mum's place for a meeting, the first in a series to discuss the draft running order they're putting together for the day. Yes, a running order. They've got copies for me and Honey and Mum. The baby gurgles and makes little grunts as we get down to business.

Page one, invitation list. I scan down fast. Familiar names, familiar names. No Craig.

Page two, the running order itself.

Five lines down, *Best Man's speech: Tully Welsh*. I'm staring at it dumbly like it's a typo. 'Who's Tully Welsh?'

Louise throws Wally a look: *We've discussed this. Remember how we decided you'd handle it?*

'He's the player development manager at Cricket Australia.'

'Best man?'

I'm trying desperately not to betray any emotion.

Wally sighs. 'It's political, okay?'

No way, brother. Not that easy. 'So, how long you known him?'

He rolls his eyes. 'There isn't, like, a legal minimum, Darren.'

'Yeah, but how long?'

Mum's frowning. 'Stop it, you two.'

Louise exhales and tries to move us along. 'So I was thinking we could do the cake straight after the bouquet throwing? Darling?'

•

As my third season in the state side winds to a close, Honey and I move in together and my single life in Richmond becomes a couple's life in South Melbourne. Just a plain, rented terrace, but it works as a moated citadel against all my baser associates. Craigo won't come near the place and doesn't trust Honey, a feeling she plainly reciprocates.

I can walk to the market to buy—ha!—fruit. We have dinner parties, not parties. I even find myself cursing when the kids with their P-plates take the roundabout too fast. I look back in wonder that I lived across the road from a heavyweight gangster for four years.

Louise brings little Hannah over every few days. They live in Kew now, she and Wally and the toddler. But Wally's increasing absences leave her in a strange kind of limbo, one she chooses to fill by wandering the cafés of South Melbourne with Honey and, less often, with me. Hannah can't say 'Darren', and chooses to replace the word with *Daddle*. Every time she does it, Louise corrects her with an embarrassed smile. But the little girl favours me in everything. When she's fed, she's fine in the presence of the women but will kick and squall for me if I'm in the house. *Daddle do! Daddle do!* Louise shifts her strategy slightly by coaching Hannah to say 'Uncle'. This works for a while—she reverts to 'Uggle', and even develops a sing-song chant about *Uggledaddle*. On the rare occasions that Wally's in town, he sits through these antics in tight-lipped silence.

Louise has risen in the development hierarchy in close parallel with Wally. To me, their lives are a sad, repetitive carousel of commitment. I'm sparing you the details of their wedding day because it felt so much like both of them were playing to a crowd, discharging obligations in everything from the invitation list to Tully Welsh's role as best man, to the name-checking in the speeches. The pay-off is, the gifts are extravagant. Not just toasters and glassware but art, electronics, even furniture. Never mind their vows to each other; it feels as though they've formalised a pact with their respective careers.

Even on maternity leave, Louise is harassed by calls from the aid organisation she works for. Federal budget cuts, trouble in Zambia. Spats over expense spreadsheets, media releases and bank managers. Her version of saving the world sounds deeply bureaucratic. And Wally isn't there. Over the summer he's become a face on the television, stripped of personality. He's a man who smiles and offers soundbites in airport terminals, wheeling his giant bags on trolleys. Even to me, the man inside him seems buried under platitudes.

But Hannah? She's a delight; a raucous, slapsticking show-off with a talent for the ridiculous. When her mangled speech and funny faces don't work, she'll disappear and reappear with something on her head: underpants, a box, a pillowcase. She tumbles and dribbles and jabbers her way through the giant world, grabbing at everything with her warm, sticky fingers. I can watch her for hours. Sometimes her antics remind me of Craigo when he's drunk—the staggering gait, the emotional outbursts, the need to be hugged. It fascinates me watching her eat. She shovels food in as fast as she can, frequently missing her head altogether.

She runs on love as much as food, but is far more delicate in the way she consumes it. She will stroke an adult ear to savour its velvety surface, then carefully compare the feel of her own. She likes to kiss faces: her mother's, Honey's, her hovering father's, and mine. She will look carefully over the available terrain before deciding the perfect place to position the kiss; left of the nose, high on the brow, out wide on a cheek. Despite her voracious attack on everything under the sun, kissing is done delicately. This tiny *peck* is yours alone in the universe.

Under Honey's influence, my game improves out of sight. Not the instinctive stuff, but the stuff that comes from being fitter, more alert. Like sleeping a full night before a game and cutting down the pharmaceuticals.

In three years, I make so many runs that the only thing preventing me from following Wally into national selection is the ongoing success of the national side itself. And that can't last forever.

Honey and I start telling people we're *trying*, an active expression for the passive reality that we've stopped trying not to conceive. Hannah doesn't know what a large part she plays in my decision to go along with the program. She's in prep now, a tiny human in her school tunic, carrying an oversize bag on her back like some comic turtle. Louise is making the cross-town trip to South Melbourne day after day in search of—what? Sisterhood with Honey? Family for her daughter? She's fraught and exasperated so much of the time.

Following an armchair afternoon conversation about Wally's and my backyard days, she asks me to make a pitch in the backyard at Kew. We sit out the back in the sun painting stumps on a compost bin and Hannah swings the miniature bat with theatrical joy. We throw a ball at each other at waist height. She can catch. She's five and she can catch.

In Adelaide I knock up the fastest fifty in the history of the four-day game. When I get home we get back to *trying*, with a mortal earnestness that is new and different. We're no longer fucking, or even making love—we're attempting to reproduce. In Hobart I take a catch at gully that for ten years will be described by pundits as physically impossible. The phone rings in my peach-coloured suite at the Casino and Hannah's breathy voice is on the line, telling me she watched it on the telly and she can do that too. *Mum says Daddy's got very good news,* she whispers. *But we can't tell anyone.* In Perth I bat for nearly two days to make two hundred and fifty and save a match. I get a call at the hotel afterwards from Wally, strained and distant. He's in the Caribbean, wants to know if I've heard from Louise, and how's Hannah? I've got my feet in the bath and a beer in my hand. I feel for him: he's a man who got the very thing he'd wanted all his life and then discovered it wasn't what he thought it was. *Why are you asking me?* I say. His answer is gone from my memory, but it was unsatisfying.

Hannah's very good news appears on the evening bulletin a few days later.

I'm at home with Honey, chopping vegies for a paella. Onions frying, two soda waters on the bench: no beer hour in this kitchen. The telly's yammering away in the background and when I glance at it I see his face, squinting in his baggy green.

'Turn it up.'

The newsreader is waiting to throw to a press conference, recounting Wally's stats and making reference to his 'humble beginnings in suburban Footscray'. She's talking about a 'bombshell appointment that will send shockwaves through world cricket'.

Wally, my brother, is the captain of the Australian test team.

The newsreader touches her ear—they're ready to take the press conference—and suddenly there he is, looking a little pink and scrubbed after training, eyes up and talking to the room, no notes. He's behind a chaotic nest of microphones, a curtain of sponsors' logos behind him. And beside him, the chairman of selectors and the outgoing skipper. Looking vanquished.

'I'm as surprised to be sitting here today as you are no doubt surprised to see me,' Wally opens with a smile.

There's an appreciative ripple of laughter.

'Circumstances have dictated that I've been promoted to this role well before my time is due. I'm under no misapprehension about that. There can be no greater honour for an Australian cricketer than to become captain of the test side. When I walked down the corridor on the way in here, I looked up at the faces in those paintings and I thought to myself, there is no way I deserve to be among these people. Bradman, Hassett, the Chappells. Allan Border. These are men of enormous character, and right now I feel very daunted at the prospect of trying to emulate their deeds. I want to thank the board for giving me the opportunity—'

'Thank Mum. You need to thank Mum.'

'Shut up, Daz.' Honey gives me a playful slap.

'—and I particularly want to pay tribute to my mother Pamela, who has done so much over so many years to make this dream a reality.'

'Oh good *boy*, Wal!'

'I want to lead a united team, and I want to listen to the considerable range of views and experiences within the squad. Anyone who knows me knows it's not my nature to try to bulldoze my way through. Anyway, there's a lot to do, so I'd better leave it there.'

He smiles briefly, shakes the hands of the men next to him and he's gone.

And at our place, the phone starts ringing.

•

Life in the state side churns onwards, largely unwatched by the public.

Then in Sydney something quite odd happens.

It's a day–night game, which we're expected to win. Small crowd, an unexpectedly cold night. I'm listed to open the batting. During the afternoon, the opposition have put on 246, a little shy of five runs an over. Thoroughly achievable. I'm putting the pads on when I'm approached by a touring Englishman called Rowan Cooper. He's a nobody, a dour off-spinner who won't play a red-ball game for us all summer. He's good for five overs of handbrake cricket if the other side gets some momentum up, which is precisely what he's delivered today. Other than that, he's inconsequential.

'Mate,' he says. 'Mate.'

So he wants something.

I keep strapping the pads on.

'Mate, I'm onto a little action.' He raises his eyebrows. 'You want in?

Such approaches happen from time to time. They're rare, but not unknown, particularly for someone like me. Anyone—players, assistant coaches or jackals in suits might sidle up at some unexpected moment and ask if you could help out a punter. The transaction's usually a minor one—just beer money for an easy stunt. No one's going to ask you to throw a game, so there's no real moral problem with it. It's just a sport within a sport. Honey wouldn't like it but Honey won't know. My attitude is, if I can fit a little wager within a credible game plan—and you don't look like you've got two heads—I'll entertain it.

Cooper very nearly falls in the two-heads category though, and my hunch is this is barely going to be beer money.

'What's the gig?'

'You get stumped. First ball you face from Alberts, after you pass twenty-five. It'll be a wrong 'un. Charge down the pitch, have a swing and miss it. Get it right and it's worth three grand. Here's fifteen hundred now.'

Three grand is a bit of a surprise from this minnow. He hands me a batting glove and I can see the hundreds tucked inside. I take the deal. Why, you ask? Because none of it matters.

Getting to twenty-five isn't much of an effort.

I chip a few around, tap one boundary out through covers and one through mid-wicket. By odd coincidence, I reach twenty-five without facing a ball from Johnny Alberts. I'm on twenty-eight by the time he comes into the attack and I'm on strike. And it's then that I realise there's a conceptual problem here. Johnny's a left-armer. And I'm a left-hander. What constitutes a wrong 'un in these circumstances? His ordinary spin would be from leg to off across me, so I figure he's going to turn one from off to leg. I stand with my bat raised, watching them arrange the field, wondering which of these idiots is in on the joke. Keeper must be. I look back at him, standing right up close at the stumps, and he makes a little smooching motion with his mouth. Not sure how to read that. Alberts is too far away down the other end to read any cues off him.

He lopes in and whips the ball into the air. By the time he's let go of it, I'm already moving, a half step then a full one, so I'm five or six feet down the track and completely vulnerable. Normally I could watch its rotation, the seam tumbling over itself, revealing which way it'll break once it bounces. The light's wrong and I can't make it out, but it should spin in towards my pads. All I have to do is play around the outside of it and it'll go through the bat/pad gap.

So I pick a line through about ten o'clock and throw everything at it, hands high on the bat handle, swinging in the very direction the ball shouldn't spin. I even close my eyes as I heave through the shot. But at the point when the ball should have slipped past the inside edge of the bat, I make contact.

Perfect, sweet contact. Middle of the bat.

Even as the swing finishes with the bat lying on my back I'm already wondering what the hell's happened. The ball is streaking through the night sky, rising slightly as the backspin takes effect. The spectators at wide mid-off are swelling in their seats as it rockets towards them. I've hit it out of the park and I have no idea how.

The keeper's remonstrating with the bowler, marching down the

THE RULES OF BACKYARD CRICKET

pitch with his gloved fists on his hips. This, to the audience, would be as they expect. He's furious with Alberts for serving up an absolute pie. But there in the middle, there's no missing his words.

'That was supposed to be a wrong 'un, you fucking idiot.'

Alberts looks back at him helplessly, shrugs his shoulders. 'Sometimes they don't come out right. Can't help it.'

They exchange a long stare, long enough to set me wondering whether the problem is something else entirely, whether Alberts is no dupe at all, but has taken a counter-wager with someone else. If he has, he's a long-odds punter, because the chances of me doing what I've just done are extremely remote. The ump finally senses there's an unusual level of tension in the air, and sends the two of them back to their posts. As the keeper passes me, he fixes me with a murderous glare.

'Not my fault your boy can't bowl a wrong 'un,' I venture.

Seeing as I've blown the three grand (and indeed I'll have to return the fifteen hundred), I can't see any reason to throw my wicket away now, so I settle in and enjoy the night. The act of batting is flowing in the same way that drinking flows some nights—unconscious ease and fluidity. Alberts, it seems, not only can't bowl a rigged ball, but struggles to bowl competitively as well. I finish with a comfortable eighty-eight not out, and we record an easy victory.

As I saunter up the players' race, kids reach out to pat my back and high-five me, but something's wrong. Badly wrong. I can see backs turned as I enter the rooms. The atmosphere's poisonous. Not the reaction I expected. It's possible this thing was a smidge bigger than I understood.

'Great win boys,' I say to no one in particular. And no one in particular replies.

Rowan Cooper's in the locker room, packing his things. He looks like he just lost his last dollar. I wonder if he has.

'Mate, I'm sorry. It turned the wrong way and the damn thing connected.'

Cooper turns and looks at me, and to my horror I can see he's been crying. 'Wasn't much to ask, was it mate. Just miss the fucking ball. Just once. But you had to be a bloody hero, didn't you.'

He pushes me half-heartedly out of his way and storms out of the room. I'm left waving the batting glove with the fifteen hundred in his direction. If he's not concerned about that, he's taken a much bigger hit than I thought.

But this is only the beginning of the weirdness.

Two hours later I'm seated on the hotel bed watching TV, eating a light chicken salad as instructed by Honey. The phone rings: it's Wally in Miami, where it's late morning. Even as I greet him he's underway, speaking firmly.

'What happened tonight, Darren?'

His thoroughness exhausts me. How the hell has he heard about tonight?

'What do you mean?'

'There's people calling me, Darren. What happened in that game tonight?'

His voice hasn't risen, hasn't wavered. It's me doing the wavering, for some reason.

'We won. It's cool. I don't know what the problem is.'

'Darren, I want you to be straight with me. Was there a fix going on?'

'*Darren*? Who's "Darren"? I'm still your brother, you know.'

His tone softens just slightly. 'Yes of course, Daz. So was there a fix, or not?'

'Not really, no.'

'Not *really*? What does that mean?'

This probing of his is beginning to make me deeply uncomfortable.

114

'Well, it was sorta waved around, you know, but it didn't come off and it doesn't matter. It was just a spot thing anyway, not the game.'

There's a long silence on the other end. Then the same cold, patient voice. The voice of a man who was my brother but is now burdened with responsibilities I can't imagine. The voice of someone choosing their words with particular care.

'You don't want to have anything to do with these people. Do you understand me?'

'Mate, it was fucking Cooper and Alberts. We're talking park cricketers here. They're muppets.'

'Do *not* underestimate them. Stuff like this can have consequences you can't see. Who knows about this?'

'There's nothing to know about. No one does. Fuck, what do you care, anyway? Carrying on like it's the bloody Mafia. How's Miami?'

'I'm not interested in small talk, Darren. I'll say it again—you're mixing with people you don't understand. I've made very sure to never get caught up in that stuff, and I don't see why you can't resist it.'

'I think your job's going to your head,' I say, and because it seems the sensible thing to do, I hang up the phone.

Squibbly

After countless attempts, I've got the shard of plastic lodged right where I need it, between the thumb and forefinger of my right hand. It's getting cold in the boot. The muscles above and below the shot knee are cramping, making the leg jackknife excruciatingly. There's no prospect of stretching it out in such a small space, no option other than to clench and writhe until it sorts itself out.

I start slowly, carefully slicing away at the cable ties with the shard of plastic. Dropping it again could cost me an eternity. An actual eternity; so no pressure or anything. I can't get my fingertips down to where the ties wrap around my wrists, can't check the effectiveness of the tiny scratches I'm making. All I can do is persist.

A smell wafts through the boot, thick and unpleasant over the exhaust. Meaty and sulphurous. Takes me a moment to identify it.

Werribee. The western sewage treatment plant. So we've reached the outskirts of Melbourne.

Another season. A home game in Melbourne, but the players get the option of a hotel room near the MCG, and Honey and I take up the opportunity.

We've talked and talked, as the city faded to silence and even as it awoke itself in the small hours. Like me, she's capable of lying awake all night worrying about the shape of the universe. So we had each other to annoy. When she fell asleep, I turned the bedside lamp on to push back the dark a little. Little thoughts and worries. Tiny dancing bears that I stop with a pill.

The dawn comes quiet. I leave Honey to whatever place she's gone to, transfixed, as I dress by the brown curve of her thigh, lit soft in the baby glow of a summer day through the gauzy hotel curtains. The early hum of traffic. Someone tipping a bin far below in the alley. Leaning in close to her cheek, I listen to her breathing. Confident, unconcerned.

This will be a Day Among Days.

Everywhere I look I see perfection. I feel it. Even my bare feet on the carpet are feeding me the ticklish static of fate. My body feels fine: not a twinge, not an ache. I plonk myself on the carpet and stretch the hamstrings. Leaning forward, legs apart, I push my hands along the floor, pulling at the muscles behind my shoulders. They spring back in response. I push the hands a little further and a grunt escapes me.

'Goo'luck.'

Her voice is smoky with sleep.

Because it's a lifetime habit and one of the ways in which I'm most like Wally, I open the coffin and run a hand through the gear: in the long compartment, three sets of pads for a lefty: buckskin, recently scrubbed and whitened by Max the property steward. One pair's still slightly damp from yesterday's sweat. Two bats, new grips on each— again, Max's hand, like one of Santa's elves while I downed a beer in the dressing room. A box, greasy and adorned with two random pubic hairs; two thighpads, again, one of them damp. The damp one's the lucky one.

Rolled up in a white towel, four pairs of batting gloves with the pad on the left thumb. Another little ritual of mine is to take the small rubber thimbles out of the thumb of each left glove. I've never understood the point of them: they take away the tiny sensations you get through the thumb, and they make your hands more bulky. The pile of discarded thimbles is on the benchtop. I interrupt my audit of the coffin for just long enough to pinch the air out of a couple of them and use the suction to stick them to my forehead. Good to have a sight gag in reserve in case your winsome bedfellow wakes in need of a laugh. The effect, I confirm in the mirror, is like a lightly sunburnt baby goat.

Little cloth bags in the outside pockets of the coffin. One contains sunscreen, zinc, Vaseline, Aerogard, glue and scissors. The other is more specifically medical: painkillers, anti-inflammatories, tape; needles for lancing blisters. These are the superstitious relics of a long career in grade cricket. The big grounds have all this stuff on tap. Even the umpires carry it in their pockets, but my vestigial self-reliance persists.

There's a brown paper envelope they gave me the night before the game that contains guest passes to the ground, a timetable and a few badly spelled briefing notes. The Queensland side, their averages, strike rates; probably dietary requirements. I couldn't say precisely what the notes cover because I haven't read them. What do I need briefing notes for? Bowl the fucking ball at me and I'll hit it.

She's stirring. I drop a guest pass in her open handbag, lean down and place my fingers lightly for a moment on her forehead. I don't expect her to turn up.

The airconditioner is grumbling into life now.

•

At breakfast in the bistro (another bistro, another eight-slice toaster), I can feel eyes on me. It's the fate of state cricketers to be perpetually half-recognised. We're the backbenchers of cricket—elected but not anointed. A kind old lady in the lift appears to recognise me, but it turns out she wants to let me know I've left the thimbles on my forehead and I look like a twat. My word. She said 'dill'.

The eyes in the bistro, however, are real. *It's him. Who? Keefe. Next big thing. Ninety-seven not out overnight. If he keeps going the Vics could win the final.* At one table, the newspaper has the back page facing outwards and there I am, taking up three-quarters of the page on one knee, smashing Wehnderfer to the cover-point boundary. Big Hans is slightly out of focus in the background of the shot, stooped in his follow-through.

When the occupants of the table have wandered off, I scuttle over and collect the paper.

Starting at the back, I read all about the game. With more tea left in the pot, I flip over and work my way into the paper from the front.

Five pages in, a one-column court report from Amy Harris. Pitbull Freer is back on the streets; he lost the appeal she told me about but he's out on parole now. A little cloud darkens my sun. Should I be worried? Wouldn't he have better things to do with his liberty? Would he even know I once spent a few vigorous hours with his special friend? His photo, like mine, is taken with a long lens but for different reasons. He's outside some restaurant: the corded neck with its chains, the spikes of the tatts reaching forward of his ear, pointing towards his tiny eye, set deep behind the cheekbone like a fighting dog.

Pitbull. More apt than I'd realised.

The waiter comes over and tells me there's a phone call. When I take the receiver and hear the scratchy noise, I know that Louise is holding the phone to Hannah's ear. So I wait patiently for her little voice.

'Mum says you have a very big day,' she says carefully. 'I hope you bat for a long time, Daddle hey guess WHAT Wednesday is the first day of school and I'll be in grade one Daddle and that means I get a desk with Charlotte and I can play cricket with the grade twos cos they don't like preps but now I'll be a grade one but I can get em out anyway cos I can do that ball you know that ball I got you out with at our place when it went under your bat? Daddle?'

'Yes, mate. That's a yorker.'

'Yorker! And we're allowed on the big playground at lunchtimes this year but not at little lunch or after school and we get to go on the tramps if you got a teacher watching and how many runs do you haf to make?'

'What do you mean, mate?'

'You know, to get in the test team with Dad?'

'I don't know, mate. Hopefully not many more.'

'Anyway I hope you do...yep I AM Mummy, *wait*...so...love you bye.'

Like all kids, she lacks a sense of the wind-up towards ending a call, and has just crashed the receiver back on the cradle. Gone.

She turns out to be the only one willing to go straight to the issue at hand. Everywhere I go this morning, people maintain a distance, like I'm busy defusing a bomb or something. But there are no nerves. I'll clear the ton with ease and I'll do a whole lot more than that.

In the dressing room, there's a brief team meeting in which the talk is about everything else but me. We're five down and we need 289 runs to take out the final, to take delivery of the Sheffield Shield.

First ball of the day, I watch Dave Pemberton in his sweatbands limbering up. I watch him like I will circle him on a plain and then tear a bloody piece out of his flank with my tusks. Long, smooth approach, upright delivery stride. Hands aligned parallel through an invisible vertical plane.

There's a faint chatter of applause as the ball is delivered. Straight and full on middle stump and I chip it out easily enough.

Second ball, my certainty about the ton nearly brings me undone. I take a wild swipe at a loose one outside off, and succeed only in getting a thick edge on it. The ball flies just over second slip and is gone. About three seconds later I hear it hit the advertising hoardings; the *clang* of hard leather on tin.

The hundred.

My batting partner Phil Herring runs down the pitch and clamps me in a hug. Our helmets bash together. There's a ripple of polite applause among the Queenslanders, and a gentle shorebreak sound from the grandstands. Clutched in the arms of Herro, somewhere mid-pitch in the centre of the MCG, I've got 956 runs for the season and a century in what is likely to be Victoria's winning Shield final. I'm averaging fifty-four, with daylight between me and the next-best number-four batsman in the country. In two weeks' time they'll announce the squad for the Ashes in England this winter, and there is nothing on the face of the earth that can prevent me getting the nod.

I break away from Herro's hug and salute the stands with a raised bat. Yes, thank you kids and pensioners. Thank you junior office workers, skiving off your Friday so you can drink piss in the sun. Thank you empty plastic chairs in your multiple colours to fool the news-viewing public into thinking there's people here. Thank you ground staff, who have to be here anyway, and thank you stoners tugging on quiet spliffs high in the northern stand. This one's for none of you. This one is entirely for me.

And then they bring ol' Feddy on. For some reason, they didn't use him in the previous innings, or indeed in this innings until now.

Federal Collins. Pride of Antigua, and the fastest bowler I never saw. A man so introverted he makes men of few words sound like gossip girls. Some burr of anger is buried between the great shoulders.

He takes the ball from the skipper as though he should have had it all along—no 'Thanks skip', no 'Can I have a third slip?' Nothing.

The keeper and slips are standing so far away I can barely see them.

Fed walks out to the end of his run and drops a plastic marker disc, windmills his arms through one quick warm-up and just starts running in.

As he gathers speed, I have a brief second to regret that someone else hasn't borne the brunt of his impatience. He's six foot four standing still. I know this because I've looked up into his eyes at social functions, and I'm six foot. In his delivery stride, leaping off that left foot and airborne as he passes the umpire, he's at least seven foot two. And as that right arm whips over his ear, the clutched ball streaking like sunlight through a thrown glass of claret, I swear that giant hand is topping out at, I don't know, eleven, twelve feet in the air.

The problem with such a high release is not so much the angle it comes down from, but the resultant angle at which it rears up off the turf. A ball pitched on a reasonable length suddenly becomes a spitting, hissing bastard of a thing that wants to get into your throat.

I know from long experience the barely detectable dropping of a bowler's eyes, the sinking of the lead shoulder, that tell you it'll be a short one. It's there too in the angle of the wrist holding the ball, the knuckles tipping forward to retain it for an extra millisecond. And from years of dodging microwaved tennis balls, I have an instinct for unnatural bounce.

The eyes drop: a jolt of adrenaline.

So I'm already half-ducked when it enters the space–time continuum fuckery that causes a cricket ball to become invisible. At first it's in his hand, then it isn't there at all, and then—apparently—it's streaking at about a hundred miles an hour through the space where my head was. But I'm squatting on my haunches by now, wondering if I couldn't take a job with Craigo at the leasing joint where things happen a lot slower.

It sails harmlessly past me. At some point I grab a single, leaving Herro to take strike and deal with the rest of Federal's demons.

He's got a great eye, Herro. Eye like a dead fish. But he's also got an unfortunate tendency to put his body in the way if he's not confident his bat will do the job. Squat, powerful, thick-limbed, he's a generous target. He wears two short ones in the ribs, with his bat (the very object that should be taking the punishment) held aloft, out of harm's way. Both times, the ball makes a hollow tympanic thud that reminds me fondly of belting tennis balls into ol' Sambo the fat staffy.

I'm about to wander down the pitch to offer support when Feddy finally finds his voice. Watching the gasping batsman from the end of his follow-through, he grabs the underarmed return throw from the slips and turns to me. Then he says, in the bassest of basses:

'You take a walk down dere and I will troe dose fuckin stumps down, *mon*.'

I've never seen a man so serious. I offer Herro a weak little *you right mate?* and a concerned wave of a gloved hand. He's grunting his way back to his feet by then.

The next one clean bowls him, and he looks glad to go.

•

Federal's first spell is a mere six overs. Through a combination of good luck and careful strike manipulation, I weather it.

By the time he starts his second spell, I've cobbled together another sixty runs and we're a mere thirty-seven runs from victory. In the moments of stopped play, I've been sneaking the odd look at the scoreboard, the sequence of lit globes making the letters: KEEFE, D. Beside it, the triple columns say 170. The highest ever individual score in a Shield final between these two sides.

The sun has passed its angry peak and is now bathing the east side of the 'G in a soft yellow glow. The grandstands bury the outfield in deep shadow. Federal's been gone from my thoughts for an hour or so now, out fielding defensively on the boundary rope. There's nineteen overs left to bowl in the last session and we've got three wickets in hand. Nothing can, or should, go wrong. And even if it does, my ticket to Heathrow is booked, because no one can take these one hundred and seventy runs away from me.

So seeing big Feddo there at the end of his run-up is disconcerting but by no means alarming. He'll be tired by now. He's been in the field all day, a glowering presence under that big hat of his. For a guy with his destructive ability, the solitary wicket of Herro would be a disappointing return. For whatever reason of internal team politics, he's been under-used.

On reflection, I should've guessed these things might've added a little sting to Fed's bowling. Maybe my mind wanders ahead, to the press conference I'll give as man of the match, charming everyone with my insouciant one-liners. To the phone call I'll receive from the chairman of selectors, asking my size in caps. Maybe I can taste the first cold beer, less than an hour away. Who knows where my mind is.

But Federal Winston Collins is still very much here.

He streams in like he just finished a morning warm-up: momentum personified. As he rears into that delivery stride, his upper body is bathed in the golden light spearing through some empty exit in the grandstand. It flashes brilliantly on the gold chains around his neck, a blinding flash of light in the exact place I don't need it.

I pull away, bat raised.

It takes a long instant for Federal to realise what's happened. He half-releases the ball and it rolls away towards mid-off, as his momentum carries him down the pitch, winding his arms to regain balance. Finally he stops, standing with hands on hips about ten feet from me, breathing hard. 'What da *fuck* was that?'

The ump's moved from his position and is rushing down the pitch. 'Darren, why did you pull away?' he asks.

'Fed's chains,' I respond. 'They caught the light. Couldn't see a thing.'

The ump looks from me to Federal, to the chains. Fed's fuming, but he says nothing. The Queenslanders are starting to gather, directing a bit of chat my way. Stuff about my mother. My poor, much maligned mother.

'All right,' says the ump. 'Let's get on with it, eh?'

I think about this for a moment, and balanced on the tiny fulcrum of that moment I make a decision that will change my life.

'Tell him to take the bling off.'

Fed and the ump simultaneously stare at me in disbelief.

'What?' they both say. Fed's taken two steps forward.

'Ditch the chains, Fed.' I lean on the bat. Brother Wally would know this stance. 'I'm not gonna have that happen again. Take 'em off.'

Fed takes three very quick steps forward, and suddenly he's towering above me, pointing a long finger deep between my eyes. 'Don't you dare disrespect me, boy!' Several fielders have darted forward to grab him by the waist. 'Don't you even *look* at me battyboy...I will fuck you up!'

'Cool it Federal,' says the ump. 'Darren, where's this light coming from?'

I point at the non-striker's stumps, which are now bathed in the heavenly glow. Over in the west, the sun is blazing through the exit halfway up the Ponsford Stand.

'Pussy,' spits Fed. 'Ain't never seen the sun?'

The ump wanders over to the square leg ump, who's been avoiding us all. They chat for a moment, then he returns.

'Take them off, thanks Federal.'

125

Fed's eyes are wild now. He fumbles around his throat, searching for the clasps, and one by one he hands the chains to the ump. Someone throws him the ball and he allows it to smack into his palm. His eyes never leave me.

'Gonna hurt you for this, little boy,' he whispers.

The urge to antagonise just gets stronger and stronger when these things happen to me. I'll never know why. So I wait until he's got all the way back to the end of his run, until he's turned, until I'm damn sure he's looking at me.

And I blow him a kiss.

Fed takes off at full speed from the first step, expressionless. I tap the bat as he runs; lift it as he leaps. He slams the ball hard into the turf—again, I can tell only because his body says he did—and it disappears. I'm inside its line of flight, because I've already decided before he bowls that a man this angry is incapable of feint: it'll be a bouncer. And it's important that you don't get a reputation for copping this sort of stuff. I have to hook him.

So in the part of that second when the ball is invisible, I'm rocking onto my back foot, tipping slightly to my left, beginning to pull the bat in a low-to-high arc that will take it past my nose. It's pure guesswork, based on Fed's usual pace, the state of the wicket and endless repetition of exactly this shot. If I'm out by an inch or two I can adjust. You sometimes see still photos of batsmen doing this, and they have their eyes closed. This is not evidence of an action reduced to forlorn hope. It is the point of total trust in the intimate choreography of the swing. Eyesight no longer matters. It will work, or it will not.

Then the ball reappears, and it's got awfully big.

It's where I thought it would be, but *so* much earlier than I'd calibrated the shot for—a mere instant from smashing into the grille of the helmet.

I jab the bat handle forwards at the ball. Two inches off the grille of the helmet: I've managed to protect a wire cage with a leather glove. The idiocy of this is unanswerable. But then, reflexes are themselves unanswerable.

There's a sickening crunch and I know immediately that the ball's caught my thumb on the bat handle, and all sorts of destruction has taken place. For a moment, though, I'm suspended in that childlike state where I know the pain is coming like an avalanche but it's not here yet. I throw the bat and start hopping away from the crease. God knows why I'm hopping. I bend double, with the hand between my knees, straighten and look at the sky. Now it's here. Nothing will separate me from the planet-size pain, the death-metal screech, coming from inside that glove. I collapse and roll over onto my back, clutching the hand to my chest. People are starting to gather. Klausner, their new wicketkeeper, looks down at me with something like pity, something like vindication. We've been shitting each other for two days out here, and now I'm writhing on the grass, a victim of my own hubris. The crowd has roared somewhere beyond sight because the ball has reached the boundary. It was propelled there by seven millimetres of bone in my left thumb.

•

The team physio waddles out with his little bag of parlour tricks. Magic spray and reassurance is about all the wobbly tit has ever been good for. Sure enough, he undoes the Velcro cuff on the glove and pulls it away, ready to hit it with the aerosol. But as the glove slides back, he stops dead and drops the can. The long side of my thumb, just above the wrist, has deformed into a nauseating sac, with a pointed angle in it where some piece of bone has been forced outwards. *First metacarpal*, I will hear over and over. Looks like something from a horror movie. The end of the thumb is turning purple and the nail has been smashed and torn back. It's crowned with a comical tuft of cotton wool from the inside of the glove's padding, like a fucked-up finger puppet. The crushed splinters of the thumbnail are spiked out of the pulp of the nail bed. The end of the thumb is already completely devoid of sensation and will remain that way for the rest of my days.

'Ooh,' says the physio. 'That's not good.' He's holding the hand as if it might try to escape. 'We've got to get you off.'

He puts a hand on the small of my back and continues to carry the smashed hand carefully in front of himself. I shuffle forward obediently, no bat, one glove, muttered profanities. Our number-ten batsman is jogging out towards the middle. From the corner of my eye I see Federal calmly take his chains back from the ump and replace them around his neck.

I can hear scattered applause as I head up the concrete race to the rooms, where there's an unspoken tension between concern for me and concern for the game, now precariously balanced with two part-time batsmen at the crease and another thirty-three runs to find. I take an icepack and gingerly place it over the thumb, then slump into a seat at the big window, swatting the physio away like a blowie. Craig appears out of nowhere—he's managed a few times lately to scam his way into the rooms. I don't begrudge him doing it, but I do wonder sometimes at how porous these change rooms have become.

Craig plonks his arse down next to me. Through the haze of agony I see that today's monogrammed polo is brought to you by Werribee Precision Exhausts. He grabs the hand and examines it.

'Fuck,' he says.

'Yep.' There's blood dripping from the nail bed.

Craigo exhales loudly through his hairy nose and looks at his feet for a moment, then from side to side. 'Bastard,' he says.

'Yep,' I agree.

'I can have his legs broken.'

'*What?*'

'Federal. I can have him fucked up. I know people.'

'Jesus, Craigo.'

'I can make it happen, completely untraceable.' He looks me deep in the eye. 'No one does this to Darren Keefe.'

'Mate,' I grunt, 'that's a fucking terrible idea. Please don't do that.'

There's two ambulance officers marching into the place like they own it. Porous rooms, like I said. Craig tries to shield me but he gets two rubber-gloved hands on his man-boobs, and against his protests they shove him in a corner and drag me out.

●

It's a Rolando's fracture—comminuted fracture of the base of the first meta-carpal...possible compromise of the nervous and vascular supply.

This is what one tired-looking doctor is telling another one. He's maybe thirty, neat haircut, bony cheeks. They've given me something in a drip in the back of my other hand, something that's dulled me. The doctor's conscious I've been listening, and speaks in the exaggerated tones reserved for the simpleton.

'It means you've broken your thumb, Mr Keefe,' he smiles. 'Right down here in your hand.' He gestures on his own hand.

'I didn't break it. Big Fed broke it.'

The doc smiles again, like I've successfully recited the eight-times table.

'Of course. So we'll need to put some wires in to secure it back where it should be. We do that under a general. Now, have you taken any drugs of any kind in the last, say, seven days?'

I think hard.

'You look really tired, doctor. Do they make you do terrible shifts here?'

'I'm fine. Now, any drugs?' His pen hovers over a clipboard.

'Christ, I'm an athlete.' I look down at the lumps of my body under the hospital sheet, the pinnacles of my toes. 'This thing's a temple you know.'

'So no drugs?'

'Just a couple of beers last night.'

'Good.' He ticks something. Puts a condescending hand on my belly. 'How's the pre-med? Feeling relaxed?'

I nod serenely.

'We're going to anaesthetise you in a moment, and when you wake up you'll be in post-op and *hopefully*'—he pats my guts—'we'll have that thumb all sorted out for you.'

The other doc has boobs under that gown and they're wonderful. I give her a wink and she responds with a thin medical smile before tweaking something on a machine beside me. She's set a trail of fluid in motion down the plastic line that leads into my hand.

Lights out.

•

Two days later I'm off to the surgeon's rooms in Windsor.

Wally's driven me there. Wally and Louise. They're worried I shouldn't be driving on painkillers. Waiting in traffic, I unload something that's been bugging me.

'Wal, do you think Craig could organise a hit on someone?'

Wally's eyes in the rearview mirror. 'What, like a gangland hit?'

'Yeah. Paid job. Break their legs, whatever.'

Louise stifles a giggle. Wally laughs out loud.

'Mate, he can barely organise breathing in and out. He's probably the most harmless person I know.'

'You remember those kids he took on after the rep game at Richmond? That wasn't harmless.'

'We were teenagers. And he didn't *organise* it, he just did it. Why are you asking, anyway?'

'Well, imagine it. It's a funny thought, the big guy going all Don Corleone.'

Inside, the surgeon's wearing a lovely charcoal suit, chair swivelled, looking at X-rays. There are photos of his very clean-looking family on the bookcase behind him. I'm looking at the giant white bundle of my bandaged hand, wrapped into an exaggerated paw shape, like a polar bear's mitt.

Surgeon drops the X-rays, looks at me. 'You lied to me about the drugs, Darren. Your bloods came back: methamphetamine and cocaine.'

'Oops.'

'It's not my job to police what you put in your body. I take it nobody dope tests you in state cricket. But you lie to a surgeon, you run the risk of not waking up from the anaesthetic. Is that clear enough for you?'

'Absolutely, doctor. Thank you.'

'The bone will knit over a period of weeks,' he says, unwrapping the polar paw. 'But what concerns me is the main nerve leading down your thumb. It was trapped in the pinching motion when the ball hit the end.'

He's reached the end of the bandage and now he peels some medical tape off the hand. Underneath is said smashed-up thumb tip, all purple and black and ballooned, but now there's a long incision, almost from knuckle to wrist, with a row of blue stitches intersecting it. He takes a needle from a tray and pricks the end of the thumb.

'Can you feel that?'

We both know the answer, but lying to doctors has become second nature.

'Clear as a Yucatan sinkhole.'

'Just yes or no, thanks. How about this?' He moves the needle a little further down the thumb. Nothing. His eyes narrow.

'This?' He's moved all the way down to the knuckle now.

'Ouch,' I venture.

'I hadn't touched you that time. You're not feeling any of this, are you?'

'When's it going to wear off?' I ask him.

For the first time, he looks a tiny bit less than infallible. He sighs. 'I don't know. We have to wait and see. I'm going to have the rehab people test it every couple of days, and if we don't get an improvement in sensation in'—he clicks a pen and starts jotting notes—'a month, I'll send you to a microsurgeon. We'll look at opening up the canal for the nerve a little more.'

Now he's wrapping the hand again like we're all done and dusted.

'If you head down the hall to Sue, she'll plaster it for you. Six weeks.'

All of a sudden, I can feel the panic rising. 'But...when can I bat again?

He's standing at the sink, washing his hands like Pontius fucking Pilate as he calls over his shoulder, 'I'm not sure. We just have to watch it for a little while.'

He dries his hands.

'Hey Darren,' he calls mildly. 'That was a marvellous knock. Well done.'

•

When the cast comes off, there is no return of sensation, no answer to the prick of the needle. The thumb will only make a vague curl, won't close with its neighbours to form a gripping hand.

Reflecting on that now, lying here with so much of me punctured, cut and broken, it's hard to recall the magnitude of this problem, but it had the potential to mean the end of everything.

So I go under again, this time for a decompression.

The results are delivered to me on a Friday afternoon by a GP on retainer with the state team. He strains for the right tone as he reads off the computer screen, choosing to look at it, not me. In a sidelong monotone he delivers the news that is no news at all: the nerve is irretrievably shot and will not heal.

'There's a guy in America who's pioneering a technique which might or might not be helpful and I'm not saying I'm recommending that but I know you want to hear all your options...' And some other stuff I'm not even listening to. I'm curled in a defensive ball within myself.

The thumb is permanently stuffed. I've lost the ability to grip anything—a cricket bat, for example—with my left hand.

The Vics keep me on contract. Seeing as the season's over, they can watch developments in the off-season to work out if I can still bat. I spend the winter swimming, running and lifting weights, buy a mountain bike and start exploring the Yarra trails out of Richmond.

In August, five months after the Shield is handed to Queensland following a tense nine-run victory, Federal Collins is attacked in a laneway behind a Brisbane nightclub by two unidentified men. He is remorselessly beaten and ultimately loses the sight in one eye. He never plays professional sport again.

England

The car's slowing, and as it slows there's a *clang* as the wheels pass over a metal speed hump. Next I feel a series of short, tight turns. Then they turn the music up very loud. We're stationary for a couple of minutes, then we roll forward, then we stop again. I can smell cooking fat.

The cheeky bastards are getting takeaway. So I do the obvious—I can't yell for help so I start kicking the crap out of the inside of the boot with my good leg. They turn the music up further, and I realise how futile this is—they're all yelling and laughing in the car now, and all I've done is increase the attendant's desire to move this carload of lunatics out of the place.

The car starts to roll again and cruises slowly forward. There's crunching gravel. I really didn't want to hear crunching gravel.

The car stops, lifts a bit as someone leaves their seat. A door slams. Within a second or two I can hear the boot lid being unlocked. I drop the holy shard again, as deep under my hip as I can get it.

Light streams in and there he is, burger in his left hand, chewing.

He surveys me for a moment as though I am a sack of potting mix or an overnight bag. Then he slams a fist down into my face with his whole weight behind it. For a second all I can see is a blinding flash of light. Pain becomes the world again. He grunts with the impact, straightens himself up and shuffles his jacket back onto his shoulder, takes another bite.

Something has come adrift in my mouth. My lovely white teeth. Two of them.

'Don't be a fucking idiot mate,' he says, with burger bulging in one cheek. He pulls a slice of pickle out of the bun and flicks it away. Slams the lid.

Five years into his test career, Wally is newsworthy mostly for not being newsworthy.

An unselfish contributor to team culture and a ferocious competitor, but someone whom the public finds unknowable. No tantrums, no binges, nothing inexplicable. Personal vendettas, lecherousness and racism have simmered away just below the surface of the sport for so long that no one knows how to take a level-headed professional with no apparent vices.

In Pakistan, he visits a women's shelter then an orphanage. In Britain, he bows for the Queen. In New Zealand, he stands respectfully before a terrifying haka and attends an Anzac service. In the Caribbean he plays cricket on the beach with the local kids.

That's the public face.

To me, there's irony in these gestures because I've had his fingers in my eyes so many times, seeking with all his will to blind me. I've had his snot on my cheek as he pressed his head into mine, trying to employ a fifth point of pressure when both hands and feet were not enough to punish me fully. And yet I don't resent him extracting what he can from those moments. He's there, after all. I admire him more for it.

He's home each Christmas; Mum, to my eye, increasingly less so, although he refuses to see it. She insists on cooking for him, burns everything and fusses dreadfully, consumed by a thousand little rituals she's invented to hide behind.

But by the third Christmas—'97, I think—everything collapses.

It's me and Honey, Wally and Louise and Hannah in the summer-lit back room at Mum's. The kitchen's separated only by a low servery, bisected by the sill of a cutaway wall. On top of the sill she's arranged a row of cookbooks bookended by a large plaster owl. We're sitting all martial and neat in our positions, paper crowns from the crackers on our heads, waiting for Mum to present the dessert. The roast's been a success—no charring this year. Louise has rifled through the old Bing Crosby vinyl, then followed up with Dean Martin, Sammy Davis Jr and Sinatra. She's trying to explain to Hannah who all these guys were. Hannah does that screwy face kids do.

I'm fiddling with my thumb joint, feeling it click when I roll the knuckle, wrestling a different kind of pain. We're a small family, always were, especially once Dad was gone and our three-cornered world was all there was. And here, at the peak of our togetherness, we amount to this: one stretched marriage, a de facto relationship, a child and a worryingly muddled matriarch. That's all. It's like we're waiting for the rest of the family to come through the door. We're vulnerable to dissolution in a way that I know families aren't meant to be. I want to hold each of them, beg them not to leave.

Straight after the roast, Wally and I duck out the back with Hannah. It's an unspoken assumption that she gets to bat. I've been over the day before, to drop off the meat from the butchers and mow the pitch, making sure everything's just so. Hannah's first flamboyant shot on the legside sends the ball into Mum's new crop of tomatoes. The smell rises from the foliage as I scoop the ball out. She's got basil in there too. Companion planter.

Wally seems surprised by Hannah's ability, her easy acquaintance with the rules. He's even more surprised when she thrashes at his long-forgotten leg-spin, lifting one delivery out of the backyard and into the Apostouloses'. This tweaks a sadistic instinct of mine—if it was me and him, and I'd hit that shot, I'd lean on the bat and tell him to go get it because it's not my fault he's dishing up shit. He'd flare at that, and there'd be a fist-fight within seconds.

So here she is, leaning on the bat for just an instant, him floundering, completely unsure of how to handle it. Did I teach her this?

Then she grins sweetly. 'I'll get it, Daddy.' And she does.

While she's gone, I can't help needling him as he picks at the weeds under Mum's tomatoes.

'Hits 'em pretty well, eh?'

'I know,' he says defensively, because we're both well aware he doesn't know.

Later, back in the house and Mum's still in the kitchen. Still won't accept any help. Wally's looking at his watch, late now for the team meeting ahead of the Boxing Day test. I'm facing the kitchen, he's facing me. Over his shoulder, I see Mum popping her head round the end of the row of books: once, twice, three times. The look on her face the first time is one of worry: by the third time it's naked panic. She's looking to my right, at Hannah, who's reading out the slips of paper from the crackers with their harmless dad jokes, unaware of the looks being directed her way.

After the third glance around the books, the panicked one, I call out to ask if she wants a hand. No, she replies breezily, but I'm going anyway. She's bent over in a cupboard, doing I don't know what.

I take her gently by the forearm and draw her up straight so she has to look at me. We can't be seen from the table. Her face is a wretched map of a confused land.

'What is it, Mum?'

She waits a long time, turning over her options.

'*Her,*' she whispers eventually, eyes darting towards the table.

'Who?'

'The little girl, darling.'

Tears spill from her eyes, from her wonderful, tired eyes.

'I know we all love her...' Her hands are up, covering those eyes in surrender. 'But *who is she?*'

I hold her close for a moment, taking in the shampoo smell of her hair, the food smells in the room. I'm not ready for the core of our world to crumble.

With my back to the opening that leads through to the table, I hear a faint noise and look over a shoulder to find Wally's standing there watching us. Mum's head is buried somewhere around my chest. She can't see him. I watch Wally's eyes for a long time and he looks straight back and it all passes between us.

He knows, he knows.

He understands, and now we can deal with it.

•

We don't, though. Life gets in the way, especially Wally's life. Cricket for him is a career, deeply entrenched.

For me, it's life with the circus: wanted here, surplus to requirements there. Dance on the highwire, then muck out the stalls. A decision's been made somewhere that I am no longer up to, or good for, the longer form of the game. Over four days, goes the medical advice, I'm likely to suffer from swelling in the thumb joint, leading to loss of grip, leading to more damage, poor performance, and so on.

Whether that's true or not, I don't accept it. No one's done a test, and I've never complained to anyone on day two, three or four. The deadened joint doesn't hurt. It doesn't do anything.

Late in a long night with Craigo, we name the thumb Squibbly. I'm not sure which of us thinks it up, but it seems to capture the cartoonish horror of a dead thumb, the zombie neighbour of four perfectly good digits.

I have lost a measure of control over the bat, though I won't admit it to anyone else. But there's no one in professional sport who doesn't carry these things, at least not after a few years at it. And this is how the mutual deception grows up around injuries: the player won't say when something's gone chronic, and management will employ guesswork about physical failings to move the veterans along.

But at twenty-seven, I'm nobody's veteran. I can run between wickets as fast as anyone, and there's nothing wrong with my eye. If anything, the minuscule interactions that flow between me and the approaching ball are finer and more subtle than they've ever been. I know a good pitch from a bad one with a press of the fingertips. I can sense fatigue in the posture of a bowler. I can count fielders like a poker shark counts cards, understanding the prevailing odds to my offside and my legside having regard to who throws left-handed or right, who's carrying a hamstring, who's too lazy to chase hard.

I have all this in me, and yet it's useless as collateral in selection. They lean on their spurious medical reasoning and they consign me to fifty-over fixtures with riding instructions to swing big and keep it interesting. The sweetener is I get to play fifty-over cricket for my country, not just my state; but it's clear, if not explicit, that I will never play a test. Not with a dodgy driving hand, and not with a chequered disciplinary record. *Be the showman*, I'm told. *Go out and entertain the punters. That's you, isn't it?* I'm an orca in a pool, cutting frustrated laps. On the handful of occasions that I try to construct a careful innings, I'm taken aside and counselled. *No one came here to watch you look after your average.*

So I swing like a madman and run around screaming. Learn to slide in the outfield. I cultivate grudges against various fast bowlers because the crowd likes to see the opposition captains bring those bowlers on when I'm around. I get to travel more, though I'm no longer sure if that's a good thing or a bad thing. Honey is tiring of it, and she senses the rotten core of the whole enterprise. These are the dying spasms of a career, prone on the floorboards in a pool of blood.

•

Craig, on the other hand, sees nothing but blue skies in this change of circumstance.

He's been busy setting up a business he calls Wattle It Be, a touring fan club for the Australian cricket side. Ahead of every international tour he buys cut-price packages for people like himself: sweaty single males who like to drink and chant while they get sunburnt in front of sport. The whole concept is horrific, but it's a roaring success. He's turning people away. After two or three tours he works out that he can recruit a retired test player to operate as a kind of figurehead and pub coach, offering special comments and war stories, and the not-quite-promise of access to the players.

As one of those players, I know there's a fair amount of effort devoted to ensuring Craig's touring parties never get that access. Craig himself does, but that's just part of his mystery. He's there after a session of play; at an official function; up the back of a press conference. Watchful, comfortable, like some kind of security expert. He looks like no one else in the room, almost irrespective of what that room might be—his physical bulk propped up by a wall. The bomber jackets, the jeans crushed into accordion pleats either side of his groin. He wears his mobile phone in a holster on his belt. Even the team manager, who takes about a thousand calls a day, doesn't do that.

When things go well for me his joy is suffocating. He hugs me, leaves a hand stranded aloft in search of a high five, or starts pounding out applause until others feel obliged to join in. He has this skill for placing himself in vulnerable positions—like the hanging hand, the lone clapping—so that others will rescue him simply to alleviate the awkwardness. But despite that I appreciate it. Honey can't come on tour. I get to chat to Hannah by phone every few days, when the time zones and the homework and the ballet and swimming allow, but beyond that I have little in the way of close personal friendship to draw upon. Wally's there for the international games of course, but his demeanour in the dressing room is dour and fixated, and he and Craig seem like magnets with opposing charges these days. If Craig crosses the room, Wally veers away.

I can talk to Wally, in a limited way. He'll discuss the day's play, the sponsor commitments, the weather, the pitch, the opposition, even Mum's increasing confusion, but it's all a disembodied drone. Watching his eyes, I can still see him in there. But the pressure he places upon himself has sapped the life from our exchanges. I'm a fellow player, a colleague in this sweaty firm, and only distantly a brother.

One night I find him by chance in the carpark under the hotel that houses the national squad. He's got a rubber ball, flicking it fast and low against a cement wall and catching the rebounds with soft, agile hands. It's a lifetime habit of his and he can do it for hours. He doesn't hear me until I'm right next to him. Stops. Looks at me a moment then resumes.

'Can't get any peace when I do this outdoors,' he mutters.

I drop into the spot that would be the slips fielder next to him, and without a word he angles his next throw so that it rebounds towards me. Catching it with a dip to my left, I fire it back slightly harder than it came to me. He moves surely, cups it and returns harder again.

This is how we talk, I'm thinking.

We're boxing sideways, watching the wall. Shuffling feet, feinting and whipping and darting. He's grunting now with the effort, runners squeaking on the polished concrete. I can feel his moves without looking at him. This one high, this one low. I'm snatching them one-handed, throwing with the wrong arm, underarming. His answer, as always, is relentless perfection. He wills me to get tricky with him and he just repeats, and repeats, and waits for my errors.

Finally one of mine hits a pipe fitting at the top of the wall and rolls away to come to rest under a car. I run to get it, come back to find him puffing, hands on knees. He takes a shot from his Ventolin and pockets my return throw. I get back in the lift, sweating in the bright light, and realise I haven't said a word to him.

And this is how I search for him every time I see him; employing the things we both know that no one else knows. Impersonating people we've laughed at, playing to his love of sarcasm. But most of the time, I'm reduced to winking idiocy. The moments falter and are lost.

●

No such problem with Craig.

A three-day exhibition match in Darwin—middle of the southern winter but a perfect thirty degrees—and Craig's busy blistering himself on the hill with a crew of diehards he flew up the night before. They're staying at the Casino too, he enthuses, when he finds me despite the exclusive high rollers' pass.

This is the night after the second day's play. They've given me the acting captaincy for this one, only because of someone's injury and everyone else's apathy. *I'm the captain of Australia!* I say to myself once or twice. But I'm not. There isn't even a team meeting. Our opponents, a Northern Territory development eleven, have put up a better fight than anyone expected. Between our insipid performance and their desperation, the two sides are quite evenly matched.

Craig orders two cognacs—no one seems to pay in this bar—and settles in an armchair beside me.

'You guys need to declare first thing tomorrow,' he says.

I smile indulgently. 'Does that work better for your drinking buddies?'

'It's not that. It's gonna rain in the late arvo. And when it rains here, it doesn't fuck around.'

I find myself laughing. 'Mate, it's the middle of the dry season in Darwin. It's not going to rain until October.'

'It's gonna rain.' He suddenly looks serious, leaning forward to tap me on the knee. I can hear the ice cubes clink in his tumbler. For no accountable reason, he's making me uneasy.

'So what?'

He reaches into his jacket and produces a wad of printer paper. Swirls and numbers and graphs. Drops them in my lap.

'What are these?'

'Weather forecasts. Metro, long range, short range, a private one and a rural website one. And I arksed a blackfella.' He seems to think this seals it. 'It's gonna rain.'

'Okay, it's gonna rain. It's an exhibition match for fuck's sake. So what?'

'Nonono, you *hafta* take it seriously Daz. Every game matters. If it doesn't matter to you, it probably matters to someone else. You're in control, Daz. This one's yours. Show some leadership.'

He takes his cognac and wanders off across the room, plays the roulette for a while. The last I see of him, he's deep in conversation with a man who approximates his size and posture, but is Indian. Craigo's probably just sold a busload into Mumbai for next year.

The following morning dawns bright blue like the days before it and I ignore his advice completely. At three p.m., and needing only fifty runs to win, we watch a giant thunderhead settle over Darwin and unload three inches of rain on the city. Play is abandoned and Craig doesn't talk to me for a month.

●

The tour to England changes everything.

It's announced a few weeks after the Darwin match, and no one's more surprised than me. The national side apparently needs me, needs a fast gatherer of unsubtle runs. *Strictly for limited-overs cricket*, they specify. Not the tests.

The money's better, and I convince myself this is a late bloom in my career. The gentle light of the northern summer agrees with me: it recalls Mum reading us *The Wind in the Willows*, that verdant buzzing insect meadow and riverbank reverie. But I arrive in the British Isles as a fully formed adult, with even more fully formed appetites, and it's Pimms and lemonade, straw boaters, blazers, picnic rugs and afternoons laced with sensuality.

Overtaken by such moments and still vaguely aware that I'm in both the twilight of my career and the peak of my physical condition, I drink it all in deeply—the afternoons in the sun at the community events we're invited to, the pubs, even the music festivals. I've rediscovered ecstasy—a little after the majority of the drug-using populace, I concede—but this summer in England it's everywhere, and so are Blur and the Gallaghers and Supergrass and the Poms have thrown out the spectral John Major and embraced Tony Blair and everything's so cool and new and possible.

It's hard, in the grip of this fervour, this whatever it is, to hold a steady line on what home means.

Not that I really try.

I call Honey regularly, but the calls have adopted a routine quality: *How're you going? Good. How are you going. Yeah good.* It's nobody's fault, but I don't have the concentration span for this. There are girls around the team as there will always be girls around teams, but now the high-season chloroform strips all accountability.

At first it's just a dance here, a kiss there. But we're moving all the time, never more than two or three days in a place, and there's no longer a need to extricate myself or even explain. I'm raving, night after night in the city nightclubs, suffused with indiscriminate pill-driven love for everything up to and including Craigo, who is not accustomed to having his embraces returned with interest.

We keep talking, Honey and I.

I can't tell what's getting back to her but something must be, because she's more distant all the time. This works corrosively on my patience: there's no brotherhood in Wally, and Mum's deteriorating fast. Conversation with her is a patchwork of ideas and loose strands, often lapsing into glum silences. It's raw and confusing and it hurts— Wally and I both depend on Louise to get to her when the district nurse can't. I'm grateful she's not wandering. I've heard that's next.

So I don't have time for Honey's *are you still taking the echinacea?* One fateful night I take a call from her while there's a girl in the hotel room, giggling and weaving her hips. I've got a finger to my lips, barely suppressing my laughter, turning away so I can concentrate on the call, but Honey knows I'm not there. She knows I'm not there and she knows someone else is. Just as the hotel-room girl takes her top off, does a silent shimmy on the bed, Honey tells me she's been at Louise's place to give her a break because Hannah's got mumps and our mum lost her car.

With nauseous immediacy, I know it's over.

The executioner is one of the tabloid dailies. They've snagged a one-in-a-million shot: the hired photographer at a coastal music festival turns his camera to the crowd for an overview of the sweating, bouncing mass and catches me dancing shirtless, sunburnt and grinning idiotically behind a cigger, with a girl under each arm. They're in bikini tops; I'm out of my mind. The picture is picked up, predictably enough, in the Australian press under headlines such as *Your Sports Funding Dollar at Work* and *You'll Keefe: Cricket's Bad Boy Lets Off Some Steam*. Honey doesn't ring. I know it's time to face it.

Her voice is tight and restrained. I can imagine she's rehearsed all this.

'So you're obviously not coming home to me, then.'

'I guess not, hey.'

'What a waste. What a...what a massive waste. Can't you see what you're doing?'

'I s'pose.'

'You've lost me Darren. You probably think that's nothing much. But all this fooling around, this...fuck. Found yourself some drugs over there, huh?'

I don't answer.

'So that's a yes. You're just, you're throwing your career away and making a public spectacle of yourself, and it reflects on me. You know that? They ring *me* up asking for comment. And what am I supposed to say? That you're a fucking idiot?'

Faint static on the line. Distance. Cicadas outside in a street tree.

'People expect me to be like this.'

'Oh for fuck's sake. That's the weakest thing you've ever said. Grow up.'

More silence. The cicadas have stopped.

'So this is it then?'

'This is it.'

There's more; there's accusations and explosions of rage and even grief. I'm sitting on another hotel bed when all this takes place, only this time there's no company, and by the time the conversation ends with her hanging up in tears, I feel about as low as I deserve to feel in counterbalance to the highs of the past few weeks.

I slam the phone down on its cradle and sigh into my hands. It is a waste, an exchange of the lasting things for the passing things. I wonder if it'd be different if Fed hadn't smashed the thumb. But I don't think that ball changed my essential character.

I dial Craigo's number as I'm flipping channels on the TV. There's a one-dayer on, Bangladesh versus Sri Lanka. Somewhere dusty. No answer from Craigo. Maybe his tourists need a booze mentor for the evening.

I dial Wally's number as an alternative to staring at the walls.

No answer there either.

•

The tour contract allows me free flights for a member of my immediate family. Due to some anachronism that dates back to the days of bespectacled gents puffing on pipes, Honey didn't qualify, being a de facto. There was a time when she would've come over anyway and that time has passed, and there's no point blaming the rules. So the only person I can bestow the perk upon is Mum.

We've started talking about her condition—we still call it 'the condition' because none of us is quite sure what it is—and when I bring up the idea of her coming over Mum swings from thrilled to reluctant and back again as she simultaneously imagines sitting in privileged seats at Edgbaston and getting lost in a London tube crowd. I assure her I can help. Inside, I see it as a kind of therapy.

There are moments when I think I'd be burdened by trailing a little old lady around behind me, but the reality is she's a middle-aged woman in fine physical health. It's an easy mistake to make as I listen to her on the phone; her elisions between adamant and addled. *Thank you very much dear,* she says. *I'll think about it.*

Wal and I have both got powers of attorney over Mum. Mine is a concession Wal grudgingly made after realising he was almost never in a position to get things done domestically. The short, terse conversation about that one was resolved in a compromise: I'd have a medical power of attorney provided he kept control of her financials.

Anyway, I get off the phone and make a note to call her GP when the clinic opens (see the little responsibilities I'm starting to wrangle?). Dr Eliza from down the road—Mum's personal physician for twenty years that I know of—is surprisingly permissive about the whole thing, right down to faxing scripts for various drugs to my hotel so I can replace them in the event that Mum loses hers. She suggests I have someone take her to the airport and collect her from the other end, and a week later I'm standing in arrivals waiting for her to emerge.

That ennui that creeps over regular travellers, you forget it's there until you see someone for whom flying's still a source of wonder. Standing in wait, I can't summon any memory of Mum ever being on a plane, let alone travelling overseas. Tired clumps of passengers wander past, searching the room and finding love, or at least a driver; and then she appears in the doorway, wheeling her luggage and beaming as she scans the crowd. A flight attendant follows closely behind her, as I'd requested. I rush forward to Mum and press her close, squishing her glasses up over one ear and drinking in the smell of her. Even stricken as she is, she somehow makes it all right.

In a cab down to the hotel, she's craning her neck to take in the Englishness, a quality I've long since stopped seeing. *Ooh,* she marvels. *Look at those dear little shops.* She was tougher than that once, tougher than words like *dear.* Back at the hotel, I take her through the lobby and up to the room I've reserved beside mine. Mercifully, she lets me take the luggage.

Knowing I have a full schedule of games over coming days, I find her a scorebook ('Reception? Darren Keefe, room 119. Can you find me a cricket scorebook?') and I even recruit a handful of junior tour officials to keep an eye on her when I can't.

The arrangement plays out beautifully: when there's time to kill I've got something to do other than indulge myself or berate myself. This is the nearest I've ever been to living as a parent—ironically of my own parent. It puzzles me when I think too hard about it: corridors of paradox that lead nowhere. I'm trying to make memories for someone who will shortly forget.

Perhaps as insurance against this ugly inevitability, I buy Mum a cheap disposable camera, and she clicks away at everything she sees: the Camden market, a double-decker bus tour, me pulling faces at the Buck Palace guards. There are even times I can look to the stands from third slip and see Mum's bright colourful presence, flanked by tour employees, perched in her seat and lifting the camera to secure proof of the world.

She's confused occasionally, but provided I'm nearby she remains mercifully free of genuine distress. Some nights I take her out for dinner—pubs mostly, because she sees them as synonymous with the London of her imagination—and other nights I prop her up in front of her telly with room service and leave instructions with that night's minder that she's to be gently rescued if she strays.

The minder shifts are shared between three youngsters with whom I have an understanding: I look the other way when they slouch behind the pillar and smoke: they studiously ignore my companions and my physical state when I come and go during the night. Looking out for Mum didn't seem, at the time, to be too much trouble to them.

•

At the start of the tour I'd got myself a little hatchback from a hire company and started driving at night. Just loops of the city at first, then further and further out, to Cambridge, even to Stonehenge. Mostly it's the distraction of dealing with the unfamiliar surroundings, but it's the lights on the dashboard too. Life. Another way of resisting the dark.

Tonight, having worded up the front desk team to keep an eye on Mum, I'm climbing into the hatch for my most ambitious nocturnal tour yet, out to Weymouth on the M3, when I hear footsteps approaching on the dark street outside the hotel.

To my surprise the feet belong to Tully Welsh, casually waving a key at his own car, which lights up and beeps as it locks. Welsh has been appointed tour manager: several summers ago, he was the object of Wally's ambition, and therefore the best man at his wedding. I haven't forgotten it.

He's in a lemon polo and slacks with a striped canvas belt. It's midnight and he looks like he's off to play golf. The coif stands high and proud, apparently made of a single piece of some polymer-based material.

His mode of dress, his hair and even speech, all of it is calibrated to career success. We, the team, are a project for him. That's no bad thing if it means the tour runs smoothly, but it doesn't breed loyalty.

He heads for the passenger side.

'Where are we off to, Daz?'

'I like to go for a drive some nights. Where are *you* off to?'

'Coming with you.'

He jumps in, studiously searches for the belt and buckles up. I haven't even got in yet.

'What's this about?'

'We need to talk.'

I shrug and climb in. I'm not a loner. The aim is to keep the darkness at bay, and even Tully Welsh is good for that. We talk shop until we reach the Chiswick Bridge and the city's edge is behind us. Bigger sky now, even in the dark. Trailers loaded with sculls on the bank of the Thames, and looking downstream I can see a blue-and-white pub, lit yellow in the night. I take a left and nose through the side streets before I find it, block letters on the façade: The Ship.

Welsh is after something and I don't know what it is. I get us two beers and sit him in the corner, try to flush him out. 'You ready to talk yet?'

'Yeah, sure.'

'Well, I'm not asking you to, but you did get in the car.'

Welsh sighs deeply. 'How's your mum?'

'She's fine Tully. How's yours?' The poor schmuck looks deeply awkward and part of me wants to prolong it. 'Come on. What's it all about?'

'Mate, you know what it is. Same thing it always is. Discipline.'

These talks are tedious at the best of times. I've had a few of them, and Welsh is not going to be one of the great practitioners of the art of bollocking.

'Go ahead.'

He takes a gulp then lowers his voice. 'You've been on tour four weeks. Played three games.'

'Not my fault. Put me in the side if you don't like it.'

'You know I don't control that. You've had a lot of time on your hands, Daz, and you've used it to draw attention to yourself.'

I'm about to flare, to defend the indefensible, when he lifts a cautionary palm to stop me. 'You smacked an opposition player at the pub after the launch party—'

'He's an arrogant shit, Tully, you know that as well as I do.'

The hand goes up again. 'You're very lucky we were able to keep that quiet.'

'Keep it quiet? Mate, tell the world. Tell 'em I'm not gonna stand there when he calls our only Aboriginal player a coon. I didn't ask you to brush that under the carpet.'

'You don't think it through, Daz. You've not only risked a frenzy in the local papers, but you've armed them with a sledge against you, and against him, for the rest of the tour. Now they know it fires you up.'

He waits a moment.

'And if that was the end of the list, I'd probably agree with you and we wouldn't be having this discussion. But there's the photograph at the dance party, you've been pissed more than once in public, they've got you smoking in the dressing room on the TV.'

'Little things...'

'We already knew you'd hired the car...'

'Not a crime. I have a licence, you know.'

'You set your pubic hair on fire in a taxi.'

'It grows back.'

'Burned your thumb for a bet at another pub...'

'I can't feel it Tully. It's a party trick, c'mon.'

'...fraternising with that bogan, the guy with the cheer squad.'

'Craig? He's completely harmless.'

'Maybe he is, but what's he doing in the rooms the whole time?'

For the first time I'm genuinely surprised. 'I don't know. You tell me. I thought he must know someone in management.'

'You've had girls coming and going...'

'Don't try to parent me.'

'I'm trying to protect you.'

'From what? I'm delivering what your bosses wanted from this tour—I'm making runs and doing the clown prince thing.'

He seems done for the moment, which is good because it means he hasn't got wind of the laundry-truck incident last week. If he hasn't raised it now, it seems I've got away with it. A thought occurs to me.

'Why'd they send you to give me the lecture? I would've thought it's Wally's job.'

He sighs expansively.

'We would've. They wanted this addressed last week after the festival photo. But we couldn't find Wally at the time and I haven't had a chance since.'

'Not like Wally to go missing.'

'No. That's your schtick.'

●

My complacency grows. There comes a night when I peck Mum on her dry cheek and leave her to *EastEnders* and a pork roast with instructions to remain in bed. She smiles sweetly as I disappear. Dinner with a publicist, followed by a bar and a club. Sex is at her place, given my parenting role at the hotel, and after whiskies and pills it's all a bit disorienting. I wait till she's asleep and ease myself out of the unfamiliar bed. Finding my pockets empty I'm forced to rummage through her fallen handbag for the purse and lift myself a few notes for the taxi ride. It's better than waking her.

So then there's trouble finding a cab, trouble explaining the way home, a short altercation over the fare, and by the time my bellhop friends have let me into the hotel it's nearing three.

'Mum good?' I ask as I saunter/stagger past.

'Haven't seen her all night,' is the reply from the junior member of the team, young Ben.

Excellent. Full degustation for wee Daz and no repercussions. Up in the lift, down the corridor and past Mum's door, I'm surprised to find it ajar. I can hear the TV and so I head in to switch it off, assuming she'll be sound asleep.

She's not there, of course.

Rumpled bed, lamp still burning. A paperback copy of *Emma* face down on the quilt. My fucking muddled head won't clear, won't focus.

My room? No. I check a few other doors, all of them locked. A voice or two in protest from behind them. Fuck.

The lift. I study the buttons: there's a gym and pool floor, and my heart jolts to a picture of Mum floating face down in a swirling white cloud of nightie amid the blue glow of the underwater lights. The lift takes an eternity and so does swiping the bloody card to get in there.

Nothing. Just the steady hum of the filter.

No one in the gym, the toilets. Fuck, *fuck*.

The damn lift descends at its own pace and I race back to her room to try the closet. Why didn't I think of the closet? Nothing but a few rattling hangers and her coat, the one she brought because she thought it would be just right for Hyde Park evenings. Okay, wherever she is, she isn't in a coat.

Back down to the lobby and a short and fierce interrogation of young Ben. He looks mortified and clueless in equal measure, but has reserves of common sense and I've all but expended mine on good times tonight. He darts behind the counter and produces a set of keys, runs me to the hotel courtesy bus with its swirly gold cursive on maroon and we're squealing over the polished concrete and out into the darkened streets.

I'm making stupid deals in the passenger seat with a God I don't believe in. *Just bring her back. I'll be good. I'll be good.* It was a nightie, wasn't it? Could she be both confused enough to wander out at night, and also sufficiently organised to get dressed beforehand? Ben cuts spiral laps around the hotel block, widening out each time—he's smarter than I gave him credit for.

One lap, two, and at a bus stop halfway round the third lap, there she is, arms bare in the nightie, deep in conversation with two girls who look very post-club. Ben hits the anchors and a second later I have the old girl in my arms.

'Hey, honey, what are you doing out?' she asks, genuinely amazed to find her boy at a bus stop. The girls seem unsure of the situation.

'She's my mum,' I tell them. Ben hovers behind me.

'I am!' She beams. 'Look—' she stretches out her right hand next to mine and proffers both to the girls. 'We've got the same fingers!'

They assess Mum and me and the minibus for a moment longer, and one of them says, 'Why's she on the street?'

'She's really cold,' says the other, and indeed I can feel Mum shivering even as she hugs me.

I mumble an apology and a thank you and shuffle with Mum under my coat back into the velour surrounds of the courtesy bus. They're probably going to ring the cops on me and right now I don't care. Get Mum to bed, lock the fucking door and drop a Serapax.

God can go to hell.

•

A week after that, four weeks into Mum's stay, I start to realise I'm out of my depth as a personal carer. The cricket does actually demand a level of concentration, and a lot of time, which come at the cost of withdrawing both from Mum.

In only two more weeks the tour will be over anyway, and I'll have to end this business of crowded streets and thin sunlight, tiny cricket grounds with their skewed histories and oak trees, all of it. The pubs, the freedom at night, the eccies. Damn, the eccies. It's going to cost me a fortune to keep this routine up at Melbourne prices.

I get the team travel agents to book Mum a flight back and I pack her off with assurances I'll see her in a couple of weeks. I arrange a bag of excess cricket gear to send back with her.

'What's this for?' she asks, as I drop it on her trolley at the check-in counter.

'It's so I can dodge the excess baggage, Mum. These days we

need three of these bags to play internationals.'

She rolls her eyes as the bags disappear down the chute towards immigration. I walk her in silence through to the security gate where she kisses me on the cheek and makes a worried frown at the doors. She's holding one of my hands, not ready to let go.

'You look after yourself,' she says. 'Stop these late nights, Darren. They're not good for you.'

'Aw, come on Mum, I'll be home in a couple of weeks.'

The frown lights into a smile like forever ago. 'I love you, boyo.'

It stabs me, stabs me straight through the heart. 'Love you too, Mum.'

She releases my hand and turns away reluctantly.

I'm doing a ridiculous movie wave as I watch her slender shoulders disappearing between the doors, trailing her little carry-on case over the tiles. Somewhere behind the ordinary walls to our left, a conveyor belt carries her luggage, her carefully selected coats and socks and thermals and an unmarked sports bag, labelled in her name, with its set of left-hander's pads, its two pairs of gloves and its three cricket bats: the two Gray-Nicolls with the white rubber grips and the Stokes & Carville with its red grip, its hollow centre and its one point seven kilograms of pink ecstasy tablets, each stamped with a tiny shooting star.

Exile

My nostrils are burning from sucking in air. My nose isn't quite clear—in part a legacy of having it broken once by Wally, and maybe the takeaway from twenty years of cocaine abuse. Each inhalation whirls and deviates over small piles of rocks inside there.

I've switched my attention to the gaffer tape, but it doesn't give at all. I try cartoonish smiles and frowns, but the muscles that should carry out these movements are clamped in position by the tape.

When I can distract myself from the gag it stops bothering me. But the instant I start to think again about my breathing, I get panicky. I suppose if I suffocate as a result of being gagged, I'm doing better than I'm likely to do at the other end of this car journey. And that might even cause some chain-of-command problems for the people in the front: damaged goods on arrival.

Death by gaffer tape. Suitably pathetic.

•

There's a photo you can find if you go through the *Sydney Morning Herald*'s archives: me in the rooms at the SCG, propped on a bench with my back to the lockers. In my whites, barefoot. I've got that scuffed and saturated look you only get after a long day on a hot ground, but more than that, my whole physical demeanour screams defeat. I've looked at it long and often—head in hands, hair poking exhaustedly through my fingers. Tangles of strapping tape on the floor. And no one within reach of the contagion. You can't tell how a photo is cropped unless you're the creator or the subject, so let me tell you that change room was packed: players, support staff, families and hangers-on, even Craig. But either side of me it's just discarded gear and timber benches.

We've lost the one-day competition in embarrassing style. I've made a duck. Big fat blob. And before the bails have hit the ground, the Board have got a press release out.

Director of Cricket Operations, Tully Welsh, told a media conference on Tuesday afternoon that management had been dealing with disciplinary issues surrounding Darren Keefe for several years. This has included offers of counselling and welfare inputs to address his issues. However, he has failed to observe the standards expected of him.

The Syntax of the Living Dead. Who writes this drivel?

Welsh described the situation as extremely disappointing. 'The Board has high expectations of its players and staff: we expect them to uphold certain standards. Victorian players and staff receive education on the Code of Conduct on a regular basis. We have attempted to offer Darren multiple forms of welfare and support in recent times. Again and again, however, he has fallen short of the standards expected of a senior player. Darren's failure to address these issues has left us with no other choice but to take this course of action: accordingly, Mr Keefe's contract is terminated forthwith.'

So let's see: the 'multiple forms of welfare and support' was Welshy gate-crashing my drive out to Weymouth last year. The 'education on the Code of Conduct' was a yellow sticky note affixed to a stapled sheaf of papers, on which was scrawled PLEASE READ.

It all feels predetermined, because it is.

I've been cleaned up by a very good delivery tonight, but others have dropped catches and tried ridiculous shots. It doesn't seem fair of them to play the ill-discipline card when today was a comprehensive team failure. I'm not the oldest guy in the side, and most of the time I've been in form. Not like the old form, not the days of great plunder. But I've adapted to my weakened grip: changed my game to do away with the big hitting and just live on a bit of chip and run. Yes, there's been trouble along the way, but minor stuff, silly stuff, and not recently. Jesus, I've even done the pointless recovery sessions at the beach, shivering like a twat with my arms folded across my tits.

The players in the rooms that day, they have their various reasons to shun me. The younger ones have their own friendships, and also the political smarts to avoid me like a turd underfoot. No debt to a broken-down troublemaker. The older one—and as I say there is only one—can't even make eye contact for fear he'll be next. So him I understand. But longevity, experience, craft…these things have to count for something. Don't they?

Instinct and love. That's what inspired all those hours against Wally. Then I'd wanted to be in this side, then that side, then the side that selects the best from those sides. The pursuit was relentless and it all led to this place. No matter how carefully a player might try to consider the reality of retirement ahead of its occurrence, it's a blindside, and a savage one, when it hits.

•

There are other changes that take place around the same time.

Little things at first.

A routine trip to the physio to get a bit of work done on Squibbly's knuckle. But at the counter the pretty girl says *cash or card?* and

I do a little double-take because there's always been some clacking on the keyboard and a smile and a *thank you, that's fine*.

'The, ah, the Board picks that up...'

This must be how it feels when the family cash card fails at the checkout. People on the waiting-room couches trying to look without looking. She makes a show of double-checking but she already knows the deal.

Then I'm asked to return a phone I've had on 'promotional loan'. A nightclub membership 'lapses' though I'm unaware of it having had any kind of term.

A handful of tiny gestures of sympathy. The feeble kind of support that will later be perfected by Facebook. One or two former players pick up the phone, wanting to talk as much about their own tortured passages into retirement as about anything I'm experiencing.

I head down to the MCG one fateful Thursday, park the car in the ample space that characterises domestic cricket, and wander through the eucalypts to the grandstand. Deep under it, at the dressing-room door, there's a security guy. Shorter than me but a lot heavier. Ten years younger and dressed in black, scowling.

'How are ya mate.' I reach for the door handle beside him. He shuffles across slightly and taps my hand away from it.

'Can't go in there. Players' area.' His mouth barely moves.

'That's cool,' I say. 'I'm a player.'

'Nah mate.'

Don't make me do this mate. I smile. I wrestle with those words, the ones you never want to use because they signify all kinds of defeat. I nudge forward.

He stops me.

Here it comes.

He's got a hand on me.

Here it comes; I'm gonna have to say it.

Yep, I'm saying it.

'Do you know who I am?'

'Nuh.'

Christ. He actually doesn't.

I'm reasonably accustomed to doing this routine outside a night-club with a small crowd in the queue. This, this corridor under a grandstand in the middle of a weekday afternoon, is an away game for me.

'Darren Keefe. I'm a former player. I'm...shit, I'm Darren *Keefe*, mate.'

'Sorry Darren. Secure area.'

He's specifically enjoying the feeling of making me feel no longer famous. He's itching for a confrontation. And so am I.

'Understand you have a job to do mate, but you're embarrassing yourself here. Of course I'm allowed in.'

As I'm talking I slip a hand round behind him and knock loudly on the door. He shoves me violently in the middle of the chest.

'Didn't you hear me Mr Keefe? I need you to move back from the door...'

'Not interested in your needs, number twenty-two.'

The door opens inwards and the puzzled face of the team property steward peers out. We both try to get the first words in, but the bouncer wins.

'I'm sorry sir, this gennleman knocked on the door. I'm asking him to leave.'

No one's ever called the property steward—Max, I think it is—'sir'. I give him a good-humoured shrug like *can you believe this tool?* and make a move forward. The bouncer's hand comes up again, blocking my path. Max looks pained.

'Well, mate, if he's asked you to go, I guess...'

Oh for fuck's sake.

The bouncer's oozing vindication and I feel like smashing him. I feel like smashing fucken Max, whose apologetic look is only inflaming me. This must be the point when wall-punchers punch walls, but I'm accustomed to looking after my hands. And so, God help me, I throw a punch at the security moron.

I know, I know.

He catches my fist easily between his hands in a clapping motion and drives a knee into my groin. And that's all it takes. I'm on the ground at his feet whimpering as the nausea spreads through my whole being, balls-outward to the fingertips.

Max hurriedly shuts the door. Number twenty-two waits a decent while before hauling me up by the back of the shirt and working me down the corridor with an arm behind my back and one of his knuckles pressed excruciatingly into the side of my neck.

And just like that, I've been evicted.

I am an outcast.

•

No testimonial match. No invitation to the end-of-season gala. The enjoyment of privileges is directly proportional to the pain of having them withdrawn, and I make mental lists of those who've crossed me. I rehearse vengeful sound-bites for interviews but no one calls. There's speculation in the press that the game's administrators are keen to mark a new dawn, start afresh and so on. Cutting me loose is apparently a motif of the New Professionalism.

After weeks of invisibility I find myself profiled in a weekend liftout magazine. Not Darren Keefe the force of nature, the crowd favourite, but Darren Keefe the 'troubled star': wayward brother of national sporting icon Wally Keefe. 'Beleaguered'—Christ, that's only a short step from 'disgraced former'. The piece is written for the non-sporting reader and does not carry Amy Harris's by-line, but it contains plenty of things I've only said to her.

Like for example a throwaway comment to the effect that, like Peter Pan, I'd taken a long time to grow up. The story repeats that assertion verbatim, along with the observation that Peter Pan is not a redemption tale—that in fact the character never does grow up.

Also verbatim is an exchange I once had with Amy. She'd commented that I'm very close to my mother, and I'd agreed. *Why then, she'd asked, don't you hold all women in the same sort of respect you have for your mother?* I'd fumbled my way through some sort of an answer, but we both knew it was the question, not my answer to it, that mattered.

During these weeks, the gear sits in bags in a spare room, old sweat and sunscreen atomising into the room's stale air. The first time I go in there to get something else, I see the bags slumped there, and just look at them without composing a thought. The second time I sit down, take a few things out, handle them. Things that have been the detachable parts of me. I can see them now for their functional ugliness, but over as much of my life as I can remember, the shapes and small noises of these things—gloves and pads and other objects in yellowing shades of white—were integral to me. I take a selection of stuff and give it to the local cricket club to auction off.

The third time I go in, I've got three generous lines up my nose and I'm twitching. I pick up a bag and throw it in the car, head for Brewer's.

I book myself a net and a ball machine, wander in there under the fluoro tubes in an ordinary baseball cap and a T-shirt, unnoticed and lost in my thoughts. I want to feel the rhythm of repetition.

I set the machine for a bland line and length on middle stump. Dial in a hint of outswing, quickish medium pace.

The yellow balls streak through the air, one after another, and one after another I drive through the same arc and deposit each ball in the same square metre of the net. The hollow detonation of bat

163

on hard plastic ball echoes around the tin and wire whalebelly of the Brewer's nets, precisely every ten seconds. My shoulders are warming up. Stretching, striking, following though, I find I can swing with my eyes closed. Next I adjust my stance by a handspan towards off and start whipping the deliveries across my body towards the legside, targeting one square in the netting.

It should be Wally throwing 'em down. Brewer's is all about him, the places he stood and worked. I'd take his feigned outrage and obsessiveness over a machine any time.

These were once the rhythms of my days, the pincer formed by my right arm as upper jaw and my left as the lower, the bat held light but firm in its apex. Exhaling steadily, *blowing not puffing*, as the movement is executed. Long years of coaches watching those physics, me watching footage, swinging through that arc again and again. When it hurts, when it doesn't, when it's boring, when it brings me comfort and when it's solely for the entertainment of roaring summer crowds. Through that arc, again.

I'm sweating now, breathing harder. Every ten minutes I scoop the balls and put them back in the hopper.

I know it's all done now.

It's nothing in the end but muscle memory. Synapses and fibres subjected to enough repetition will reproduce the same effect on cue and without conscious intervention. That source code is buried in my body and will persist until the very end. Until they take me out of this boot and shoot me in the head.

But that day in the nets I knew. From that point forward, none of it had any practical function.

•

Craigo says I've got it all wrong. In the sun-drenched resort pool bar of his mind, retirement is the best thing that could have happened.

We're at a dance party in Byron when he lays it all out for me: the two oldest men in the place, plonked on our arses on the lawn under a giant inflatable Chairman Mao. We exist outside of the communal thrall around us, though Craigo has done his best to medicate us both. He's wearing scallop-leg tennis shorts from the seventies, a polyester shirt with nauseating geometrics all over it, huge mirror sunnies and a terry-towelling headband. He is beyond ridiculous, has entered another realm that might even be cool.

I struggle to hear him over the thudding bass, which only makes me feel older.

'You can't *afford* to keep playing,' he's insisting. 'There's all sorts of stuff waiting for you—TV, radio, a book. Shit, I'm surprised it's taken you this long to get to this point.'

He's thinking celebrity appearances for his booze tours, which, if I'm to live to old age, sounds like a terrifying way to spend the next fifty years. He can see me thinking this.

'You need to be realistic about who you are, mate. You're not Wally. You're not going to be part of the club. Ever. Not a coach, not a selector, not an administrator. And fuck 'em mate, who wants that? You're the people's sportsman, the guy who can hit a ball out of sight and still front up for beers afterwards. You're a naughty boy, and the public love a naughty boy, cos he's the guy living out all the shit they can't get away with. They've got wives and Saturday morning sport and home loans and they look at you and you set 'em free...can you see it mate? You set 'em *free.*'

He pats the dome of his gut.

'You need to trade on that, my friend. Don't be something you're not.'

The Fall

The top right corner of the gaffer tape is not quite stuck on. A tiny triangle, about four millimetres on each side, pokes free from my cheek where it never quite adhered.

It's teasing me.

My hands want so desperately to take hold of it and pull. The thought of ripping it free, hauling in great heaves of air, even this boot air—it's almost like sex. The relief would be incalculable. Thoughts curled into a tight fist around the problem, the solution comes to me spontaneously.

I press my cheek against the carpet as hard as I can, so hard that the fibres make stinging little impressions in my skin. Once, twice, three times there's no effect. But after a couple more attempts, the corner of tape grips the carpet and tears away from the skin just a little.

I repeat the process and it tears a little further. The triangle of freed tape is now about an inch along each side. I press down again as hard as I can. I want the adhesive to grab the carpet as firmly as possible. Then I pull my face away like a lion ripping flesh from a carcass.

The tape tears this time, tears in a straight line, leaving the little triangle of tape stuck on the carpet.

I want to cry, but I fear if I do the flow of snot will drown me.

On Saturday November 13, 1999, Wally is on tour in India, two tests into a three-test series blighted by disharmony and poor performances. Louise is at home in Kew with Hannah, or at least I assume she is.

And I'm at the strippers in King Street with Craigo.

He calls me quite unexpectedly during the afternoon. As though he knows I'm cut adrift these days, especially these Saturdays. That's always been his talent, the ability to appear from nowhere with a straightforward solution for some absence or hankering in your life. Craigo, like nature, abhors a vacuum.

So he turns up in a gleaming coupe—I've given up trying to identify them—laughing and wanting hugs. His new sunglasses make him look like John Goodman, simultaneously menacing and comical. His things in the centre console, a random sampling of the Big Guy's world—CDs from American west coast stadium rockers, paperclips, a Zippo, more sunglasses, mints, a roll of black roadie's tape, business cards from one-bogan computer businesses, radio stations and night-clubs. Pens. Nail clippers. Panadeine.

He sees me rummaging as we roll towards the city, gives me a slightly paternal frown. I tweak the stereo until it gives us Bryan Adams and he's happy again.

When we reach the club, I watch with amusement as Craigo passes up two perfect parking spots directly in front. He hovers in the left lane next to the vacant spots, looking up, looking down, then revs away muttering, 'Nah.' He passes up another space, a free one since a construction crew have removed the meter, and his anxiety mounts.

Eventually he parks a block away.

Now I know what you're up to in these moments, old friend. Context is everything.

He checks his watch once he's heaved himself from the driver's seat and feeds coins into the meter. The machine spits out a printed receipt which he carefully places near the air vent on the driver's corner of the dashboard. The robust happiness resurfaces as he waddles beside me down the empty street, scorched dry by the long summer.

He's greeted at the door with more hugs, copious backslapping. He gives his bomber jacket (*Matson Rebuilds*) to the girl behind the reception desk. The car keys in the pocket jangle loudly as he drops the jacket on the counter. The only things he keeps with him are his wallet and phone.

I grab the drinks and a table side-stage, nod to a couple of barflies who've recognised me. Craigo is no sooner seated and two gulps into his scotch than he's up again and wandering around the room, greeting people. The girls are on, the music is thumping and he's still at it. It's over the top, even for him, and more than a little awkward for me, sitting there sipping away at a beer on my own.

After an hour of this—me watching the girls, Craigo entertaining the room—he finally settles and dumps his phone on the table between our drinks.

'Anything wrong?' I holler over the music.

'No mate, great!' he mouths.

The young thing, stage name Desiree, is winding herself around a pole, eyes cold.

I'm bored. Despite myself, I'm bored.

Craig's looking at his watch.

The phone rings.

I can still see his face, from the cheery *Ellow?* through the long silence that follows. I see that face rearranging itself into something darker.

'When?'

His eyes dart to me. 'Why don't they know?'

He rises in his seat. 'Where's Louise?'

A name that doesn't belong in this air. Craig's standing now, reaching out a hand almost unconsciously in my direction. It hovers over the table; a finger curling, beckoning me, though his gaze is still directed to some point halfway between him and the dancer. Time is slowing down.

He's taken me by the arm to pull me up and we're running between the tables. People are staring. Craig brushes a bouncer aside, sweeps a hand past the front desk to collect the jacket, keys jangling again as he hits it running. The phone's still pressed to his ear and he's barking short responses.

'No.'

'Coming now.'

'Yep.'

'Yep.'

He cuts the call as we're running along the footpath, pockets the phone and looks at me. His breath is short.

'Hannah's missing.'

'What?'

'Missing. Gone.'

His jacket's flapping all over the place.

'When?'

'An hour ago. Someone got into the house. Hit Louise. Took off with Hannah.'

He's looking sidelong at me, gasping for air, rumbling and lurching all over the place. I can't compose a question to ask him; the shock has robbed me of speech.

We reach the car, throw ourselves in and he reverses out so violently that a passing vehicle has to take evasive action.

'W-where we going?' I finally stammer.

'Wally and Louise's.'

'Who rang you?'

'Police. They couldn't find you. They're at the house. Louise is—like—she's not hurt but she's a mess.'

By now I'm seeing Hannah's face, the gravity of the situation scrambling my mind and tearing at my heart. How could someone steal a perfect and perfectly blameless child? To what end? Is this the random selection of some predator? Is it something to do with Wally's fame? A mistake! Yes! She just wandered off...and will return tired and sorry in the morning.

'Has someone told Wally?'

'They can't find him. I'm sure they're doing everything.'

It's still hot outside and despite the roar of the aircon on full, I lower the window and look at the passing houses. Someone somewhere has her. For reasons that would already be playing out, too terrible to contemplate. The awful possibilities fill everything.

Craig is driving feverishly, punching at the gearstick, swooping past slower vehicles, forcing roars and rubbery squeaks from the car. We both know there's no point in it. Whatever has been done is done, leaving only the dread that chokes the day.

•

At the Kew house, there's roadblocks on the street. Media and police cars. It's well after sunset now and there are lights on extendable arms pointed at the house, bathing the whole place in a welter of savage white halogen.

We're ushered through the concentric rings of people who are there to secure nothing at all, concerned with an absence, not a presence. At the door there's a tight cluster of men in suit pants and shirts. We're stopped, quizzed. Craig's taken aside. Eventually they let me through but Craig's made to wait, despite his protests.

I push down the hall past whispering people.

No signed pictures, no framed memorabilia. There's almost no trace that a professional athlete lives here. No sign of cricket beyond a neat row of yellow Wisden spines in a bookcase—Wally's thing for history and rules. It bespeaks his bitter distaste for sentiment, his nagging aspiration for social advancement.

Louise is sitting at the kitchen table, hair backlit by a table lamp. Traces of Hannah's life are everywhere: her school photos on the fridge, a drink bottle with her name written near the neck. Her handwriting. And outside the back door, near the dog's water bowl, her runners placed neatly side by side, waiting.

Louise is upright, elbows on table and chin on fists. She's been crying but she isn't now. There's a welt over her left eye, extending diagonally back into her hair. In the centre of it a dressing's been affixed, and there's a small spot of blood in the centre of that. Her left eyebrow is swollen and there's blood in the eye, giving her a strangely combative look.

Her eyes—the red one and the white one—follow me. I can't imagine what physical contact is appropriate—a hand on the shoulder? A hug? Her demeanour does not invite touch. So I sit there, half looking at her, half trying not to.

People come and go—detectives, mostly. They keep their voices low, don't smile or laugh. They're combing their way through everything, using little stepladders and lights, photographing, brushing. All of them wear bright blue disposable gloves, as though fearful of contamination by grief.

Louise is still watching me but there's barely any recognition there. I'm conscious that two of the male detectives have moved closer, looking

171

at random objects but apparently waiting to hear us talk. I watch one of them long enough to make eye contact. He retreats a little.

'Should you be in hospital?' I venture.

She shrugs, infinitely uncaring.

'What do they know?'

'Not much,' she begins slowly, quietly. 'Rang the doorbell and I just opened the door, like a fool. They had'—she waves a hand over her face distractedly—'balaclavas. We'd just been for a…a swim.'

Her face begins to crumple. 'She hasn't got anything warm.'

The tears flow like she's bleeding them. Her face is veined with the pressure. Her breath hisses forwards as she sobs. I can't even begin to think how much pain she's in.

My thoughts are taking on strange shapes, turning on me like they just noticed me in a crowd. And their mood is turning ugly. I was at the strippers. I was at the strippers with a no-good friend who works part-time as a gangster I think, but I don't really know. I was drinking beer in a dark room with a whole lot of failed humans while a handful of girls—empowered or disempowered, I don't know—took their clothes off for our gratification. Outside the sun burned down on the rest of the world while Louise took Hannah swimming, a mother and her daughter engaged in the happy cocoon of their rituals, while I was ogling someone else's daughter.

Someone came here and did this to my family. While I watched the strippers.

After a long time her weeping subsides, and she goes back to staring, the wakes of the tears shining across her cheeks.

'Wally?'

'They've found him,' she responds, absently. 'Hyderabad. There isn't even a fucking test in Hyderabad. I mean, what was he—?'

'Could've been anything,' I offer feebly.

'Yeah, anything with *him*.' There's a nasty edge of sarcasm in her voice that's new to me. The anger is unmistakable in her eyes. Two rings on the third finger of her left hand. A green stone, sunlight sparking in it. A child has been torn from her mother. Something elemental has been severed.

'They're putting him on a plane.'

There's movement among the nearby cops: a woman's whispering to the two suited men. After she breaks off from them, one leans forward.

'Mrs Keefe, we'll be telling the media that you and your husband will not be paying a ransom under any circumstances.'

She suddenly looks hopeful. 'Has there been a demand?'

'No. I'm telling you this because we may have to make some preparations. Now we do want you to have money ready, because what we tell the media and what we'll do might be two different things. Could you get access to a large amount of money quickly?'

'What's a large amount?'

He rolls his eyes, searching for a random figure. 'A million dollars?'

'No,' she says firmly.

'Couldn't you mortgage this place?'

Seems like a good idea to me. Four bedrooms, a pool, views over the city. Wally would be making a fortune.

'It's already mortgaged. To its limit,' says Louise, enunciating each word coldly.

'What?' The detective is visibly shocked. 'Why?'

'You'll have to ask Wally.'

The detective wanders off to relay this news.

'Where will you stay?' I ask, again seeking to push back the silence.

She shoots a look at the nearby huddles.

'They say I have to be guarded until Wally's back.' She snorts disdainfully. 'Watched.'

'Who on earth—?' I begin, but she cuts me off.

'Don't.' Her fingers splay into hard white stars like she's pressing them on an invisible screen between us. 'I don't know. I can't imagine...' And then, curiously: 'I just don't understand this life.'

•

The media interest over subsequent days is unrelenting and predictably divorced from reality. The police are working on a theory, they say. The police have a suspect, they say. The police have no idea, they say. They hold hopes the girl is being held, alive, for ransom. There has been no contact as yet from anyone claiming to have the girl. There have been claims which they're seeking to verify. There have been claims that have proven to be callous hoaxes. Illustrated liftouts in the daily papers suggest everything from a serial killer to a paedophile ring to an international conspiracy. Her school photograph becomes a permanent fixture behind the shoulders of the city's newsreaders. There is an aerial shot of their neighbourhood in one newspaper; I can see the pitch that Hannah and I mowed and rolled together, a pale scar on the vivid green of the landscaped garden.

No stone, however awful, is left unturned in the lather of their speculation.

Perhaps one stone.

In the free-association vacuum of their ideas, they note Louise is thought to have a history of depression. She was once investigated by an international body (she in fact gave evidence to a Dutch inquiry into NGO employment practices). No one goes so far as to say she is a person of interest or that she is 'helping police with their inquiries', but nor do they take care to exonerate her or pay any heed to her obvious distress. Meanwhile, Wally is accorded gravity, sympathy, respectful distance. The notion of questioning his absence from his family, and simultaneously from the team, never occurs to anybody.

I don't disagree he's blameless, but I'm struck by the lack of critical thinking when it comes to a man like him.

Craig gives a statement to the investigators explaining our afternoon at the Fillies Bar. It all checks out and he's left alone, which for a man with his recreational pursuits must be a considerable relief, but he disappears for a while anyway.

Wally rings me in the middle of the night, eighteen hours after I walked into his house. The detectives have allowed me to sleep in the spare room there, once they've satisfied themselves that I had no role in the incident. Their preference is for everyone to clear out completely, but as Louise has refused to leave they grudgingly agree I should be there with her until Wally arrives.

It twists the blade inside me: she wants to be here when they bring Hannah home.

Wally's call comes from Singapore, where for these last few hours I imagine he remains a figure of no public interest. He's awaiting the last leg of his flight home and wants me to get him from the airport.

Entering the cavernous building, it's immediately clear that there's been a tip-off: a black and silver knot of photographers and equipment completely obscures the entryway from the arrivals hall. A call goes up from among them and a few spin around to get their shots of me arriving. A few more rush forwards with microphones, their voices cancelling each other, a formless blur ricocheting off tiled surfaces.

I look over their heads: the board indicates the flight is yet to land. And so I spend an awkward half hour seated on a café bench, flicking away journalists while we all wait for the main game. Darren Keefe, alone on a bench with his despair. I don't want to give them the pleasure but I don't have a choice.

Eventually the mob rises and clamours as the first passengers come through. I'm so accustomed to footage of Wally in airports, pushing his trolley loaded with equipment bags, that at first I don't recognise him with only hand luggage. He's well dressed but not in team gear, his head slapped and pulled by the long-haul drag. Exhausted and depressed, without concealment.

His eyes swivel, looking for me. The cameras crunch one after the other, flashes firing from outstretched arms. The yelling is obscene. *Wally! Any news? Have you had a ransom demand? How are you feeling?*

That last one stops him in his tracks. He searches the scrum.

'Who said that?' he asks.

Woman in a suit, dressed and made up for television. The cameras now turn to her. She loudly announces herself and her network. Wally's baleful eyes fix upon her.

'How the *fuck* do you think I'm feeling?'

His venomous stare holds her as her mouth opens and shuts.

There's stunned silence for several seconds before the roaring begins again: none of these people has ever seen Wally Keefe uncomposed, unrehearsed. In the last frame of the silence I manage to call, and he finds me by voice, veers my way. We move through the pack towards the exit, the shape-shifting mass re-forming itself around us, a shoal of mackerel cut by two sharks. Wally pays no heed to them, nor to me. His head's down, pushing grimly forward.

We run in front of a rolling taxi which lurches to a halt, cutting the pack from behind us. Their numbers thin as we scurry into the carpark building and across the carpark floor. I unlock the car and Wally throws the small bag in the back seat. He slumps into the front, slamming the door behind him.

'Thanks for coming,' he says quietly.

'Are they telling you anything?' I ask.

'Police? No. They don't know, or they're not saying. You?'

'Same, really. I think they've genuinely got no idea.'

We drone south down the freeway, both of us staring straight ahead. I can see out of the corner of one eye that he's trembling slightly.

'You all right?'

He's studying his phone, hands bouncing all over the place.

'I'm fine, all right. Just...fucking fine.'

I decide not to push him any further. He makes three calls while we're driving. One to Louise ('Yep. Me. Twenty minutes.'), one to the police to tell them he's headed for Kew and one that I'm guessing is to team management, about retrieving his gear from India. He finishes by ordering someone to 'get the fucking media off my back'. There's a barely contained fury about him, from his frantic rubbing at his swollen eyes, to the tone of his calls, even the way he's sitting. It's been a long, long time since he and I have engaged in the combat that framed our childhoods—the blue over my state selection was probably the last decent tangle we had. I'm remembering now that Wally's response to emotional pressure is to lash out.

And there are others out there who don't even know, given his carefully controlled image, what Wally is capable of.

Somewhere around Mickleham Road a hatchback pulls alongside us and lingers just long enough in parallel that Wally and I both look across. It's a rental: the guy driving it gives us a guilty glance, then the back window comes down and some idiot points a camera at Wally. Big, professional lens. Wally looks around inside the car and finds the coffee mug I was using on the way out to pick him up. With his other hand he stabs at the armrest until he finds the window switch. Down goes the window and he hurls the mug at the hatchback, striking it directly in the centre of the driver's window. Mug and window shatter completely, revealing the driver's shocked face, the glittering shards of glass on his shoulder, as the hatch drops speed and retreats.

I'm left staring straight over the top of the steering wheel at the freeway ahead. Wally and Louise are being subjected to an intensity of suffering that I can't experience because I'm not a parent. Watching them is pure helplessness. I want to clutch at him, to find my beloved brother in his sorrow, there beneath his rage.

Outside the house the cops have set up a card table on the front path, stationed by the most junior of them, a kid with no stripes writing on a clipboard. At either end of the garden, motionless figures dressed in black. Helmets, heavy boots. Rifles, for God's sake. Wally's eyes are wandering over the scene, as if determining which side of his personality to engage.

'Don't come in,' is all he says as he steps out of the car.

I don't want to come in. I don't want any further part of this. The presence of the men in black is feeding a restless animal in my mind. Whoever's got Hannah is not a lone freak, a street-roaming predator. Whoever's got Hannah orchestrated this for a reason, and they're an ongoing threat.

•

As the weeks wear away, Wally and Louise gradually shift from bewilderment to insistence that Hannah will be found. A handful of the boldest journalists point out that the lack of a ransom demand, particularly in the case of someone as famous as Wally, is surely a bad sign. One openly suggests: 'It is likely the police are investigating a homicide, despite the poignant refusal of Hannah's parents to accept that reality.'

The journalist in question is Amy Harris.

I've refused to take her calls throughout. I assume Wally has done the same. I know viscerally that she's right to hypothesise in this way, but I'm not going to assist her. Within hours she's being pilloried by other commentators, some bizarrely suggesting such speculation is 'un-Australian'. Australians, of course, being known for their restraint when speculating.

Wally and Louise take to wearing purple wristbands ('Hannah's favourite colour') with 'HOPEFORHANNAH' stamped in them. People buy them from a newspaper website out of...what, solidarity? I don't understand it. I feel guilty not wearing one.

If Honey was still part of my life, she'd be urging me daily to talk to her about it. She sends me discreet texts, warm and supportive. But I don't want anyone's sympathy. It's misdirected when applied to me, to the dead cavity within me. I can't backfill it with talk.

I have a persistent feeling Wally isn't talking to Louise about it, beyond the show of unity they contrive for the cameras. The rest of us, crippled and strangled by the horror of it, will also endure by staying silent.

The certainty settles over me, accumulating day after day like a blanket of ash. Hannah's not trapped or held, reaching out to us across some formless void, willing us to find her. Hannah's dead.

Among the countless offers of support, I start to find the beginnings of some career opportunities. I greet them with an enthusiasm that is cheap, cynical and also desperate. I'm using more and more coke to get through the days; find myself turning up to meetings with fingers all over my nose, twitching like a fallen bird.

A cable channel called Globe Sports offers the best terms—all they want from me is night-time commentary of some pretty inconsequential one-day cricket. Good money, no great effort from me, and the rest of my time is my own. The role is a perfect fit for both parties. I'm both the garrulous court jester and the wounded emissary of the Keefe clan. Only on television can these contradictory personas converge. When I offer my schtick, an eyebrow or a smirk, the panellists laugh twice as hard because...well, *you know.*

I stumble once or twice, but the weight of public sympathy is such that it's almost impossible to alienate myself. One morning I'm part of a live weather cross to a breakfast TV program—the foreshore barbecue launch of some health initiative, people in message T-shirts, balloons, donation tins. I'm just about to go live with the weather guy when this pest appears out of nowhere and starts abusing me. I'm only catching some of the words over the various community-oriented noises around me, and fuck knows what his point is—some sort of conspiracy—but he uses the word *Hannah*.

Crystal clear and no mistaking it. I look directly at him—he's standing about twenty feet away, and I see him smirking, aware of the power of that word. For a few seconds I wait to see if I am mistaken, or if he's going to back down. I am not, and he doesn't.

So I charge him.

Just run headlong at the bastard and collect him around the middle. There's an audible *oof* as we collide, then we're both on the ground and I've got a forearm across his throat, choking the life out of him. He's going purple, his eyes bulging and—I imagine—gradually haemorrhaging into the dark recesses of his ugly head. I want the fucker to die, and I don't care that dozens of people are watching us and there's cameras everywhere. I want him to die by my hand, right here.

Eventually the crowd intervenes and I'm hauled off him, still trying to stomp his balls as we're being separated. He chokes and splutters, takes an eternity to get to his feet. They drag him one way and me the other. The live cross is cancelled, obviously.

But here's the illustration of my newfound identity. It's reported that night that I was approached and insulted by a renowned serial pest, and that I acted under extreme provocation. And the network, as rapacious and grubby as any other, 'has elected not to broadcast the incident, which was captured on camera, out of respect for the Keefe family's privacy'.

The job with Globe is just about perfect, though perhaps not entirely fulfilling. They fly me to domestic games: eight or ten international one-dayers for the season, along with a handful of domestic fixtures, some exhibition games. Easy.

I can carry out the role with all manner of intoxicants on board. The best combination is a couple of lines and some champagne. Yes, I'm looked at askance in various stadium bars, ordering the bubbles while I fuck around with my feral beak. But I tell you, it works: getting loaded makes life less of a chore. Management know I'm doing it, but they also know they'd be running on four flat tyres if I didn't.

The arrangement works fine for about two years. I get my teeth done, on the producer's advice. Little place in South Yarra, espresso while you wait in their renovated terrace-house lounge room. Espresso is probably what turned my teeth beige, but I'm not complaining. By the time they're done, my smile flashes in the blue shades of a glacier.

I even do some footy, boundary-line stuff, for Globe in the winter. For the live crosses I team a scarf with a pair of designer glasses I don't need. I'm putting a light blond rinse through my hair. Nothing radical, just a shade or so. Meanwhile, I owe a few people some money here and there—bets that went down, cars I've leased, things like that. But overall the living is surprisingly stable.

Then comes the night when it all gets upended again.

Rhapsody

The face again.

I just know this can work. It needs to work—it's literally life and death. I get the irony—'life' probably only amounts to an extra twenty minutes or so. But the instinct to prolong and preserve it is stronger than I realised.

Where I think I went wrong with the gaffer tape was in the pressing on and ripping off, because I only had to get the angle of rip away slightly wrong and the tape would tear laterally. It's not very good quality stuff.

So I've come up with a new approach, scuffing my face across the carpet so the exposed edge of the tape catches and pulls.

It's soon apparent that this technique works better, but is a lot more painful. You'd think I had bigger fish to fry, pain-wise. But the small agonies, like the small indignities, are cumulative.

Scuffing away, the skin on my cheek rubs off and melts into a sticky, raw wound. The tape has indeed caught and is pulling away by the centimetre now. I can sip tiny gulps of air through that side of my mouth. I imagine I look like Groucho Marx working a cigar, and that makes me laugh unexpectedly, wheezing in and out through the tiny aperture I've made.

The bag of cricket gear's at my feet. I've had to explain it several times since I came into the stadium—just felt like a net session, gonna give it away to some kids, it's a charity thing...I really would've preferred to do this somewhere more private.

To my left, his earphones resembling two giant novelty mouse ears, is Christopher Wilkington, former captain of England, Oxford double blue and fantastically boring human being. Had a terrific test average, built entirely on flat tracks and selfish not-outs. To my right, some drone from Globe. Mike or Mick or Nick or something. He seems bearable.

It's a night game at the SCG between two celebrity teams, for a charity called Shine a Light or, no that was a Stones song...Shining Path? Shiny something. It's grinding its way into the thirty-third over of the first innings. There's a plastic biro lying on my notes and I'm feeling the urge to stab it into Wilkington's left eye. I want to watch him scream and lurch back in the chair and pull it out with gelatinous eye-goo dripping off the end.

There's a push to cover and someone ambles in to field, heaving a lazy throw into the night sky. The backdrop to the arc of the ball is hundreds of empty seats. No one's said anything for a while, when there's a tapping sound on the rear glass wall of the booth: looking around I see Craigo grinning like a croc, beckoning.

Craig's been away for months, one of his mysterious disappearances. The first time he went, Wally and I thought he'd just moved on from our lives. Then he reappeared, and no amount of questioning could elicit an explanation. 'Just stuff,' he said. Another time: 'Checkin some opportunities.'

After further disappearances passed without explanation, we gave up asking. Some of it, I figure, was his 'Wattle It Be' tours, but they've mostly been outsourced to bomber-jacketed minions by now. Anyway, here he is, back from wherever he's been.

'How the fuck did you get in here?' I ask him.

He looks a little beery. 'Dun matter mate. Doworry. Hey, you wanna get in on some action?'

He's got moleskins on, tweed jacket and a straining chambray shirt. He's dressed, in other words, to fool someone that he's an Old Boy.

'What is it?'

'Little spot wager. The ol' guy, the CEO of the charity, whatever it is. To score more'n forty. Hundred to one.'

He raises his eyebrows foggily. 'It's good, mate. Good odds.'

I sigh and try to think for a moment with a hand in my hair. 'I'm sure that's because he's shithouse.'

'Heeeey...' It's his look. The one that says *trust me*.

'Okay. Gimme half an hour.'

'How much you want on it? I can do you credit.'

Craigo's bloody credit. Last thing I need.

'Just wait will you, mate? I'll have five hundred. I need to see a guy.'

He shrugs and ambles off. I duck back into the commentary box for the bag. Producer's flapping his arms now and urging me to get back in the chair. He'll be right. I'm headed the other way, down the office-lined corridors of the media centre and out, into the cool stale tobacco of the members'-stand bar.

First things first. I swing left into the gents and get myself a cubicle, chop up a line and snort it home. As I come out, a thousand angels sounding triumphant bells in my ears, a kid wanders towards the urinal, fumbling for his fly. He sees me—*sees* me for the darting, twitching middle-aged caricature that I am. Hope, disappointment and resignation, combined in three seconds of a twelve-year-old's face. How cynical he must be for a young fella. I throw him a gedday champ and he smiles uncertainly.

Out into the boozy light of the bar, and there's the guy. Reefer jacket, hand around a beer. I plonk the bag down, sniff my happy nose back and shake the wet hand. Derek. He looks through the bag: two bats, one used and covered in red cherries, the other brand new. Pads, gloves, sweaty old thighpad. Lastly—and I arranged the bag so the theatre would unfold this way—out comes the Australian jumper. He holds it up to his chest as if to check the size, but actually, pathetically, imagining himself. The crest is facing towards me, and inside the neck I can see the name written neatly in finepoint texta on the label, the way he's always done: *Wally Keefe.*

'How much do you want for it?'

'It's taking up room. I'll take eight hundred,' I say, feigning disinterest.

He looks troubled for a moment. We both know what's going on here.

'I mean Darren, I'm very grateful. You've lugged it all the way in here and my son, he's a good kid, but it'll take him forever to repay me that much...'

He looks hopefully into my eyes. 'I don't want to let him down.'

'Okay,' I sigh. 'Seven-fifty.'

'I could do six hundred?' He proffers the notes.

'Fine.'

I take his money, another quick handshake and I'm off, his request to say thanks to Wally ringing in my ears. Like, right.

Minutes later, I'm back on my arse in the commentary box,

bouncing off the vapid Yorkshireman. Right on the thirty-minute mark, Craigo reappears, tapping the bloody window again. I pass him the six hundred: he counts it, winks at me and disappears.

The wickets fall rapidly. There's two overs left, they need forty-eight to win. And onto the ground waltzes the CEO.

The ground PA greets him: 'Please make welcome the Chief Executive Officer of Shine for Kids, and former captain of the Danish World Cup team, Ole Terjessen!'

Oh captain, my captain. Craigo didn't mention he had form.

This could be interesting. Big man, thick moustache, swinging the bat around in circles as he adjusts his eyes to the lights. He looks thoroughly at home.

First one he watches through outside off. Second one he deposits halfway up the sightscreen with a loud bang. It seems Ole has a straight drive, and it's a monster. Third and fourth clear the rope at mid-on and backward square respectively. Fifth is a classical late cut through backward point for four. He closes out the over with a single to third man so he retains the strike. Been around the block, this fella. He's already on twenty-three.

The other mob have saved their opening bowler for the final over, but he looks tired. He trundles in and lets go a straight one, which big Ole slams directly back, nearly taking out the umpire at waist height. Two bounces into the fence and the thin scatter of spectators have come to life. I've even got some repartee going with Wilkington, whose version of exuberance is, 'Well by golly, he's hit that.'

Next ball, another pull shot. Four more. A glance to fine leg brings another four, and everyone, including me, is now on their feet. The Dane seems composed, unhurried. Next ball he drops to one knee, looking to hoik it over square, but only succeeds in getting the toe of the bat on it. It smacks into his front pad off the edge and squirts out to point as he ducks through for a single.

Shit.

The Dane's off strike. Twelve to win. Two balls left. I'll have to pinch some more of Wally's gear to recover from this.

But then a little crickety miracle: a no-ball. And perhaps sensing the crowd's eagerness to see the Dane do the business, the other schmo ambles through for a single, putting Ole back on strike.

He stands there with the bat on his log-splitter's shoulder for a while, surveying the field. There's nothing much to see out there—a standard six–three spread, four inside the restriction circle, the rest on the boundary. He thinks about that for a minute then rests the bat on the ground and taps gently as he waits for the bowler.

I've got the call of the delivery. I bring it down a notch, talking the bowler in.

It's a flat, hard full toss outside off: Ole lifts it up and out and into the stands and I'm screaming and jumping as though they've actually won the game with that mighty hit. Of course they haven't but I've sure won as the Dane is now forty-two and my six hundred bucks has just become sixty grand and I can't believe I'm lucky enough to have mates like Craigo who seems to know just where to be and when and how. Oh man, and how.

It matters not that next ball the Dane is bowled middle stump trying to repeat the shot, or that the game has now been won and lost and I should be commentating it and announcing the man of the match and talking through replays of the wickets and throwing to ad breaks. It matters not that in walking out as I'm doing, I've probably squandered the Globe job and with it any hope of securing a permanent gig calling tests next summer.

Sixty grand buys a lot of good times.

Wandering the carpark in search of a taxi, I've signed half a dozen autographs before I see Craigo, relaxed and proud, leaning against the grille of his new wheels: a heavy, low-slung black Chrysler that looks like it's been pimped out for a drug lord. He's grinning like a little aths parent at the podium, and he extends his arms, looking for one of those hugs.

'Bring it in!' he rumbles, and I'm swept up in his suffocating grip.

Desperately in need of a breath, I pull back. 'I didn't even know Denmark had a World Cup team.'

'That's the magic. Nobody bothered to check.'

'So how'd the ground announcer know?'

'Little something I arranged for your amusement. You like that?'

'Much. Where are we drinking?'

'New place in Elwood. Very exclusive. You got any better shoes?'

•

Four a.m.

Craigo and I are laughing it up with these two girls. We've just finished with a thing we call the Mister Joshua routine. We saw it in some eighties movie. Craigo gets his lighter and I hold out my left hand, with the thumb, ol' Squibbly, stuck out parallel to the floor. Craigo puts on his sinister voice:

'Mister Joshua here has forgotten more about pain than you and I will ever know.'

I do a tough face. He lights the Zippo.

Puts it under my thumb and holds the flame there until the skin begins to bubble a little. Normally he'll wait for a little wisp of smoke to curl up from the burning skin. Master of stagecraft, Craigo.

The girls shriek in horror. I stare back at them deadpan. Craigo produces an ice bucket with a sweep of his arm and I plunge Squibbly into it. One of the girls takes my arm tenderly, concern all over her lovely face.

'It's numb,' I assure her. 'Can't feel a thing.'

We all laugh and throw back a tray of tequila shots.

Later, I'm dancing with her and she's twirling, pouting, grinding against her friend. There's a lot of hair flying around, lights in my eyes, more hair brushing my cheek. She's young, but so am I. The hammer blows from the speakers stop a moment and she's pushing me, squirming with animal intent. There's perfume, faint cigarette smoke and sweet, sticky alcohol. With a hand on each of her slight shoulders, a finger on each strap of her black dress, I pull her in and against me. Now she's grinding again, breaking away, laughing, swirling back in. The friend is hovering nearby, a half-smile on her face. This could go anywhere.

I am the sixty-grand man.

Her friend is taller. Athlete's legs in stripper heels.

Anywhere.

The music explodes and the lights blast everything into a raging white cataclysm. The bass is thudding into my chest and I'm swinging my arms in the air like I can make it all go faster. Craigo appears, a tray of shots held high and raining on us as tranced revellers slam into him. I sweep one off the tray, slam it and throw the shot glass into the darkness. The nymph does likewise. Craigo leans into my ear and yells.

HOW YOU GOIN?

SWEET! I'M ON HERE BUDDY. ON!

YOU GOOD TO GO? He raises those eyebrows. NOT FADING A LITTLE EH?

I wobble an outstretched hand in his direction. WHAT YOU GOT?

NEW STUFF. STAY THERE.

He points and winks. I pull the girl in close and talk under the sweep of her hair, ask her if she wants to party. She does. I want to stay under the hair. I stick my tongue in her ear, bite her earring as my fingers trace the contours of her neck. The other hand finds a thigh, smooth and hard and angled towards me. For a moment, I cannot imagine a more perfect human form.

Then we're up and rising to it again and the last shot, it turns out, was tequila and there's a hot numbness in my mouth and the taste of her still, or maybe it's the smell, and the girl, the friend, the whole seething, crushing mob of the nightclub, we're heaving like we're tied to something gigantic. Great cities could run on this.

It feels like he hasn't been gone more than a few seconds, but Craig's back. Never caught on a dance floor, always the one guiding on and off, now he takes the nymph under one paw and her friend under the other and swings them both away. We're cutting through the crowd, half of whom seem to know him by the way they part as he advances. Or do they know me? I am the sixty-grand man, after all.

There's a booth clear against the wall. We slide in and I look up to see heavy men close the space through which we passed. We are enboothed. I look at Craig with new eyes, new wonder. He *knows* people. The human wall obscures us from view. He hands us little vials, plastic or very thin glass, my fingers can't tell. There's clear fluid inside, visible only by the air bubble that recalls a spirit level.

He looks at us paternally.

'Now kids,' he says. 'This stuff is called rhapsody, and it's got some kick. No more drinks, okay?'

We nod solemnly.

'And get out of here. I don't want anyone falling over.' He casts us a benevolent smile and pats me on the back.

I'm grinning like a fool. He slips around me, headed towards the adjoining booth. We pass each other sidelong, two shits in the night.

The girls haven't got up yet. The nymph has peeled the strap off one shoulder with an easy tilt of the hip, and turned the black dress down to reveal a breast in a black strapless bra. She pokes the vial under the fabric and it's held in the gleaming satin curve. Her friend is still watching: watching me, watching the nymph's long fingers tug the bra back into position. The nymph's eyes lift from there to meet mine. The friend's still smiling, and she leans on the nymph and whispers something that makes them both giggle. She's put a hand on that bare shoulder. Softly.

I'm in a fever. They're so young. I just want to get the hell out.

She's yelling to me across the booth table. Her teeth, so white, so straight and perfect.

'One more round! Go go go! Whooh!'

There's a waitress, three vodkas, deep lowball glasses. As soon as they're on the table the girl's got one of those fingers in her glass, dipping it and streaking the warm fluid down over my lips and chin. She leans in, draped across the table.

'I'm Emily,' says that mouth.

'Yes you are,' I agree, and she smiles.

We throw the vodkas back and stand to leave, and I remember the lights and her extraordinary arse, them walking arm in arm, her friend's hand resting just where the high curve of her buttocks meets the small of her back as they stride regally through the void ahead of me. The thudding sound from within and without. The blurring roar of the crowd.

And then there is nothing more.

•

Next there's me in a car in a state that's not me at all. I'm in the passenger seat. Someone's in the driver's seat and I don't know who it is. We're parked, I think. I'm warm and content.

But someone's crossing the road towards us: the fleeting sight of them makes me feel protective of the other person in the car. They're crossing the road and it isn't good and they're walking towards the car and the figure is a man, tall and thin, in a suit. The suit's pale, and he's wearing a hat with a brim like a fedora, and it obscures his face as he skip-walks lightly across the road towards us. He's approaching the driver's side, approaching the door, where he slows, looks in briefly, then changes his mind. He's moving around the front of the car now, slower and more deliberate, turning past the front corner of the bonnet and angling towards me when a feeling of total dread consumes me. This man fills the night with a cold menace: the atoms themselves have turned sour. And I know as he approaches that he can feel my fear and takes pleasure in it. The fear and his pleasure are escalating in unison. He is nearer, leaning down and looking in and I lurch for the door lock, reach out a hand to snap it downwards, but I'm too late, and in a light-fingered instant he's opened the door and I find myself looking up at him and he has no face. Not darkness beneath the brim of the hat, just nothing at all. And somehow he's taken my left hand in his hands, holding my forearm firmly and I can see one of his hands and it's finely sculpted, cut from square angles, and the flesh is not the colour of the living but the colour of some kind of meal or grain, sandy, unliving and scattered with hints and faint shadows like I'm looking straight through his skin and into rotting flesh or a writhing mass of larvae. And I don't want him to touch me more than anything I do *not* want him to touch me but he has my hand and now he is reaching out his other hand to touch me, simply and deliberately on the forearm with his fingers, and as he does so I feel a satisfied smile that I can't see, because his pleasure has found a new height like laughter or even orgasm because *he has touched me* and now I can't be untouched, and I'm still trying to get my arm away from him but he doesn't even notice my efforts, because he has touched me. And I'm screaming and screaming and screaming and none of it will make the slightest difference because he has touched me.

There's stillness and silence. There's darkness, then there's movement.

Violent movement, and I want to resist it.

A crushing feeling in my throat but it's still dark. I want to gag, can't gag. Voices: calm, determined. Pressure on my chest.

There's something in my throat. Food maybe. I know there is, and now I'm focusing on it. That, and the terrible weight on my chest. Someone's hitting me. Hitting me hard in the centre of my chest.

My legs aren't there. I think my way to them and they don't respond. I try to fight back against the hitting and the voices tell me not to. Voices not raised but forceful nonetheless. I'm trying to see the owners of the voices but I can't see. Male voice, female voice.

I'm floating.

Now I've got light. I'm on my back, something soft under my head. I'm reaching for my face, fingers finding my mouth, the source of the gagging sensation. Hard plastic.

There's a tube in my throat.

They slap my hands down. Tell me to relax. What? How do I relax?

The faces belong to uniforms and the uniforms are paramedics.

'He's conscious.'

'Get the ETT out.'

I'm coughing as they handle my mouth and suddenly the object is gone. The woman's all business and she's pulled out a bloody great curly tube like a plastic shofar.

'What's your name?'

It takes me a moment to process this. People normally know who I am.

'What's your name?'

'Darren Keefe.'

It means nothing to them.

'What've you taken?'

'Whah?'

'You took something. You and the girls. What was it?'

Who took what? *Took*. Took, like stole?

'Oh. Fuck,' I say, grinning sheepishly. 'Ravage me.'

'What?'

'Rabitty. Ratshitty. Rap city.'

The female ambo is peering deep into my eyes, moving a penlight torch between them. 'Concentrate. This is very important. What did you take?'

Something about the urgency of her manner pulls me back.

'Rhapsody. It was called rhapsody.'

'We're working on you right now, Mr Keefe.'

I look around. I'm next to a wall. Pinpoints of hard fluoro light and open sky. There's a small crowd of people around the two ambos, but they're all in…Shit. They're all in scrubs.

'Hospital?'

'You're at St Vincent's. You're in the carpark. Someone dropped you here. You and two girls.'

Dawning horror.

'Where are the girls?'

She looks at the bloke. He says—

'*One two three.*'

And they're lifting me onto a trolley and we're clattering over asphalt. There's trees and darkened cars going past. And the world is unscrewing itself again.

•

This time I'm in a bed and there's even white light all around me. A drawn curtain. A man standing beside the bed.

'You look Indian,' I say. I know that's a daft thing to say, but someone's cut the lines to my verbal brakes. His slight smile corrects me.

'I'm Dr Khan, you're in the Emergency Department, and I'm a registrar here. How do you feel?'

I know the question's medical, not social. I try to think it through.

'Sore throat. Head very foggy.'

He reads a chart as he talks to me.

'All right Darren. You were dropped in the hospital carpark at 5.58 this morning by an unknown vehicle, along with two young females. On emergency admission you had a blood alcohol count of point two-two. That's very high, okay? Glasgow Coma Scale ten...You also had at that stage unknown drug toxicity, which we've now established to be a combination of some cocaine, but also ketamine and pentobarbital, okay? Now do you know those substances, you know what they do?'

'Well, the coke I do. How are the girls?'

I can see his face change faintly.

'You've also got a large burn on your left thumb. Do you know where that came from?'

I shrug.

'Mm. All right, well look, you'll be fine. We'll keep you in here and get you rehydrated through that drip and by this afternoon you should be free to go if your obs are good. Now there's a man here who needs to talk to you. He's from the police, okay?'

I can't answer. The walls are closing in.

'Okay?' It's that medical *okay*, the one that indicates things are not okay. 'My job is just to check that you're clinically all right to talk to him. I can't advise you about what to say, of course.'

He finishes with a small brittle smile and writes something, left handed. Then he's gone, and I can hear a few murmured words outside the curtain. Another man enters, neat and compact in a suit and tie, a blue-and-white chequered lanyard around his neck. He draws the curtain back after himself and sits in the chair by my bed, carefully places a black zip-up satchel on the floor by his foot, then watches my face for a while, his own face neither hard nor relaxed.

'Now, Darren,' he says simply. There are almost imperceptible movements of his head from side to side as he studies me, leaning forward in the seat. He's young, but he's watched Christopher Walken.

'I'm Petro Salinas. I'm a detective sergeant of police.'

He watches me again, searching for a reaction. Finding none, he continues.

'I know who you are. Obviously.' He smiles. 'Cricket fan. Now we need to talk about last night. Before we do, I need to say to you that you are not obliged to answer my questions, but that if you do, anything you say may be recorded and given in evidence against you. You understand?'

My mouth clacks as it opens, dried and plasticky. 'Yes.'

'Fine.'

He checks his watch elaborately with a raised forearm. 'The time is now 11.27 a.m. Now the two girls who were found with you early this morning. Do you know who they are?'

He's picked up the satchel, unzipped it and started writing on a pad inside it with a cheap blue biro.

I think hard but nothing sticks.

'No.'

'Well I'll tell you what we know. One of them is Keely Detheridge, nineteen, retail assistant. No ID on her, but her mother reported her missing and she matches the description. So working assumption is, that's her. She's conscious now and able to talk, but she has severe amnesia.'

Thank God for that.

'They're watching her liver and brain for any indications of permanent damage, Darren.'

He searches my face again.

'Now the other girl is Emily Weil, also nineteen, physiotherapy student from Berwick. Very bright kid, apparently.'

Why would you throw in a detail like that, I wonder.

'She's on life support as we speak, Darren.'

He looks deep into my eyes and I can't hide in there.

'No signs of electrical activity in the brain.'

The watching, again. I don't know what I'm conveying, because the world is hurtling through me and around the cop and me and I no longer know what on earth I should say. *Life support.*

He's seen something, because he leans back and writes.

'She was clinically dead when she came in, Darren. No pulse, no breathing. Her parents are at her bedside on the floor above us,' he points at the ceiling with the pen, 'but it doesn't look good.'

He sighs. He watches.

'You know this stuff you'd all taken, this...' he checks his folder. 'Pentobarbital. I had to look it up. Not something we see every day. Vets call it euthasol. As in euthanasia, Darren. They use it to put dogs down.'

I can see her now, the black dress. Her mouth.

'The Yanks use it to execute people.'

The long fingers, the gleam of fine sweat on her chest. The sleek muscles of her shoulders as she danced. Devoid of all erotic context, now I'm seeing an overexcited kid. A daughter. Me and people's daughters again.

'So why would you take such a substance?'

Part of me won't answer. The rest of me can't answer. Why *would* you take such a substance? He waits awhile. I'm imagining her in the ward on the floor above us. Stuffed with tubes, crowded by machines.

Her lips are blue. Not a corpse in the strict sense of the word, but her face is a story told, a movie watched. All of her that was promise is now realisation.

'Are you refusing to answer my questions here today, Darren?'

'No. No, I just. I just don't know what to say.'

The cop carefully writes this down.

'Who did you obtain it from?'

'I don't remember,' I say, but of course I do.

'If you can give us a name, we can step in and get the rest of this stuff off the street, maybe save lives. You want to think about that answer again?'

I do. I think about that answer, and what I come up with is that I value friendship above everything. Loyalty is all I've got these days.

'I'd love to help, but the whole thing's just a blank. We were in South Melbourne after the charity game. Nightclub in a back street in Elwood. Called Moss, I think.'

I can give him this, because I know any number of halfwits are going to come forward and say they saw me. He writes the answer down, but he's read me well, clearly unimpressed. 'It'd be really good to get a name...'

'Sorry.'

'Mm. All right. Look, they'll have to consider, if things don't improve this afternoon, at some stage the, well, the parents are next of kin obviously, and they'll have to review the continuation of life support. You...follow me?'

I'm falling, through the bed and into the centre of the earth itself, where it turns out they also have fluoro lighting.

'And if that happens, if they—er—let her go, then it'll be over to the homicide squad and you won't be dealing with me. So good luck, anyway.'

He delicately places his card on the bedside table. And with that he snaps the satchel shut and he's gone. The curtain swings lightly in his wake as the chair sighs and resumes its shape.

•

The continuation of life support. It must be a wrenching, terrible thing. I try asking the nurses as they come and go about the girl upstairs in ICU, the one who was brought in with me. I try to make it sound like neighbourly concern, and I'm disgusted by my tone even as I do it. The answers range from patronising (*let's just focus on getting you well, hey!*) to icy (*that's not your concern*).

The hard reality, delivered to me by the wall-mounted television, is that Emily Weil is dead by the following morning, and with her a part of me that I can't define.

In the days and weeks that follow my instinctive response is self-preservation, and if you think you'd be any different in this situation, don't kid yourself. It's like someone's trying to shove your head underwater, and of course you fight back. You strive for air, you suck and slobber on the breaths you can steal, even if the logical response might be to accept the blame and slip under.

It's strange how some of it, no matter how frightening or hysterical, just bounces off. The tabloid piranhas parked outside the house. The rolling scrum of microphones and cameras that follows me everywhere. The mysterious demonstrators who seem to have a matching cause for something so randomly hideous; in this case women's rights tied into a weird alliance called COSI, the Coalition Opposing Sportsmen's Impunity.

It takes six months for the thing to work its way through the system, to finally manifest in a courtroom. For the four days of the inquest I endure the hate-filled stares of the parents. But it's late on the third day that something gets under my guard.

The barrister acting for the family has the mother in the witness box. She is, I don't think I'm overstating this, a wreck. She weeps and sobs and chokes and it takes hours to get a simple few words from her. So it's hard to know why the barrister feels the need to ask her, just as things are winding up for the day—

'What disappoints you most about Mr Keefe's conduct that night?'

There's a brief stoush between the barristers about whether the question is permissible, and in the end the coroner lets it in just because she's curious about the answer.

Which is this: she understands her daughter might have been starstruck; that maybe she was a willing participant in the drugs. But she was a young girl, barely more than a child, and I am a grown man—physically at least. One who got himself into such a state that he couldn't help her daughter when she might have been saved.

'He abandoned my girl.' She forces the words into the room, almost incoherent. 'And now she's dead.'

And until that moment, through all the questions from the media and the police, from Wally and from Mum and the whole fucking lot of them, it's never once occurred to me that this is what I did. I abandoned Emily.

•

After dwelling on it all for another four months, the coroner delivers her findings.

She reads, eyes down, in a monotone. The judgment is in the words, not the inflection. Next to me in the gallery, Mum sits in a skirt and jacket that she probably would've preferred to be unveiling as mother of the groom. She's grief stricken. In the car on the way in, she's been blaming everyone but me.

'Well, these girls will throw themselves at sportsmen, won't they.'

I tell her I don't think that's much of a justification. And besides, I haven't been a sportsman for some time.

'All I'm saying is they know what they're getting into,' she hisses.

Now she sits stoic among the wreckage of her son's reputation as people examine her for traces of emotion. Her hands are laid neatly on her lap, but they're trembling. At first I think it's the stress. But the top one appears to be pressing down on the bottom one to contain it.

Tremors. Through my distraction, I realise I need to talk to someone about that.

The coroner finds that I was present when the substance was purchased or otherwise obtained, and when it was administered. She finds I most probably had no active role in the girls' decision to take the substance. She takes particular care to single me out for refusing to give evidence on the grounds I might incriminate myself, noting simultaneously that it's my right to do so but that it's my own con-science I have to grapple with. She concludes that Emily Weil died by misadventure, having been administered a toxic quantity of a con-trolled substance, causing respiratory failure and eventual death.

The substance can't have been controlled very effectively if a delusional man-child and two hyped-up kids can get their mitts on it in a nightclub.

The coroner refers the matter of my involvement to the police, and by late July I'm facing charges of using and possessing a controlled substance, to wit, pentobarbital.

I'm inclined at first to fight the charges. There's enough money sloshing around to pay for the sharks, even though the owners of Globe confirmed within hours of my discharge from the hospital that I was now on indefinite leave, to enable me to get all the help I need. I take this as a boning.

But Wally works his way into the mess: phone calls here, coffees there. I would say it's his permanent role in our family, being the titular CEO of the enterprise. But it's also his permanent role to be the face of Australian cricket. It does him and the sport no good to have me staggering perniciously around on the public stage. Another instinct reminds me that nothing from my brother comes freely: he's either repaying a debt he perceives he owes me—or he's setting up a debt to call in later. It's the way of all politics, as I'm starting to learn.

The advice, he tells me, is to let the charges go through. Look as sorry as hell and cop it. Despite the gravity of the outcome, according to Wally's best bureaucratese, the penalty could be quite minor. They're not saying you killed her, he assures me. They're saying you took drugs with her and she died. I think about the Weils. I doubt the distinction would mean very much to them.

So Wally arranges a fantastically dreary barrister to come along to court one bleak Tuesday morning and say a little piece about me, what a decent man I am. How it's hurting me, how I've changed.

We cram into an interview room adjacent to the court, streaked with the scuff-marks of a thousand other miscreants. The barrister goes through it all, glossing over the squalid bits and looking for redeeming features, which we both know are morbidly outweighed by the squalor. He has a complete copy of the prosecution brief, and I thumb through the photo book, reconstructing a night I barely remember. Handbag contents, my wallet and phone, the hospital carpark, tyre marks. Then, working backwards in time, the front door of Moss, an image of an alleyway I don't recognise, tin and timber fences stretching away towards a vanishing point.

The photo is in there because it shows a spray of vomit on the fence and the ground. Indeed, the following photo is a close-up of the same thing. How many people vomit, let alone piss, fuck, shoot up or even take a shit in laneways behind nightclubs, I wonder. It's hard to know what such an image could prove.

Tin fences.

I stare a little harder at the photo. And there, on the right, I can see a spot where the timbers run horizontally, forming a rough capping above the tin fence. And on the horizontal timbers, a series of hand-painted black letters.

I have to squint to make out the name, but there's no doubt.

Hope Sweeney, Bootmaker.

He's long gone by now, I imagine. But his grim scepticism about the graceless prodigy who was Darren Keefe, that outlives him.

An hour later in the courtroom, the magistrate calmly points out that I'm yet to cough up the name of the person who supplied the drugs, and that doing so might be seen as evidence of contrition, but my learned counsel is all over this. He produces a report from a toxicologist to say that the stuff we'd taken, thanks again Craigo, causes severe amnesia in most cases. *Of course he'd name such a person*, says the barrister over the top of his notes. *He wants to see this dreadful stuff taken off the streets as much as the rest of us. But he literally can't remember.*

The magistrate sighs in a tired way and says things about my public profile, my diminished status as a role model to children, my lack of maturity for a middle-aged man. He says he must impose a penalty that reflects the need for general deterrence, as if there are queues of people thinking about behaving like me. He makes clear that he's not penalising me for Emily Weil's death, but for possessing and using the drug that killed her. He fines me two grand and puts me on a bond.

And there it is: my reckoning with society is complete. Brisk, efficient and entirely devoid of any proper sense of damnation.

But of course, that belongs on the streets and in the living rooms of the nation, where a fallen sportsman of any hue is a sinkhole for righteous indignation.

•

At his insistence, I meet Wally at a café in the CBD. About the *public side of things*, as he delicately puts it.

My brother turns up in a suit and sunglasses, his half-hearted camouflage. But he is unmistakeably himself—the set jaw, the square posture, his tendency to duck-walk. People crane their necks as they pass, particularly when they see that he's talking to me. The bad brother. He deserves credit for meeting me out in the open, for allowing some of the stain to rub off on himself.

Three seats at a table by the window, a sugar dispenser and napkins in a stand. We order and while he waits he carefully works through the whole thing. I'm leafing through the sports pages of a curled breakfast-shift tabloid while he talks, reading the form guide through a coffee ring. The inattention bothers him, I can tell.

He wants to know how I met the girls, who their families are. How did they recognise me, or didn't they? What was the drug? What's the last thing I remember? I can't help feeling he's assembling something, some kind of Meccano assault vehicle for unspecified later deployment. I remind him that these are the very matters I was coached not to talk about under the counsel of the lawyers he hired for me.

Just as Wally turns the topic to the person he wants me to meet, said person appears. Corpulent, blood-red in the face, silver hair. Maybe fifty-five, with a half-sneer pre-formed under the moustache on his slabbish face. He looks like one of those hideous political operatives. He's eating a banana, for fuck's sake. I check Wally as though this is his first-ever practical joke.

'Really?'

'Yep. Really. You want help here, we do it my way. Alan's been doing reputation management for the Institute of Sport and he helps out with Cricket Australia from time to time. He's got some stupid people out of some nasty scrapes.'

I shake the boneless mass of his hand. 'Thank God I'm neither stupid nor nasty.'

The great oaf almost purrs with pleasure, and I can see that my early resistance is part of some inbuilt checklist he encounters with all his clients. The Kübler-Ross of public shame, with me stuck at denial.

The coffee turns up. It's scalding hot and milky. Wally pushes his across to Alan, untouched. He gets up and excuses himself, leaving me and the oaf to get to know each other.

'So,' he begins. 'Let's cast an eye over your particular shitstorm.' He sheafs through some papers with the air of a bored factotum.

'You've no-commented the police, which is good. Exercised the privilege against self-incrimination in court and blamed your lawyer outside court, which is also good. You were seen throwing a frisbee at St Kilda beach during the first weekend of the coronial hearing, which is bad. Photo in the *Herald Sun* wearing a T-shirt with the word *schadenfreude* emblazoned across it, which is also bad. Do you actually think through the implications of these things?'

We both decide it's a rhetorical question.

'You're yet to talk candidly about what went on, and to some extent you're prevented from doing so by the very real risk you'll put your foot in it. I don't ever want to know who gave you that horse juice, but they'd be feeling tetchy about their customer right now.

'Despite all that, we'll need you to do a confessional. On tabloid TV, someone soft. We'll train you up for it. Shed a tear or two, make it clear you want to set the record straight once and for all, yada yada. There's *shitloads* of money to be made if you do this right. You understand me? Shitloads.'

Wally never asked me who gave me the drugs. Why wouldn't he ask me that?

'What about the girl's family?' I ask.

The oaf is clearly baffled. 'What about them?'

'Can I approach them? Try to apologise personally? Check how they feel about me doing media?'

'*Ohhhh*. Sorry, I get you now. No. That would be a fucking stupid thing to do.'

'Don't patronise me, you fat fuck.'

The insult washes over him without a ripple. 'You need a prepared statement. To stop you ad-libbing in front of microphones.'

He opens his computer and fiddles around for a while. Because Wally had been sitting opposite me, he's plonked himself in a chair almost beside me, and now that Wally's gone he's uncomfortably close. I watch the screen as he clicks his way through his various rabbits and hats. A list of folders: *assault, bust-up/creative, bust-up/management, bust-up/partnership, chemical leak, financial default, hit and run, infidelity, sexting...*

'Here,' he says. 'Post-sentence.'

'What are your qualifications?' I can't help asking.

He takes out a cigarette and lights it, drawing thoughtfully. 'None of your business,' he exhales.

'Well, do you know what you're doing?'

He turns the computer so it's facing me directly. 'Go on then, you run it.' He waves a hand at the keyboard and ashes the smoke, just a touch prematurely. 'It's not about age anymore, Darren. Not about fame either. You're on the scrapheap, and I'm the recycling guy.'

I watch him sullenly. I'm reflected in the glass door behind his head: deepening valleys forming an arch from the base of my nose, the softening shape of my jaw. There are little silver hairs growing out of my ears. I've taken to snipping them in the bathroom mirror. Men with silver hairs in their ears do not belong in nightclubs. Rampant virility is behind me now and I misused it. Oh fuck, is this all there is?

And the clincher arrives, as I watch this turd working the mouse with his slug fingers. He turns the screen back to face himself.

'Now how do you want it?' he asks. 'I can do sullen and wounded, slightly defiant, ambivalent, sincere or grovelling.'

This is unbelievable. 'Sincere.'

'Okay. Good choice. How's this?...*aware of my status as a role model...became vulnerable to these influences once I was removed from the disciplinary structures of...what was this one? Oh yeah, first-class cricket... sorry to anyone I may have hurt or offended...Horror and revulsion at my involvement in these tragic events...*You like?'

'What about *Please respect my family and their need for privacy at this difficult time*?'

'That's for the bereaved.'

'*Obviously have a long way to go to regain the public's respect*?'

'Yeah, I can put that in.'

He finishes typing and snaps the laptop shut. Then, tucking it back into a bag, he leans back and squints into a pull on the cigarette, studying me.

'What?'

He bares his teeth to hiss out the smoke, offers me a hand. 'Cool. We're on. Consider me your misrepresentative.'

I ignore the hand. He ignores the gesture.

'How do you feel?'

'What do you care?'

He smiles maliciously. 'Oh I *don't* care. It's just that I need to know, so I know how much truth I've got to work with.'

'I feel like shit. Now if you're done, can you fuck off please?'

He rises with a contemptuous snort, and I'm left alone at the table, trying to piece it all together. I am a man who retains a public profile, but with all the good parts eaten away. Flyblown or something. How I continue through my life in this state is unclear: the talent I had for pleasing people is gone, and if I can't please them, then the current situation will prevail all the way to the grave.

Former cricketer Darren Keefe. *Disgraced* former cricketer Darren Keefe. The most conventional way to defy public expectation from here would be to go religious. Get redeemed, praise the Lord. Find some good clean folk who like to happy clap and dress young. They have such nice glossy hair.

I wouldn't last. I can't sing for starters, and I'm not a stayer. Particularly not when it comes to abstinence, and I'd surely have to abstain from something.

So assuming the public can never love me again, is there anything worth striving towards? Can I rely on the love of family? Mum adores me regardless, loves us both, in fact. She won't hear a bad word—said to Wally after the charges were laid that I'd just fallen in with a bad crowd. Bless her—I *was* the bad crowd. So setting aside for a moment the culpably naive, that leaves an absent father, possibly deceased by now, and a brother who has the hardest job in the nation and is probably a little busy for a hug.

A man needs friends in such straitened circumstances, and here comes one now.

Ambling down the street, happy as a lark: Craigo. He's wearing the work outfit that used to be his everyday before he discovered gangster chic: bomber jacket and jeans with runners. He's looking into the middle distance, but then swings his big head just at the right moment to clap eyes on me and make a great display of his surprise.

'Daz! Me boy! What the hell? I was just—'

He points further down the footpath as though some other errand brought him here, then closes in for the obligatory squeeze, leaning over me in my seat as he does so. Smell of aftershave and leather. But his hands are odd: he's feeling me up, like he's searching for breasts. Is this sexual? I rear back a little, then he sits himself down, fishing for a menu.

'Just passing by, hey mate?'

He looks guilty. That hug was weird.

'Yep. Well, sort of.'

'Were you watching me just then?'

He chooses not to answer, orders a milkshake.

'So who was that guy, anyway?' he asks. Can't help himself, the big dill.

'I dunno. Graham or Bernard or something. Wally's fed me to the PR people.'

'Excellent. At least the quality of the lies should improve.'

He guffaws and slaps the table hard enough for nearby diners to flinch. Then he closes in. 'Do they want you to do a confessional? Current affairs telly? Eh?'

I look down awkwardly and shuffle the condiments around.

'Mate, I know you came under a bit of pressure to, you know, to say where the gear came from. And I know you didn't say nothin. I appreciate it. Times like, like that night, I just get so excited for ya. So excited. Y'know, I just wanted you to have a great night, do somethin special with the girls. It was for you, mate. For *you*.'

'Please Craigo, I don't wanna hear it. I haven't said anything to anyone and I never will. I just don't want to talk about it anymore. It's over, okay?'

'Jesus. All right. You're not gonna cry, are ya?'

He's tilted his head, looking up under my eyebrows. There's a lecture coming, I can sense it.

'The public can't remember anything for more than a couple of days, my friend. So unless this fuckup's got some new chapter in it, the whole world just forgets. You can rely on someone to drop their pants, or some Lebo to shoot some other Lebo in St Albans, or a politician to get caught in a public dunny or a ferry to flip over or, or, airliners, fuck! Who'd get in a plane these days? Doesn't matter what it is. The entire world's like a budgie with a fucking mirror now. And you, you're just famous. Doesn't matter for what. You're now operating on a level where the crap that destroys ordinary people, it just gets brushed over. Once you get through the apology thing with Ian or whatever his name is, you'll get a B-celebrity makeover, renovation show, dancing with the wheelchair kids, something, and away you go. People don't like their celebrities to just disappear. They wanna hold 'em close. Even when they fuck up. They're still happy if they're hating them. That's the modern truth, right there.'

He seems satisfied, and the dreadful reality is that he's right. I've never seen a moral stand-off in public life that didn't end in a shambling bloody compromise. Moral insistence went the way of pistol duels.

'I got something for ya.' He produces a large black briefcase I hadn't noticed he was carrying. Reaches inside and throws a taped-up plastic bag onto the table. I study it for a moment without taking it. There's branding on the outside: *Hook Line and Sinker—For All Your Boating Needs*. Has Craigo ever even been fishing?

'Careful opening that,' he says, looking both ways.

I work my way through the tape and plastic. Inside there's bundles of used notes. The sixty grand. I try pushing it back across the table to him.

'Mate, you earned that money legittermantly.'

'Take it back mate,' I sigh. 'I didn't earn it. I won it in a bet, and it's a night I'd rather not be reminded of.'

Craig looks wounded. 'I can't. I'm not walking around with it. It's your money. Mate, if you wanna get through this shitstorm, you gotta be more commercial. Take it to the track, use the on-course bookies—you wanna blend of box quinnies and nose bets for the favourites. Don't keep the slips, mix it around. You don't wanna bet consecutive—'

It seems the chief punishment for my sins is going to be the amount of bullshit I have to endure. I take the plastic bag and walk off on Craigo, mid-sentence—something I would never have dreamed of doing prior to this moment, but the balance of pity between us has shifted. I've spent my life pitying the silly fat man: being his famous friend, giving him marquee access to a world his own talents couldn't command. Now he pities me: it's time to go.

I can hear him calling out *gimme a ring* as I wander off, down the busy city street. Then he's in his pimped-up Merc, cruising by with his mouth opening and shutting silently behind the clean glass, pleading with me to accept a lift. But I've reached a tram stop, back turned on him.

I wish my brother was here. All of a sudden I really do, as strange as that probably sounds. His dour instinct for what the moment really means. I wish I'd stayed at the table and he had too; and the PR ghoul and Craigo the Affable Fat Man had never materialised. We could've just talked it out: me and Wally against the world. Somewhere underneath it all we're still ourselves.

The yelling from behind me continues. Pleas and entreaties— louder now because he's got the window down. Stupid fucker. I get up off the bench and storm into a lane of traffic, causing the nearest car to squeal and slide a bit, and next thing I'm in Craigo's driver's window, head and shoulders, right up in his face.

'You can keep your fucking cash,' I hiss at him, and throw the bag into the back seat.

He's snookered. He can't reach around quick enough to get it, can't abandon the car in the middle of the road. The last I see of him is the face of a hurt and confused child.

Thankfully a tram rolls up, a tram to anywhere. I dart onboard and sit in a corner as it rumbles downhill, people coming and going while I remain, a mute island among them.

Resurrection

The carpet's wet where I've been rubbing; a gelatinous slick of my skin and blood. The tape is halfway off, hanging limply from my mouth. I can probably get by with just half of it off—the breaths are deep and good now, but I want complete release. I want to be able to answer back when they get me out, say something witty and daring before lights out.

Je ne regrette rien, fuckers.

But I've hit an obstacle: I've lost face. The slick is too wet to create friction against the tape now. It just slips over the surface and no longer pulls free when I rub my face on the carpet.

I try for a while to catch the loose end in my teeth, swinging my head back and forth like an idiot. Eventually I catch it, then I have to do some serious thinking about how I can pull on it. I roll my tongue over it, tasting the blood and glue and filling my mouth with carpet fibres. I pull faces, trying to find the purchase that will allow me to rip more of it free. But all of the exaggerated grimaces and pouts and kissy faces are worth only a couple more millimetres.

My tongue's cramping. I may have to mumble my last words through half a mouth.

Within weeks of the conversation with Slimy Al, I'm plonked in a swivelling makeup chair at a TV station. Al's hovering at my side in the very same suit. We've practised my lines half a dozen times. He was disappointed the network wouldn't give him the questions in advance, but he seems happy with the general tone of the station execs, who assure him they want this to go well, for everybody. The station owns the broadcast rights for domestic cricket. These days they run ads for their lifestyle shows during the game, digitally superimposing pictures of buff young home renovators on the televised outfield. Lifestyle is sport is news: baubles from the same showbag.

My interrogator will be Elizabeth Brookes, the hard-hitting screen journo who shot to prominence on the back of a rare interview with Taylor Swift, followed by cross-promotional puff pieces on the wedding episode in *Family Bay* and the winners of the reality quest *Café Love*. She owns a Sunday seven-thirty slot in soft focus and hasn't asked a penetrating question in fifteen years.

'You know she'll flirt,' says Alan.

'Okay.'

'You'll flirt back, right? And cry. The minute she gives you an opening, fucking go for it. You understand? You're not live. They can cut it while you recover. Snot, makeup everywhere, I don't care. Just get the fucking waterworks going, okay?'

I nod, causing the makeup brush to stray onto my hair. The technician sighs irritably.

'That's my boy,' he says, clapping me on the back as he leaves. I call out after him as he retreats into the gloom.

'I'm not your fucking boy.'

But right now, I most certainly am.

.

Elizabeth Brookes is there in the small studio when I enter. Power suit, cloud of hairspray as she reads her notes. She's elegant and sternly beautiful.

She flicks the hair-sprayer away and stands to shake my hand, a heavy gold fob swinging on her wrist.

'Darren! Thanks *so* much for coming on.' Her voice is confident and unexpectedly deep. 'You wouldn't believe the level of interest in this.'

She looks to the heavens like I'm manna from them.

'It's a pleasure,' I reply, then lower my voice to a conspirator's whisper. 'You know we specifically asked for you.'

She looks at me sidelong with a painted nail hanging in the air, eyes narrowed. Then she throws back the head and horse-laughs. 'You're a charmer, just like they said! Let's get down to it, hey?'

She resumes her seat and the crew closes in around us, silently raising and lowering the cameras. There's a soft lamp beside us and a small table between our knees with two glasses of water. The lamp is purely for effect—there's lighting rigged everywhere. Someone calls action and her pupils dart. I realise there's a teleprompter behind me, but none behind her. In the darkened depths of the room, Alan's propped against a door jamb, watching.

'Darren Keefe, thank you for joining us.'

I focus on the two words Alan has hammered: *grave and subdued.*

'It's a pleasure, Elizabeth.'

'I want to start way back, Darren, and ask you: what were the first indications that you had a special talent for the game of cricket?'

She smiles generously. I'm safe here.

'Well I'm not sure that I did have, Elizabeth. But if you play enough backyard cricket against the future captain of Australia, some of it probably rubs off.'

She laughs. 'Well, you say that, but the numbers suggest otherwise—sixteen thousand first class runs, thirty-two centuries, the fastest fifty in domestic history...these are amazing statistics.'

'I faced some awful bowling, you know.'

The laugh again. 'You once hit—I'm reading here—you hit an English county bowler onto the roof of the Glamorgan Members' Stand. No one's ever hit a ball that far in the history of cricket. I mean, *how*? What's the magic?'

Oh, you dreadful sycophant.

'That was 1992 or '93, I think. It was downwind, okay? People have exaggerated that over the years.' *No they haven't. I hit the fucking cover off the thing.* 'It was a bit lucky. You put it up there and sometimes it sort of lodges in a jetstream and...' I make a rocket motion with one hand, 'it just keeps going.'

She lowers her brow ever so slightly. 'But it hasn't always been good times.'

'No, certainly.'

'Let's go back to March 1996 at the MCG. The Shield final against Queensland and you were in the form of your life.'

I nod and smile ruefully.

'West Indian fast bowler Federal Collins was playing for Queensland, and you—'

'We had an altercation.'

'Quite a big one as it turned out. Tell us what happened to your hand.'

'Well, Fed crushed my thumb.' I hold the wonky digit up in front of my face and regard it sorrowfully. 'It's not clear whether the ball hit the end and drove the bone here down through its socket, or whether

215

it just got crushed against the bat handle. End result was the same. It didn't mend well after the surgery, and I can't fully bend it.'

I give it a wiggle to illustrate the problem.

'What effect did that have on your career?'

I shrug helplessly. 'There's no feeling in the thumb—it never came back. As I say, I can't form a complete grip, and that fine motor control, well, it's everything. So my days were numbered. I struggled on for a while, but it was basically all over from then on, so, yeah.'

I look straight down the barrel of the camera with a larrikin grin: 'So, kids, don't ever modify your batting gloves like I did, okay?'

'And don't taunt fast bowlers,' chimes in the lovely Elizabeth.

'Absolutely, don't do that either.'

We both have a gentle laugh as the exchange fades.

'Times were tough after your retirement?'

'Yes they were. Looking back on it, there wasn't the support that athletes get these days. The money stops coming in, and you're released from all those disciplines you're accustomed to. And you know, people have been saying yes to you all your life, and then the music stops.'

'You seem to have taken refuge in the arms of some very glamorous women.'

She's arched one eyebrow.

'One or two. We're not naming names, are we?'

Laughter.

'There were drugs?'

I let all the levity wash off me, as visibly as I can.

'And booze, yes. It's a, it's a hard thing to describe if you're not wired this way, but...I just...needed more and more of everything. Excess. I just wanted excess.'

'There was the tragic disappearance of your niece, Hannah Keefe.'

I suck in a sharp breath and look down. She watches me for a few moments.

'What do you believe happened to her?'

'I just know that we lost the most beautiful child, someone who was...innocent. Completely innocent. Beyond that, I don't know anything. It's baffling and it still hurts.'

She's found a segue in that. 'So let's move to another innocent girl. The night when it all came crashing down.'

I need to relax. This is why we're here, after all.

'Emily Weil was nineteen when she died of an overdose after a night of partying with you. What on earth went wrong?'

She's put it open-ended, nice and fair. No kind of ambush, this.

'I was at a nightclub. I met her there, her and her friend Keely, and we danced a bit and at some stage we wound up with these drugs, this pentobarbital in little glass vials, and that's—I know it sounds unlikely but that's all I remember.'

And I don't know if it's the lights or the knowledge that I'm being laid bare, or the invitation in her voice to do it, but without warning I'm sobbing. I'm just plunged into a slobbery fit of weeping, head bowed and face in hands. I know they've left the camera running because this is what the punters want to see, but here and now, in the boot that is my deathbed, I promise you the tears were real.

After the storm subsides, I squeeze out my eyes and mumble an apology. Deep breaths.

'I failed that girl terribly. I mean, I'd only known her a couple of hours, but I had a...a responsibility to them both. Christ, I'd been so indulged for so long that I'd lost sight of consequence, you know? Someone else always took care of everything. I can't imagine the sorrow I've caused, can't fathom it. It's a stain on my soul that I can never be rid of. I'm so sorry. I'm...'

The blubbering starts again and this time they cut after a minute of it.

'Terrific Darren,' coos Elizabeth. 'This shit is *gold*.'

But I can't stop, and now she seems surprised by the notion that the grief might be real.

'Have some water?' she asks meekly.

The rest of the interview is more straightforward—what the future holds, what I think of my brother's career, more flirting. The tears are forgotten, and along with them, Emily Weil. I can feel Elizabeth winding up to a conclusion, when she asks me a surprising question.

'So Darren, your agent has negotiated a hefty fee on your behalf for this interview. What are you going to do with that money?'

'He has?' I blurt. Then I look out into the darkness to see Big Al frantically nodding. 'Yes, he has. We did that so we could donate every cent to the Weil Family Foundation. And I urge any family who's been touched by the scourge of drugs to do the same.'

'Darren Keefe, it's been a pleasure.'

'Thanks Elizabeth.'

They cut the cameras and Elizabeth lets out a whoop of joy.

'We fucking *smashed* that!' she screams. And before the words are out of her mouth, Al's lumbering in, those porcine eyes wide with fury. 'What the *fuck* were you thinking? You reckon I work for free? You miserable, self-indulgent cunt...' He's grabbing at me, flapping, tripping on cables, losing his shit. I peel the little mike off my lapel and throw the cord at him. His abuse fades to background noise as I slip into the fire escape and down into the street.

•

It gets easier from there, just as Craig predicted.

The network picks me up, first in a handful of guest reporter slots on *Boarding Pass*, the travel show for the cashed-up and unimaginative. All I have to do is lie on banana lounges and grin while I read a script. Now and then I liven proceedings with a spot of paragliding or heli-skiing. The contract is for an annual salary, so occasionally I roll up for an MC gig, or maybe a Christmas special, but none of it's too onerous.

They send me to a warehouse in Thomastown to pick out some suits. So far in life, I'm a guy who's only worn suits to court. Nothing looks more pitiful than an athlete in a borrowed suit. But these ones are magnificent, even to my untutored eye. The company people walk in small circles around me, dropping pins in the hems and peering intently at the seams. They smooth their hands downwards over the lapels, hitch with thumb and forefinger at the waistbands of the trousers until they're completely sure everything hangs as it should.

When they feel the climate is right, the network brings me back into cricket, this time as part of a well-informed expert panel, talking about the game before and after it's happened. I've got the suits. I've got the teeth, and they spend ages on the hair, which is getting just a little blonder. I've discovered spray-tanning: a light golden glow for those times that I'm doing public things but I'm not in TV makeup. Trust me, you can hardly tell.

The highlights are sliced up and fed into blog posts and other smallgoods. When controversies arise—a drug bust, a late-night-car-crash-and-fail-to-report, I write in a major daily. Vague homilies about personal responsibility, calculated to provoke outrage because outrage sells. *How dare he lecture anyone*, etc. Then back to the cocktail bar.

I get some more fantastic suits out of it. Just a little glossier than the previous ones. The sheen works well under the lights. I get free flights, hotel rooms. The money isn't a fortune, but when you're not paying for much else it's certainly enough.

•

Wally calls a press conference one dull April day and announces he's retiring from test cricket, effective immediately.

It's been coming, of course. His movements have lost their feline fluidity, and his air of serene permanence at the crease has been replaced by something more like stubbornness. There's constant injury speculation, to which I mischievously contribute now and then. *He's had dodgy hamstrings since we were kids.*

Sitting there in a Cricket Australia polo shirt encrusted with logos, he reads from a statement. His head is down over the microphones, his brow tense with strain. I know that look, though you don't see it often. His voice, his worried face, carry into millions of Australian homes and cars, into sheds and kitchens and print media and syndication globally. Over the smell of the evening meal browning on the stove, Australians will learn that their monarch has abdicated. The Governor-General could take a walk and it would be lesser news. Adults will feel their own mortality just a little; kids will mourn. He must choose his words carefully.

'It has been the greatest honour of my life to captain my country. So many kids dream of the opportunities that I've had, and I am well aware of how lucky I have been. I have had wonderful support from the game's administrators, from my family and from my team-mates. But I must be conscious at all times of what is best for Australian cricket, and I now believe it's best that someone else steps up and takes the national side forward. My passion for the game is undimmed, but time stands still for no man. And I need to consider the welfare of my family, who have made sacrifices for me to occupy this role. It is a matter of public record that the captaincy of Australia has exacted a terrible price from me and from my wife Louise...'

His voice cracks, just enough, just enough.

'From here on, I wish to focus on the various charities I am now involved with, and yes, I can confirm that I will bore you all with a book about myself, just as my predecessors have done.'

There's a ripple of polite laughter at this. He answers a few questions in brief and clinical terms, then climbs to his feet, scooping the papers as he goes. Shouted questions erupt as the pack clamours for just that little bit more.

But he's gone.

•

The board arrange a testimonial dinner at the Ambassador in Sydney and the network quickly closes a deal to have me compere it. In media terms, this is a dream combination. The graceful retiring captain, feted by his incorrigible kid brother in front of a room of five hundred and a live television audience. Are the rumours of disharmony true? Could Darren Keefe say something wildly inappropriate on the night?

The board wouldn't have dreamed of having me near a thing like this only a few short years ago. But such is the effectiveness of my redemption tale, not to mention the magnitude of the rights deal struck by the network, that they're powerless to intervene.

I get a few shots beforehand: over the eyebrows, under them, and a few around the corners of my mouth. Within hours, the poison has pulled my face back into an approximation of what it looked like at twenty. Like a chord with one bung note in it: you can just hear it but you can't quite identify it. Still, it's better than looking my age.

On the night I manage to silence the room by talking of the awe in which I held him as a child, the dreamlike state we both emerged from, the jousting and punching and the heckling and the endless repetition of the same series of physical acts to tune them to perfection. I tell them that seeing this as a grudge, seeing it as disharmony, is to fail to understand how brothers operate. I tell them it took two of us for one of us to emerge fully formed in the world. A sacrificial anode, drawing the corrosion away from finer machinery. A second vehicle, pilfered for parts. I tell them I understand my place in the world as that lesser being and that it doesn't trouble me, but in fact fills me with pride.

I tell them about the day of his asthma attack and how it felt. I am standing at a podium in this vast stage and when I look down I am looking at a few sheets of white paper, blinding in the technical light. When I look up I see a dimmer glow, a sand-scattered ocean floor, those faces in their hundreds. And no one is speaking. I have them, I have all of them for this moment. The eyes look back at me as I remember him going white, going silent. *This is a thing you didn't know about your captain, a thing he carefully hid from all of you.*

He's at the front table, looking up at me in his tuxedo. Composed, dignified, still. Somewhere between man and middle-aged man. His mouth is a fixed line of authority and calm. A mouth I punched many times, a mouth I watched that time, gaping for air, reaching for life. I can't tell from up here whether he desperately wants me to shut up, or whether he's comfortable with me trawling through such things. Louise is beside him in a scarlet gown that lends itself to the occasion. She's reaching over his shoulder towards a waiter—not listening, I'm sure—pointing delicately to her glass. A flash of jewellery. Her hair. A refill.

I free them from the silence with some laughter. This is a man, after all, who once rang me from Karachi in the middle of the night to complain to me that a regional newspaper in Quetta had got his batting average wrong (by zero point oh three), and needed to be reminded that there was a military coup going on. A man so impervious to sledging that it was often left to me to tell close-in fielders to shut up, even when it was him at the striker's end. A man so particular about his health that he used to carry around a tiny square of paper with his blood type, asthmatic status and a history of all known illnesses written in minute script. Once, when he had it out to show someone, I whipped it from the palm of his hand and ate it.

When I'm finished I call for him to come to the stage and I watch him walking towards me, strong and centred. He smiles generously as he reaches me and shakes my hand, and says something in my ear, quite loudly, which I can't hear at all over the applause that's covering my exit, his entrance. I nod enthusiastically and do a little point and laugh thing. Our eyes are dancing frantically, trying to find each other as our bodies pass. *Are you in there?* his eyes are asking, and so are mine.

We never connect.

I flow on down the vast steps from the stage and take my seat at the front table next to Louise. There's handshakes and laughter at the table, and she puts an affectionate hand on my thigh as she congratulates me. I can see their ring on her finger, aglow in the half-dark. Her hand is shaking slightly. She smells of chardonnay.

Wally's reached the podium, waited for the applause to subside and thanked me. There's kind words about my free spirit, my example of living for the moment, my capacity for fun. All of these things, I know and the room knows, are euphemisms for my inability to keep a lid on it. He swiftly moves on to wider themes. And as I listen to his summation of an entire career, I sense no pathology, no wear and tear. There's Hannah, of course. But if Hannah was going to break him, he would be broken by now. For someone with such obvious resilience—a facet in which the public can see what I see—the passage of time would ease the pain, not compound it.

So why is he retiring?

He talks about completing the circle. Says he's achieved what he set out to achieve, has left Australian cricket in better shape than he found it, and other such roll-the-credits clichés. But you don't live as competitively as Wally and then one day just lift your foot off the pedal. Devoting himself to his charities? I don't think so.

He's finishing up. A smile, a hand modestly raised in half-protest as the applause swells and fills the chamber. Hands are thrust forward. Cabinet ministers and rock stars; other veterans of the public gaze. As though each might ease his transition to the afterlife, these are the coins for his eyes, these pecks on the cheek and handshakes.

He's inching forward, coming down the wide steps, moving at glacial speed towards our table. The throng around him shows no sign of dispersing. Louise watches, looks away, sighs. He's laughing politely at something someone's said. She's checking her phone. He accepts a glass of champagne from an outstretched hand, still shuffling gradually forward. Her face is awash in the phone's bluish glow. Godawful triumphal music fills the room and a floor producer is throwing to a break and people are milling around, heading for the bar, streaming to the bathrooms. And I'd join the migrating hordes but I've already snorted every trace from my little bag in anticipation of the speaking gig.

Now I can sense Louise looking at me, and for a second I'm reluctant to acknowledge this by returning her gaze. But I do eventually, and when she's sure I'm looking and she's locked me down firmly with her eyes much darker than I've ever noticed she says the words, or maybe just mouths them over the white noise.

'It's always been like this.'

There's a tiny smile of apology maybe, or resignation. I know she's near to crying, and for a frantic moment I try to imagine why. Hannah? Wally and his perpetual *other*ness? The ceaseless pressure of her life, with its public requirement of practised grace overlaid on clashing tectonic plates of managerial bullshit and human crisis? It's a wonder to me that she's not curled up foetally in a stairwell somewhere, rather than looking, as she does, like a statue perfectly carved to reflect the dimensions of her tragedy.

As I rise from the table there's backs to slap and hands to grab, but nothing like the intensity of what's going on behind me. I take the jacket from my chair and stab my arms into the sleeves as I push back through the crowd. Five minutes later I'm twenty-seven floors above the mayhem in my hotel room, hoofing scotch from the mini-bar like a dying man.

•

So the 4.15 a.m. knocking is a surprise to me, but probably not to you.

Loud, persistent, beyond ignoring. I reach the door, still in at least half the evening's clothes, and it's her.

Louise, alone and hopping slightly to remain upright. My head's swimming, not hungover yet, just not present.

I bring her in, looking like a guilty man both ways down the corridor, and she mumbles something about the bar downstairs. She'd waited for hours and eventually got a text message from her husband's manager to let her know he'd got a late flight back to Melbourne.

She stares at me with frightening intensity.

'C'mon,' she slurs, holding the front of my shirt. 'Fuckin tell me. You thing you know? Who the *fuck* is he? Fuck is he, Darren? Slept with him twelve years I dunno. Huh? You know? You ever...punch it out of him? Eh? The boys!'

She makes an exaggerated, sarcastic salute to a grandstand located somewhere near the airconditioner. I can hear a faint hiss as her body shifts in the fabric of the scarlet dress.

'Keefe boys! Fuckin jampions. Oohyeah. Jesus, whas in the minibar?'

She bends down, staggers a second on one bare knee and a hand and swings the fridge door open. I'm watching her arse, because the animal in me never quite sleeps. She finds the half-bottles of white, takes a slug out of one and slumps against a cupboard with her wrists on her knees. As she swallows then exhales, the tears follow her breath down and over her chest, flaring red where her skin's exposed.

I'm not going to lie here and tell you I've been a moral man, but I want you to know that I'm struggling in this room, on this night. If I'm lecherous enough to be wrestling with certain desires at this point, faced with my own brother's wife in a state of distress, having

225

come to me in this hotel room; does that make me a bad man? What if I feel that charge in the air and somehow evade it? What does it matter anymore? Her husband isn't here, doesn't care; mightn't find out anyway.

Half-sleep and alcohol have got me running in deep sand. Louise can't be another object of this endless bloody brother-angst. Yet she sits at the hub of our concentric circles, at the core of it all. And what does *she* think about it? I can't form a coherent thought.

The storm is passing. She's gathering her breath as she looks up, and through the wreckage I know she understands what's going on. She works her way onto one hand, one knee, finds her feet and totters towards me. Three steps, slightly taller than me in her heels. She reaches me, places a hand on each shoulder, eyes unfocused, but directed towards mine. And as she leans in, pulling me closer with the ends of her fingers, she takes back one hand and draws her hair behind one ear with a smile that says comfort, says trust. The world again, swirling inwards with all its permutations, a record playing backwards as consequence rushes to meet its cause.

Then she trips slightly, at the last possible moment. I take her weight, ease her onto the bed and watch her curl there. With her long exhalation, the moment is gone. She closes her eyes, an earring lying on the edge of her cheek.

Three hours later I can see her from the couch, tiptoeing through the door, her shoes held low in her left hand, stepping over the newspaper with a silent *morning* to the maids in the corridor. They look at her without surprise. Everyone knows who she is, and whose room this is not, but hotel cleaners have seen everything.

•

Mum's in a hospice by this stage. Louise did most of the organising. Nice place in Kew: third floor, peach walls and bluish pastel prints from the eighties. An aged-care facility, though she's not old enough to belong in one. Aged care in such places is defined not by chronology but by the scale of indignity: incontinence, dribbling, weeping for ghosts and ultimately dying. If you're twenty-two with a brain injury, or (like Mum), fifty-six and ragged with Alzheimer's, you're aged.

We've been talking over hours, over days.

To an unknowing observer, she would appear fine. She's remembering Wally's debut century for St John's, his first innings on turf. I was furious at the time, comprehensively outshone with a miserable twenty-five or so. But she saw the day differently.

'I was so proud of you both heading off on your bikes that day. I was tired, you know, and I'd see you come in from the fruit shop and you'd shower and change and go back out to play cricket all day in the heat and I remember thinking I wish I had that kind of energy. It leaves you at some stage, doesn't it? You can't feel it happening but it leaves you.

'You both needed new gear for that game. Grown so much over the winter and I hadn't even noticed. I'd got you these pads that were far too big because I thought you might get a couple of seasons out of them and I felt guilty sending you off with these pads, knowing they'd be flapping all over the place.'

How does she know what it feels like to run between wickets in too-big pads? From obsessing about us. Watching us with forensic attention to detail.

'But I sent you off in new pads, and Wally had the new bat, the Gray-Nicolls that he made the ton with.'

'You didn't see it, did you?'

'No, I was back at work. But I rang the grandstand a couple of times from the phone in the bar at the Commercial. They'd give me updates.'

'Shit, you missed out on a lot, Mum.'

She seems baffled by this. 'What do you mean?'

'You worked so much to get us those things. I'm only realising it now. Bloody dreadful. Did I ever say thanks?'

She makes a scoffing face, waves my concern away with a frail hand. 'I got a lot of pleasure out of knowing it was going well for you boys.'

'But how the hell did you afford it? You must have had to go without all sorts of things.'

She's puzzled again. 'No...no, I did better than the other girls.'

She's drifting.

'It was a pub, Mum. Weren't you all paid the same?'

'Well downstairs, yes. But I did better upstairs.'

The notion flies straight past me, kept separate by a locked door in my mind. *Upstairs?*

'Anyway Mum, you did a great job. It never felt like we were missing out.'

But she's watching me now, a half-smile forming. 'You didn't know about upstairs, dear.'

She's pushing at that door.

'No. What do you mean?'

'I did some other things for the money, you understand.'

'Mum, what are you...'

'Gratifying the men.'

Yuck. Oh Christ. *Yuck.*

'Mum, don't.'

'Don't be immature, honey. Goes on all the time. You need to know it. You're old enough to know it. '

'Mum, stop.'

But she's on a roll now and she's not stopping. 'Perfectly natural. The hotel was on the interstate highway. Lots of truck drivers, salesmen. Even policemen, if you can believe it.'

'MUM, STOP IT.'

'Oh come on, dear. There was no way I could support you two without a bit of cash work. I made too much at the pub to get the dole, but not nearly enough to pay the bills.'

I've got my head in my hands now.

'So we could only do it when we were working two-up in the bar. And never when I took you to work, by the way. You used to cook the thermometer, didn't you? Used to get fevers of sixty degrees or more, you little scamp. Anyway, one girl would watch the bar and the other'd nick upstairs for a bit. I mean it wasn't full lying-down sex of course. Didn't have the time, for one thing. Usually it was just a quick handjob or a—'

I try to block the sound of her with an anguished groan.

'Oh you're such a baby.'

Now I've got my fingers in my ears but she's so blithe she could be discussing the football.

'The owner never knew. He only used one of the upstairs rooms as an office. The rest of them were empty, but they all worked off the same master key. Did it for years.'

I'm looking out the window, wondering if she can be distracted. Nothing presents itself.

'We even had the boys doing it in the end. The young ones. You know, some of the men have…preferences.'

I'm up and heading for the door.

'Of course, if it was anything too elaborate we'd have to send them down the road…'

•

It takes me two weeks to get an appointment with her neurologist.

He's Dutch. Tall and very mild. He observes me drily while I explain what's happened.

229

'So what do you want to know?'

'Is it true? What she told me?'

He laughs lightly. 'I don't know.'

Shuffles forward in his seat, fidgeting with a pen in one hand. 'There's two phenomena at work here: confabulation and disinhibition. The confabulist on the one hand is constructing patently false stories because the processes of memory and active cognition are muddled. That person is articulating something they imagined, but which they think is the truth. A non-malicious lie, if you like, simply making a new reality inside your head. Mm?'

I nod. It seems to satisfy the *Mm*.

'Disinhibition, on the other hand, can work in the other direction. Have you ever been very drunk, Mr Keefe?'

'Oh, I've seen drunk people.'

He misreads my smirk.

'Yes, they can be quite a handful, can't they? Well you know that "truth serum" thing about being drunk. It's just the loss of inhibition that brings everything out. Now Alzheimer's and other dementias can have a similar effect: the social conditioning that keeps the truths inside has been stripped away, and it all just tumbles out. So your mother may be inclined to invent things, but also to drop her guard about sensitive things.'

'That's not a lot of help.'

'No, I imagine it isn't. The best suggestion I can make is to gently examine your mother's story and see whether it makes objective sense. Look for corroboration.'

'Will she admit it to me if she's lying?'

'No, of course not. Because in her mind she's telling you the truth. You'll only distress her. Look outside her if the issue is really troubling you.'

As I'm walking out the door he ventures an afterthought. 'Your mother is an old lady, Mr Keefe. You could just let it go.'

'She's fifty-six,' I snap back at him.

But it really doesn't matter.

•

Despite his advice, I can't let it go, and the temptation to take it up with Wally proves to be too much.

I wait until mid-afternoon to call him because I've heard he's in Dubai, from where the new barons run cricket. I can tell from his greeting that he's distracted, tetchy. Good sense would be to ditch the planned conversation and just keep it social.

But as we know by this stage of the car ride, I'm not a practitioner of good sense.

'What is it?' he demands.

'Good thanks mate. And you?'

'Darren, I've got people here. What do you want?'

So he's done with the niceties. Down to business then.

'Do you think it's possible Mum could have been a hooker?'

'A what?'

'Hooker. Prostitute.'

'Darren, what the fuck are you talking about?'

'Sex worker. Mum.'

He releases a loud sigh of exasperation into the mouthpiece. 'Where the hell have you got this idea?'

'She told me. Says she used to turn tricks at the Commercial. Upstairs. For truckies.'

He doesn't reply, but I can hear him moving about, hear a door closing. His voice returns, lowered to a vicious hiss.

'Listen you fucker. You've done enough to smear our family name over the last twenty years. Enough, you understand? You want to drag your own reputation through the shit, that's your life. I don't give a fuck. But you're not traducing our mother's character. And I'll tell you something else. I've worked hard to build a reputation that's the exact inverse of yours. I go through life making sure people understand that I'm not like you.'

He's waiting in silence because he wants that to sink in.

'So I take it you don't believe her.'

'It's not a question—' he stops, realising he's raised his voice. 'It's not a question of what I believe. It's a fucking ridiculous story. Our mother is a decent person who made sacrifices to give us a life. You want to bring her down? You want to go talking to your media mates? Huh? Need another revelation to keep yourself in the news?'

'No.' He's driven over me. The brute-rational bulldozer. 'I just want to understand it. I really don't understand those years.'

'Yes you do. What you don't understand is how you turned into such a fuckup. You had a good start, and Mum had everything to do with that. So leave it alone.'

I can't answer.

'Are we done?'

I still can't answer.

'Good.'

•

Another time I turn up at the home, come out of the lift and take the left turn that leads to her door. It's late afternoon, and someone must have left her door open because a bright square of golden light falls on the peach wall opposite the doorway. I'm stopped mid-stride in the sad corridor, because there are shadows on the bright square. Hands. Hands working themselves into shapes.

A fierce-looking dog. A goat. Then a whole lot of fiddling around, the creatures half-emerging from the curl and stretch of fingers and then rearranging themselves. A short, fat rabbit becomes a camel. The hands rest in camel pose for a moment as though satisfied with their work, then they drop away abruptly, and the square of light is just a projector screen after the slides are done.

I round the final corner and there she is in bed, propped up and beatific, head still inclined towards the patch of light on the wall. The hands have retired to lie on her lap, over the fold of the blanket. I scan my childhood and realise it's another thing I didn't know.

Her voice appears mid-sentence as though I'd been sparring with her all along.

'You're still not understanding it,' she says. 'You come to a point where dreams and memories just merge into one another. For all the good they're worth, they're the same thing.'

I hate it when she talks this way, when she accesses some spooky zone of insight that cuts across her practical self and reveals someone else.

'What do you mean?'

'I mean that knowing something happened, and *thinking* it happened, the difference doesn't matter in the end.'

I don't want to grapple with this but I can't help myself. 'Isn't that what photos are for?'

She looks at me like I'm a child to her once more. 'You can show me a photo, but photos aren't proof of anything. Have you ever looked at a photo and felt that tugging feeling, that you want to climb back into that image? When you were young and beautiful? When you were doing something graceful?'

The pointed look again. 'Your playing days. The photo's as elusive as the memory. Just ink on paper. It's a rough estimate of a thing that might or mightn't have occurred. God, I can scratch it off with my fingernail and it's gone. You can't climb back into those clothes or hear that song or kiss that girl. You can't hold that child...' She sobs briefly and starts chewing a nail. '...severed from now. Scary, isn't it?'

A clock grinds away somewhere. People talking in the corridor.

'Some things happened when we were awake, and some of them happened when we were asleep. In the end, they're just images that you make up in your mind when you're sad, or sentimental. Or lonely. Oh honey, lonely. Once you've got no plans left, all you've got is memories and dreams. They're made of the same stuff. You stop worrying about the distinction, love.'

•

The thing with the truckies and the gratification isn't the only time it happens.

A little later on, a little further down the slope of her senescence, I find her sleeping when I walk in and I take a little while to survey the room. Wally's paid for everything. His flowers stand in a vase on the shelf at head height, but he's never been here. I can imagine what you think of me by now, but you might be surprised to know I've been the most frequent visitor to this awful place: watching her sleep, reading to her, sorting her damn pills and smiling while she pats my hand and calls me Warwick.

Did I mention? Warwick was Dad's name.

When she wakes and sees me, I'm brand new to her. That small mercy of the disease: the rendering of everything and everyone as new experiences.

Mum's lost weight. I know her hands, the spots on them, the curl of the veins. Their grip is as resolute as ever, but the tendons show now in a way that frightens me. *Darling man*, she murmurs, with her cosmic smile. I don't know if that's an acknowledgment of the adult me or another rewind to Dad.

She peers at me with that sweet little smile, like she's choosing from a box of puppies.

'Ooh, wait wait wait,' she says. 'I can do this.'

Her nose scrunches with the smiling, her eyes overbright. 'Yes!' she exclaims. 'You're the good one!'

'That's me, Mum. Other one's a rogue.'

She waves her hand dismissively. 'Oh he's all right, just no self-restraint. *Self-restraint*, darling. That's all it takes. We all get those feelings, all of us from time to time.'

'Who did your hair, Mum?' I ask, rummaging through her top drawer.

'They have a lady come round.'

There's a will kit. Who the hell would take a will from a woman in this state? I'm tempted to open the folder but I don't. A copy of a power of attorney underneath it, made out to Wally. That's as it should be, but I make a note to myself to ask him about the will.

Smokes. Lighter. I take two and light them both, hand one to Mum.

'Thanks, darl.'

She's forgotten none of the ritual—draws deeply with her eyelids lowered, pours a jet of smoke towards the window. I hurry over and open it.

'How's the cricket, love?' she asks, cigarette pointing from the back of her hand at the ceiling.

I haven't picked up a cricket bat in nearly three years. 'Terrific, Mum. Hitting 'em real sweet.'

We fall silent for a while.

'Mum?'

She's wide awake, alert.

'How did you do it all on your own?'

'Do what?'

'Raise us. How did you pay off Fernley Road?'

She looks startled for a moment. 'I didn't. You know that.'

'What?'

235

'Warwick paid it off. Lump sum, before he left.' Her fingers are absently straightening the fold where the bedsheet crosses her chest.

'Dad? How?'

'With the payout, honey.' She's looking at me like it's me that has the memory problem.

'What payout?'

'Well, when the army pensioned off your dad, he used most of the money to pay for Fernley Road. Then he took off.'

I'm confused now. Maybe it is me. Maybe the chaotic state of her mind is heritable and I'm already coming apart.

No. She's confabulating.

'Dad was in the army?'

She sighs with exasperation. 'He was a conscript. Nasho, went to Vietnam. He had a bad time of it and he, well, he broke down. The way his ankle was, they should never have sent him in the first place. So they paid him compo and that was that.'

'So he wasn't just depressed?'

'He was certainly depressed. He saw awful things, I imagine. Never talked about them.'

'Mum, I don't know where I got this from, but I thought he was just a drip.'

She smiles, more generously than I deserve. 'He was a marvellous man. So interesting and funny. He was very spiritual, a great learner and reader. Life just got the better of him. It happens.'

'Do you know where he is now?'

'I've got a fair idea.'

Maybe not confabulating. Maybe disinhibited.

She goes no further. Something about her face changes, the line of her mouth. The topic's closed.

I turn on the TV, in time to catch the last half of the local soaps. Mum in her heyday, even Mum five minutes ago, would have scoffed at this rubbish. Now she's enthralled, lost in some childish fantasy world where I can't reach her. The only sign of her real self, strong and true, is the pulse in the side of her neck, between the columns of flesh descending into her old-lady nightie. Dear God.

The news shines in at six; swirling chrome fragment animation to a newsreader I found interesting at a launch a year ago. Over her shoulder, the editorial image is a badly confected bat and ball on grass. I turn the volume up and this is what I hear:

The federal government has announced a judicial inquiry will be held into corruption in cricket. Speaking today outside her electoral office, the Minister for Sport and Recreation said the inquiry will be far-reaching and will spare no one.

The minister in pearls, a guy nodding in the background:

'This inquiry will call in current and former players, coaches, celebrities, whatever it takes. The Australian public deserve to have confidence in their sporting heroes, and this government is determined to stamp out the cancer of corruption in our sports. Cricket is the major national sport in this country, and that's why we've decided to start here.'

Stamp out cancer. Nice. Back to the newsreader with the half-smile and the big hair.

Although the minister didn't specify what prompted this announcement, it's widely believed to be connected to revelations earlier this week that Indian bookmakers have turned their attention to domestic cricket in Australia. Illegal bookmaking operations have been offering bets on domestic fixtures over the internet for some years now, although there has been no recorded instance of a game being thrown as a result...

Mum's ashing on her bedsheets.

'Darling,' she says sweetly, 'where's that pretty girl?'

'Who's that? Honey?'

She creases her brow. 'Was it Honey?'

'We broke up, Mum. Years ago.'

She's silent for a moment. Groping for something.

'No, the little girl. She came to Christmas.' Her face brightens. 'She played cricket!'

A sudden choking-up, and I can't respond. God, if I could have some of the erasure she has.

'Such a lovely little thing.'

I scoop up the ash carefully into the side of one hand and throw it out the window, along with our two butts. Shut the window. Grab both sides of Mum's head and plant a big kiss on her forehead. She looks up at me with that translucent glow.

'The good boy,' she beams. 'So kind.'

Decline

The tape's off my mouth and I feel like singing.

The answer, after all, was very simple. There was enough of a free end that I could tuck my chin into my collarbone and trap it against my shoulder. By unhappy coincidence the tape was unfurling towards the side of my ribs where there's been some other damage done. Each grind of my shoulder against the tape released a chorus of crackling and popping down the side of my chest.

But it's worked—with a little more contorting I've ripped it free. I roll my jaw around to reawaken the muscles, mouthing word-shapes like *yaw yaw yaw.*

If I can roll my head over and put my mouth to the tail-light I can yell at someone.

Mummy, the car in front's yelling at us. But who would I yell at? And what if it didn't work?

I don't understand why things are the way they are for Mum.

She has a disease that affects memory, so why is she in a bed?

There was never a day she was unavailable to us. Never a task she was physically unable to perform, from rolling pitches to retiling the shower recess at Fernley Road. She smoked when we were kids, loved an occasional beer, yet she flew serenely above any physical retribution from her own body.

So why is she lying here? The Dutch neurologist told me a disease that affects memory thereby affects daily functioning—hygiene, cooking, financial management—even the problem of just wandering off. Kindly old people called Gwen or Aldous found decomposing in parks or dismembered by trains. So the price of managing this head sickness is the imprisonment of the body.

Now some malevolent speck of her food, ingested somehow into her lungs and setting off an infection, has triggered the start of her destruction. She hasn't spoken in weeks, a curled creature gone to shelter. She's like paper these days, and the sight of her breaks my heart.

She is dying.

When she coughs, they come rushing in and wrestle a drain tube into her, and I'm back with Emily Weil and the hospital carpark. They roll her with scant regard for her dignity to alleviate the bedsores. Her grey and blonde hair falls foolishly over her face while they work. Robbed of recollection and therefore of the evidence for love, she has no will. Her eyes on mine are a plea for release.

Wally comes when he can and we sit in silence, watching her fade. He's been back a while now, found conversation with me as though we never talked that night on the phone from Dubai.

Louise turns up occasionally, fractured and stern. Sometimes with him, sometimes alone. Sometimes clear and functional, usually smelling lightly, under the perfume, of stale booze.

Public recognition has recruited the three of us into other people's families. Louise is the face of an advertising campaign for a cruelty-free moisturiser, a Clean Water Week, a Domestic Violence Memorial. Her gravitas, her solemn and indisputable words, are responsible for a tide of donations. Surveys indicate she is among the most trusted faces in the media.

Wally occupies a different space. A former captain of the test side is conferred a kind of tenure. For a former prime minister, there's a car and an office and a lifetime of air travel. For a former test captain there's something less tangible but equally valuable—an intimate space in the lives of the populace. People can map their own lives by reference to Wally and his feats: the century he made here or there, the transcendent moments of heroism. His press conferences. He's perennial, leathered by sun as though for all of us. His televised moments can be tied to the index points in any ordinary life: a kiss, a fight, a holiday, a night on the couch.

And there's me, known for wearing a high-gloss suit and delivering easy platitudes to camera these days; perhaps distantly remembered as an athlete. I've become a Twitter celebrity, firing off one-forty-character ripostes with links to cute things and aspiring actresses, endorsing everything from spec builders to footy betting. It yields me a constant haul of free stuff, a delivery van every couple of days, and I hoard the loot in a spare room, where it piles up like the gold in Smaug's cave. Beneath the home gyms and mountain bikes and cartons of wine somewhere are the bags of cricket gear that started it all.

The Twitter following, coupled with my real and imagined misdeeds, qualifies me as a *larrikin*. It's a euphemism, larrikin, a kind of willing blindness about character flaws.

He's a lad.

He's mischievous.

Clown prince.

Of all these dishonest labels, 'bad boy' is the one that troubles me the most, implying as it does an inability to grow up. I've got a bald patch fading its way through my crown, for God's sake. I'm no one's boy, 'laser hair treatment' notwithstanding.

Craig is gone from our lives now. The closest friend I ever had, driven away by Wally's disapproval, by his own unsettling transformation into an 'industrial mediator' in pinstripes and cowboy boots. Rumoured links to bikies, belly laughs at the races.

He makes regular appearances on the news now, appearances of the 'colourful identity' type. He hasn't rung since Emily Weil, and the string of text messages I didn't return: streams of his life, deals, night-clubs, dreary shit about women and drugs in ranting, shouty capslock.

FKN AWSM HERE MAD CHIX FROM SPANE.

His tone became wounded as I failed to engage. Hard to explain why I didn't, other than to say I'd outgrown him.

My life outside the media has become smaller with the Big Guy no longer there.

The three of us prop around Mum on the sticky vinyl chairs but we're not enough to form a circle. For all the strangers we've attached to ourselves over our lifetimes, we are a constellation of three now, with a frightened, broken matriarch at our centre.

•

One still, slate-grey autumn afternoon marks itself as the last time I ever spend with my brother and mother. Our last moments as a family, fraught as always with the conflict that I choose to see as our bent expression of love.

She lies between us, her breath rattling.

She's unconscious, alive by medical definition only now. Her hair's been cut shorter than she ever liked to wear it—nobody asked our permission—and her mouth hangs slightly open. I'd found the gaping mouth unsettling until I got used to it. Looking at Wally, seated across the bed, I can see it's still worrying him. He tries gently pressing her lips together, gets dribble on his fingers and the mouth reopens. He takes a tissue from a steel dispenser mounted on the wall and wipes his fingers. He flicks the tissue at the bin, irritation mounting to rage.

'They can't keep her like this.'

'Like what?'

'Like *this*,' he gestures angrily towards the bed. His suit and hair are immaculate. He is a man at the peak of his personal authority, staring at something he cannot possibly control.

'It's not a care problem. She'd be like this if she was at home, or in a hospital, or in fucking Borneo, pal.'

'Don't get smart with me. Look at her.'

I've looked at her, hour after hour, for weeks. What I see is the patient body working by increments towards its own conclusion. Terminal decline. Can't fight it, can't change it.

Wally stands up abruptly. Starts pacing. His voice is clenched to a fierce whisper. 'She's got no quality of life. She'd be hating this.'

He turns his back on Mum and me, plants both his elbows on the high windowsill, stares out at the baleful sky. The backs of his legs are outlined the same way in suit pants as they once were in whites.

He drags a hand through his hair, leaving it standing on end. He remains perfectly still at the window for a long, long time as the afternoon darkens. The ceiling light isn't on; the gloom descends. By the time he turns to face me, his entire expression has changed. There are blotches of red on his throat and the bags under his eyes are starkly apparent.

He walks past the end of the bed, takes the other guest chair and puts it against the door. He leans over Mum. Gently slides the second pillow out from under her head.

I still haven't caught on.

He stands above her holding the pillow by its ends, looking at her with a heart full of hell. And I still haven't worked out what he's doing.

Then he lunges forward and presses the pillow over her face. Pulls the ends down over the sides of her head with his mouth pressed in a grim line of determination. I'm transfixed by a squiggled vein in his temple, the sinewed ferocity of his hands. He'll break her neck before he suffocates her.

It takes me an eternity to move.

Then I'm on him, round his ribs, trying to get enough purchase to swing him over the far side of the bed. But his weight is forward, his balance perfect, and I can't get him to budge. He's moved his grip so his elbows are pinning the pillow and his hands can grasp the metal crossbar over the bed. And while I'm looking at that I see the big red alarm button and slap it with one palm.

It lights up but there's no audible sound.

He's still going. It's been so long now.

I punch him hard in the jaw and he slackens, has to regather. I hit him again in the ribs and this time he straightens up, a knee either side of Mum on the bed and gives me one back, catching me in the side of the throat. I grab his wrist on the downswing and pull him towards me. He doesn't move until my weight falls to one side and the collective mass of both of us is too much for him. There's a huge crashing of furniture as we take out the bedside drawers and the chair I was on a moment ago. His fingers again in my eyes, and a lamp on top of us. I can feel the hot bulb near my cheek.

Then there's other noises, changes in the weight on me. The cavalry are here, two big islanders in orderlies' shirts. They heave away at Wally until they've separated us, drag him out of the room and down the corridor, from where I can still hear him yelling. A young female nurse has appeared and is tending to Mum, who remains in unconscious suspension but appears to be breathing.

The nurse hisses at me furiously, 'What the hell's going on?'

I'm gathering my breath, can't respond.

She's still muttering. 'Fucking Keefe boys. Everything they say's true, isn't it.'

•

In the midst of these bewildering days, a headline appears: *Fall of the House of Keefe.*

I don't need to look at the by-line—it's Amy Harris.

She charts our rise, subtly paralleling it with her own ascent through the ranks. *I was a cadet journalist when I was first sent to profile two unknown sporting prodigies from Melbourne's gritty western suburbs.* She talks cricket with confidence by now. Explains Fed and Squibbly and treads gently through the loss of Hannah. She commends Wally on his professionalism and dedication, defends him against the allegations that he was boring or mechanical, rationalising that his dour approach was exactly what Australian cricket needed at the time—was what the Australian *people* needed at the time, because none of us can differentiate our sporting fortunes from our real ones. She charts my countless acts of idiocy, pausing to reflect on the untold damage left behind after Emily Weil. *An unmitigated disaster.* No argument there.

Then come the paragraphs that must have caused migraines in legal: my association with *a known organised crime figure, Craig Wearne.* His colourful career, his remarkable good fortune in evading prosecution for anything. The stultifying effect that friendship had on my playing career, his extraordinary access to state and national players and his links to Asian bookmaking syndicates.

Asian bookmaking syndicates? When?

There's a row of mug shots to emphasise that Craigo has chosen some highly inadvisable friends. Two of them are no longer with us.

And here I am: shortly to become the third of Craigo's friends with *(deceased)* under my photo.

She mentions that close observers believe I am trying to pull away from the pernicious influence of this 'small-time gangster', but that the damage was done long ago.

All of these things I can bristle about, but they're more or less accurate. Then comes the part I really didn't see coming.

It has been widely known but not reported until now that Pamela Keefe, the mother of these vastly different brothers, has battled dementia for many years. She is now close to death in a Melbourne hospice. The relevance of this news? Simple: the major moderating influence in Darren Keefe's life is no longer there to protect him from himself.

Throughout his various troubles, Darren has pulled off a series of soft landings, in part due to Pamela's efforts on his behalf, and in part through the influence wielded by his highly decorated brother. Now there is only Wally to fill that role, and there are signs, since his release from the world of cricket, that he is tiring of the responsibility.

And who could blame him—particularly after Darren's conduct at the testimonial event following his brother's retirement. Anonymous onlookers have commented that Darren remained deep in conversation with Wally Keefe's wife, the well-known charity CEO Louise Arnold, throughout Wally's valedictory speech, and that he left the room with her. Both were said to be intoxicated, Keefe in particular being described by one onlooker as 'an improbably frequent visitor to the bathroom' that night. This newspaper is in possession of statutory declarations from two eyewitnesses who report seeing Louise Arnold leaving Darren Keefe's hotel room just after 7 a.m., shoes in hand.

Three heroic women have propped Darren Keefe up all these years: his mother, his former long-term partner Honey Nicholson, and his sister-in-law Louise Arnold. You could say he has a heroine habit.

And this latest incident, after all of the odium that has littered his public record, may well be his greatest betrayal.

I read it over and over, the first time racing ahead, unable to accept that she is going to do what she does. The second and third times, I'm looking for some other interpretation. After that, I'm thinking about the legal implications. I'm smart enough to know the idea here is that I sue them for libel and they defend it, and then build sales on the ravenous media interest that would attend the fracas. A dignified denial from Wally only buries me further. They can't lose.

I can't believe the scale of my misjudgment about Amy Harris. There were times along the way when I felt I was doing her a favour talking to her. Hey look, you've got access to the Keefes. And this is how she repays me.

That's what I'm thinking as I sit there reading the paper. What I think now, crumpled here in the boot of the car, is that her assessment of the night with Louise was an incorrect but reasonable inference, and the rest was a sterile lancing that was long overdue.

•

The winter is the end of Mum. It seems fitting. She represented summer to me all through the years in which memory has edited out the winters.

She stops late one night; just ceases to be. The only perceptible sign of death is her gradual cooling. This great engine of love, ground to a halt.

Her eyes are closed, the thin eyelids wrapped papery over the orbs and mapped by capillaries. Her mouth is set in a gentle curve that over my remaining days I will construe as a smile.

The staff at this place have never had much time for the Keefes— even Wally, since the incident. And now, with Mum lying newly deceased in her wretched bed, a thin man in a nursing-home uniform stands tentatively in the doorway with a folded plastic lump under his crossed arms. He's just present enough that after a while I look at him properly. Blue plastic. It's a body bag, fuck him. He's standing there with a body bag.

•

We send her off on a midwinter Wednesday, brittle and harsh, from a brick veneer funeral joint on a main road. It looks like a motel, like there'd be a bistro nestled among the landscaping somewhere. A sign saying *Vacancy*.

A brief Catholic service, short and uninspired, a product bought out of a catalogue. Then we're standing around, the three of us, working one another quietly for conversation on the damp ground. Louise is beautiful in a charcoal suit and skirt, solemn and contained. Grief is her constant companion: a day like this is her natural context. I can feel the chill coming up through my shoes as we stand by the grave and watch them lower the casket. I know that casket's over-generous, because in the end there was so little of her, as though the departing memories took the flesh off her bones as they went.

Looking around, I'm shocked at how little her life amounted to. The sun in her eyes, that easy capacity for love. The patient dedication, the humour and the toughness. She was such good company; where the hell is everybody? Maybe this happens to all of us: despite the thousands of hands we shake, cheeks we kiss, quiet favours we bestow, you wind up with a handful of gloomy stragglers by the hole.

And here in the dark, living through my own hearse ride, I can picture the human trash in the front of the car, the lot I drew for graveside company. They'll be smoking and flicking butts on my battered corpse as it disappears under shovelfuls of earth. Drinking beer maybe, cans carefully thrown in the hole because you can't be too careful with DNA; standing aside to piss and watching the steam rise in the headlights as I go under.

Mum mightn't have got the numbers, but at least she got some love.

•

The wake is at Wally's.

The house is bright and civil, as always. A house where no one leaves a phone bill on the bench, no one writes reminders to themselves on the wall. It's a big house for the two of them, but they must entertain all the time—clients, benefactors, politicians. A gleaming coffee machine squats on the counter like something medical. Pipes and tubes and beakers. Polished expanses of marble benchtop. White on white, artful fruit in a bowl.

How far we've come, Brother Wally.

A handful of Mum's old friends, couple of Wally's cricket mates, the one or two survivors among the nicotine-stained regulars she was feeding beer while we were in primary school. It's catered: food's small but exquisite, handed around by girls in black aprons.

When I've thrown back a few champagnes—Mum loved the stuff but always denied herself the extravagance—I wander back up the hallway towards the front door and take a left between the bedrooms, heading for the bathroom. Piss into the immaculately white, advertisement-grade toilet and take a line off the vanity.

Tidying up and regarding myself in the mirror, I pull the cupboard door open a little, and the angle reflects the hallway, the door to Hannah's room. The wooden lettering still in place spelling her name in lolly-shop calligraphy, backwards in the mirror. A cold draft of grief extinguishes the rip of the coke. A gaping hole in the world. Outside of myself, I step forward and push open the door. The room, untouched, smells clean and cared-for. Her posters, her sporting gear. Her bat, the one we duelled with in the backyard at Mum's. A hand-drawn chart above her desk with a homework timetable: *Term Three, 1999*. The lamp she read by. CDs in a row on a shelf above the bed-head. Oh Christ.

'It's nearly eleven years.'

I spin around and there's Wally in the doorway, watching me.

'She'd be twenty now.' He breathes a dry laugh. 'Driving; probably finishing uni.'

He looks older in here, emptied somehow. He rests his forehead on the door jamb, regards his shoes. 'The counsellor doesn't like us keeping the room this way. I think I'm ready to pack it up, but Louise...'

'What happened to her, Wally?'

His head jolts upright, his eyebrows raised. 'Hannah?' Drops his head again. 'That's why the room's like this, because it doesn't make sense. This is Kew. Warm, safe corner of a terrible world. We don't have any idea what goes on out there. I can try to imagine it, but then I reach a point where I don't want to imagine it happening to Hannah.'

'Have you let her go?'

He dwells on this for a moment.

'At a logical level, yes. But I go through times I think she might walk through the door. Is that what you want to hear, that I'm hanging on?'

'Just asking.'

A faint nod. 'Never leaves you. Feels like, like everything that happened somehow comes back to *me*. Even though Louise was the one doing all the parenting.'

'The story wasn't true, you know.'

His eyes meet mine. 'What story?'

'The one in the paper, Amy Harris. About me and Louise.'

'Oh, that one. Yeah, I know. Lou told me. Don't worry about it.'

'What are you going to do about her drinking?'

Normally he'd flare at such a question. But he's all punched out.

'What am *I* going to do? Mate, she's not going to listen to me. Or you. Numbs the pain I guess, and most of the time she's under control. Worst stuff's within these walls. Doesn't get out.'

He wanders past me, sits on the swivelling chair at Hannah's desk. Spins slowly from side to side. The gesture looks oddly disrespectful to me. But taking it as an invitation to do likewise, I sit myself on the edge of the bed.

'The inquiry starts this week.'

I nod.

'It'll be a nest of fucking vipers.'

'Why?' I'd never considered it anything more than a political stunt, a minor diversion from the government's poor polling. Wally sighs.

'Well, I was there. You were there—some of the time. You can make anything look bad if you talk to the right people, the *wrong* people. There's been fools punting on cricket since time began, and they're not going to stop. Doesn't mean the game's rooted, or that we're all on the take. Just another way people enjoy their sport. Some play it, some watch it, some punt on it.'

Faint squeaks as the chair rotates. I've never felt so clearly that Hannah is dead. Her ghost pervades everything in this room.

'I mean, you were never...' He's fishing for reassurance.

'Yeah I was. Remember that day-nighter in Sydney, '95? Rowan Cooper asked me to get myself stumped and I accidentally hit it out of the park. You were fucking furious.'

He seems to be straining for recollection, wants me to see that.

'Oh *that*,' he laughs eventually. 'I don't think they're interested in that sort of shit. That was a juvenile prank. I think they're after bigger fish, somehow.'

'Felt pretty fucking big at the time. I don't think I've ever heard you so angry.'

He eyeballs me, management-style. 'I'm sorry, okay. I'm sorry I did that to you.'

He's picked up a Hello Kitty hole-punch from the desk, is idly squeezing it.

'You been subpoenaed?' I ask.

'Well, yeah,' he replies. 'But only because I've been a senior player through all those years. There's no suggestion, of course...'

'Of course.'

'You?'

'Not yet. I don't know, you might be right. I'm small-time.'

'You were always closer to Craig than I was.'

'Yeah, but maybe they'll just go direct to Craig. I still can't help thinking that despite all the carry-on, he's just a big stupid bogan. Have you asked him if he's been called?'

'You kidding? I don't think I've even got his number these days.'

He slaps his knees, a habit of his that indicates the end of a discussion. He starts to get up, but fixes me once more with a deeper look. 'Okay, so you're not talking to them.'

'I'm not saying that. I haven't been asked to talk to them. I dunno, I'd probably talk. Trying to get my life together, Wally. Do the responsible thing. But like I say, I haven't been asked.'

He moves back to the doorway, stops momentarily. 'Yeah, but I'm hearing you. You haven't got much to offer them anyway.' He flicks the light switch on, flicks it off. Gestures to the doorway.

'You done?'

•

The conversation bumps around in my mind for a few of the sad weeks after Mum's funeral, as my former teammates start to receive subpoenas. Then the coaches, industry people, a few well-known crooks. The media are talking about *massive revelations*, and *a sport rocked to its foundations*. Everyone's paranoid. No one talks.

It's around this time I start to receive the text messages.

Blocked number. Muddled, usually late at night, in no apparent order. Sometimes they look as though they've been typed by an over-large finger that trips several keys in reaching for the right one. There's never any numbers or symbols: the sender never leaves the first alpha screen. Sometimes they look like a code, or a madman's ramblings. They don't make any sense.

Not until the one that arrives in the early afternoon on the Friday before Wally's due to give evidence. I'm in a hotel in Sydney, bright yachty view across to Cremorne Point. I'm looking out at the sunlight chattering on the surface of the harbour. Looking back at the screen. Standing there like an idiot in my underpants and socks, shirt on the ironing board. About to put on the suit to call a game that evening.

Clear typing this time, no fumbles. It says:

Matthew 18:15–20.

I don't have any friends who are religious. Well, I wouldn't, would I? And as far as I know, I don't have any enemies who are religious either. But I was sufficiently brutalised by Brother Calumn to recognise a scripture verse, and this thing looks to me like scripture. I scout around until I find the Gideon Bible in the bedside drawer. Flip through the virginal tissue of the pages, print smell fanning back at me.

Kings, Psalms, Daniel, Zechariah...

Matthew. With a finger down the column I find it quick enough.

If your brother sins against you, go and point out their fault, but do it alone. If he listens to you, the matter is at an end. If he does not, take one or two others with you, so that every matter may be established in the presence of those witnesses.

It nags at me for the rest of the day, through the evening under the lights and across a succession of beers and a gram of crank at an Oxford Street bar afterwards. What have I done to my brother? Or what has he done to me? And who cares enough to send this?

We rationalise the inexplicable because we don't like it occupying that infirm ground in our hearts. So I laugh it off, shooting tequila with a couple of fuzz-cheeked Navy cadets. Do-gooders and happy clappers have tried to redeem me before, proselytisers. Try saying that after a brace of firewaters. Not their business. It's my ongoing project and I'm doing my best, I tell myself as one of the sailors flames his lower lip on a burning tequila shot.

Then comes the day it all changes fundamentally. Headlines aren't typeset anymore, but if they were, they'd choose the giant font for this one.

Wally's fronted the inquiry and refused to testify on the grounds he may incriminate himself.

Louise

Having ungagged my mouth, I feel a surge of liberation within the wider reality of confinement.

I take to the cable ties with renewed enthusiasm, able to breathe deeply and grunt now and then with the effort. Fingers down and wrists bent, I can apply pressure to the ties with the fragment of tail-light lens, though it's impossible to measure my progress.

To stop my hands cramping, I make six firm passes at it, then rest and count to ten, try to pull my clenched fists outwards a couple of times. And somewhere around forty-eight attempts, the cable ties give up.

My pectoral muscles are burning with newfound cramp at the shock of these free-swinging arms, but now I have hope—and two major advantages.

Now I have hands.

The divorce is handled with trademark cold precision.

An email appears on my phone at 7.32 on a Friday night, just after the ABC news has gone to air and just before the footy starts. Match of the round: a preoccupied public. Bullseye.

The message has obviously gone to a mailing list, the identities obscured. It says:

You may be aware that Louise and I have struggled with our relationship over recent years, due to a variety of pressures in our lives. We do not need to recount to you the enormous trauma we have endured over the loss of our darling daughter Hannah. You are receiving this email because you have been close to us through these years, and we thank you for your loyalty and your support.

However, these pressures have become more than we can bear. Despite the best efforts of both of us, we are no longer able to remain married to each other and have decided—amicably—to separate. We intend to continue supporting one another in all our endeavours, and we remain deeply respectful of each other and proud of each other's achievements.

We plan to say nothing further than this publicly. We will be notifying media outlets by press release immediately after you receive this email. We would be grateful if you would maintain your loyalty to us by refusing all media requests, although we are willing to discuss the matter privately with each of you in due course.

Thank you.

I can imagine her face during the drafting. A meeting room somewhere, the management company maybe. Alan the PR grub smirking away throughout, jabbing at that laptop of his.

Her jaw set, across a table from Wally, her silence a scathing indictment of the whole thing. Her eyes would be red-rimmed, the crying done somewhere out of sight, her pride now a barrier to all. She'd watch her hands, a thing I've seen her do under pressure; straighten the fingers and study them as though the rings had something to say about permanence.

And Wally. A suit with open collar, calm and immovable. His

need to interpret every adversity in life as a contest, a binary struggle of wills between him and the opposing force. Right down to the cellular level, his need to *win*. Aiming to come through this as the sole survivor of his own marriage.

The email is no shock to anyone.

Louise moves out of Kew, and shortly afterwards she moves to Seattle, where a punch-drunk NGO needs rescuing. Flight from herself and the rescue of others are the twin poles of her existence.

I've missed her every day since she left. Her damaged perfection, her dignity.

What was irreconcilably different about her and Wally was her ability to accommodate weakness, her acceptance of her own fallibility. Her alcoholism is a private reality that Wally sought to suppress out of existence. I've gone through adult life actively exploiting my mistakes—behold the dancing bear!—while Wally would have the public believe he's never erred. Steering a straight line between our two approaches, Louise has calmly prevailed.

And so our family continues to disappear. Dad, so long ago. Honey, because I pushed her. Then Hannah, Mum, now Louise: our fucked-up family tree turns out to be deciduous, and it's mostly the women who've fallen to earth.

It's down to me and him. And when this car reaches its destination, it will be down to him alone.

He's survived us all. Wally Keefe, captain of Australia and family of one.

Cornered

They come for me in the early evening, which is of course contrary to type—supposed to be in the dead of night. Maybe they figured I'd be out then, given the media's portrayal of me as a lecherous insomniac.

I'm in Geelong, having agreed at the last minute to come over and do a sportsmen's lunch. This is not as much of an imposition as it might sound. They pay well and it's the softest room imaginable: the usual war stories, then questions from the floor—*what's it like to face Warnie? Who's the best sledger you've ever heard?* At the end, I sign some merch and they auction it off. There's no Craig at this one, no stifling embrace. Just handshakes all round, an offer of dinner or a bar somewhere, game over. They've sent a cab to collect me, and put me up in a nice apartment.

Which is where I currently sit.

I'm trying to install a pirated copy of Windows in a laptop.

I got the computer months ago, through nightclub mates who knew someone who was 'moving some units'. Why did I need a new computer? Because some fucker broke into my apartment and stole the old one. Jemmied the door, turned a few things over and took the computer. Also took some of Wally's test stuff—a jumper and a bat that I was keeping to sell in the event of a financial rainy day. Oh come on, he wasn't using it.

Aside from what they pinched, they left only one calling card. Took me ages to notice it. On the fridge door I'd collected photos over the years: teams, parties, public occasions, girls. The black backgrounds of flash shots at night. The fridge is clad in black and brown like a Doberman, with sparks of colour here and there like the dog rolled in confetti.

In the middle of the clustered photos, because the older images were at the centre, was a photo of me and Wally taken in the change rooms after one of our very rare appearances together for the state team. Arm in arm, triumphant. I can give you all the records we broke that day; highest partnership by two brothers in the history of Shield cricket, highest one-session total, highest season total (me) and fastest hundred against Western Australia (Wally). Two red, glowing faces, two blazes of teeth. My arm around his shoulders, lockers behind us, the blue vees on our jumpers forming a *W*.

Some unseen hand had burnt this photo.

Two scorch marks tapered upwards across the print, the distinctive teardrop shape of an applied cigarette lighter. His face gone. My face gone.

The pigments of the print bubbled and crazed into frozen rainbow droplets at the margins of the burn. My eyes scanned across all the other shots, looking for more damage, wanting the pattern of that damage to tell me something about who and why. But the shot of me and Wally was the only one torched.

So that was the night I lost the computer, and here I am trying to reload my new one.

Which is when they turn up.

They've come in through the locked carpark entryway, two blokes who don't smell good. My first reaction is to wonder how they've got in without me hearing anything.

Heavy one and a light one, but not exactly panthers, either of them. One minute I'm trying to type an eighteen-number string into a box, squinting like a fool at the screen on my knees, the next there's these two lumbering slobs in the room, one at each of the two door-ways leading out.

They close in.

I don't know the room well enough to plan an escape. I look furtively at the window, one of them sees me doing it and then without a word he hits me with something, swift and blinding across the left side of my head. No idea what it is—do they still have ashtrays in these places? But the sound inside my skull is like breaking glass, and my vision is a billion swimming points of light.

The blow leaves me kneeling against the wall. One flank's exposed to the heavy guy, who aims a huge kick at my ribs. Now I'm down on all fours making a desperate *wh...wh* sound, trying to get some air. The other guy's got a pool cue and he's smashing the computer, coming down on it again and again, as though furious that it won't disintegrate into flying shrapnel.

I look up at the guy who's attacked me: he's wiping his nose with a finger. Baby-faced, thirty-odd, hair in a neat, nerdy kind of Lego Man clump. But his mouth's a piggy dint, the forward thrust of his short lips making his nose look snouty.

Bodybuilder's shoulders, big sloping trapezoids that nearly connect his ears to his torso. Loose T-shirt, cargo pants, cut short to reveal the tatts on his calves. Runners, ankle socks. He's wearing some sort of shithouse men's cologne. Lynx or something. The peanut.

The other one's shorter, scruffier, nastier. Got a meth look about him; straggly beard, deep, pitting acne scars, lanky black hair. Thin and furious, like he should be chasing a huddled woman pushing a pram. Oh God, tracksuit pants. Of course.

Two thugs in a hired room. How randomly horrible.

Two or three others.

Dots to join here somewhere. But not yet.

The air's returning in short gasps but it hurts like hell to pull it in. Babyface has hit me with a pool cue too, I can now see. He's swooshing it lazily through the air as he steps towards me. He brings the cue down across the middle of my back, dropping me to the ground, completely prone. He stands above me a moment or two and I feel the inevitability of all this. All the things that led to this. These cheap louts don't understand their role as the consequences of my sins, but that is what they are.

He's dropped a knee on my head, just where the jaw meets the skull. My face would look hilarious right now. Once he's satisfied I'm completely immobilised, he goes through my pockets, finds my wallet and peels out the driver's licence. He flicks the wallet away, hasn't even looked for cash, then holds the licence up against my face and checks for a moment, apparently unconcerned that the face under his knee doesn't now look much like the one on the card. The licence goes in his back pocket.

This isn't a garden-variety burg, because Meth Man's smashed the one electronic asset of any value. It's punishment. A B-grade contract hit. But surely it comes with a message of some kind, a parting insult, an explanation?

He produces a bag of cable ties, plucks a couple out and then stops, sticks them in his teeth and unbuckles my watch. Lovely titanium Longines, presented to me at the Vics' Team of the Century night. He stuffs it in the pocket where the cable ties came from and rips the ties onto my wrists, one looping under the other, so tight I can feel my pulse in the heel of my hand.

'Gis a hand.'

The first words anyone's spoken since these two appeared. Meth Man joins him and together they drag me by the bound hands towards an armchair in the next room.

Who are they? I'm scrambling for a connection. Who have I offended? Okay, who have I offended *most*? Pitbull Freer? Christ, it'd be a bit overdue. Would the Weil family pay someone to do this? No, that's ridiculous. Maybe they're debt collectors. I genuinely have no idea who I owe money.

I'm neither limp on the floor nor quite walking, but pedalling my feet slowly in an effort to make the dragging into something conscious and deliberate. They pile-drive me head-first into the armchair, and for a second I can smell the upholstery. Cut moquette, Mum liked that. My arse is in the air, and buried as I am in the heavy fabric, I take a second to think it all through. It's just the head and the ribs at this stage. There's undoubtedly worse to come, but they haven't killed me and there must be a reason for that.

The pain's so bad I can't roll myself into a sitting position, but Meth Man does that for me, taking one leg of the jeans I'm wearing and one of my ears as handles, pulling me round into an approximate slump in the chair. I'm pointed now at Babyface, and he's seated opposite me, dialling a phone.

'Mate. Yep. Ready when you are.'

He hangs up and pockets the phone. I want him to engage me in some sort of banter, want to work out what I'm dealing with. But he's staring vacantly into space now. Meth Man is walking around the room, smashing things at random. A hole in the middle of the telly. A print on the wall, a scattering of neat looking objets d'art, all trashed with a short vicious swing of his pool cue. He tosses it aside as though the exercise bores him.

Then he walks towards me.

I can feel my pulse bass-drumming in my neck. He's looking at me in a disjointed way, a little unfocused. Then he reaches into his tracky dacks and pulls out his dick. Even Babyface now looks disconcerted. Meth Man inhales, shuffles slightly closer and starts to piss on the floor, just in front of my feet, swaying the stream of urine from side to side with a wave of the pallid-looking slug. Exhales loudly. Waits for the flow to falter and expire, then shakes a drip or two off the end and stuffs it back in the trackies.

'Fucking pig,' says Babyface.

Meth Man doesn't respond. I can hear a car pulling up in the carpark outside. They both look at the door. Babyface goes to open it. He greets someone without fanfare, someone I can't see because of a dividing wall in the hallway. The someone trudges in heavily, appears in the room, large and slow in a bomber jacket and jeans.

Craigo.

He seems genuinely sad to find me in the chair. 'Shit, Daz. You look awful.' He looks to the other two. 'He didn't give you any trouble?'

Nup, someone murmurs.

'All right. Okay. Can I—' he indicates Babyface's chair politely before sitting himself down with a sigh. Settles his hands on his lap, then wrinkles his nose in displeasure.

'Smells like cat's piss in here.'

I try to laugh but the ribs get me and I wind up grimacing.

'C'mon mate, doesn't hurt that much, does it?'

'Get him to do it to you then.'

He laughs at that. Easy and relaxed. I haven't seen the Big Guy for a few years now, but he's grown into the role. Whatever the hell he's been doing, he's ascended to senior management.

'What are we going to do with you, Daz?' he asks, sadly.

'Good question, Craigo.' My left eye's closing.

'You know why we're here, don't you.'

'Got a, a general idea I deserved a beating; but no, mate. Not a clue.'

He smiles again, quite menacing now. Gone is the gormless lug he once was. 'Take a guess.'

'Really?'

He smiles again, this time like he's toilet training a small child. 'Go on. Give it your bestest guess, Daz.'

'The rhapsody thing?'

'Emily Weil? No, not at all. I'd say that was one of your better efforts. I know you didn't squeal. What else?'

I've been a naughty boy, off and on, but I can't see how any of it relates to Craigo or his interests.

'Did I owe you some rent from when we lived together?'

The laugh again.

'No. No no no. Come on. Try harder.'

'Have I fucked up something you're doing? Something I haven't realised?' I can't believe I'm being made to think up my own confession, or that I'm trying so hard to please him.

'Oh no mate. I think you're perfectly aware of what you're doing.'

'I'm *doing*, like on an ongoing basis?'

He nods slowly.

'Something you've promised to do, Daz. You can stop dancing around it. The Burrowes Royal Commission.'

It takes me a long moment to process this.

'Match fixing? This is about *match fixing*?'

I can't believe what I'm hearing, but he's still nodding slowly. I feel like laughing despite it all. 'What the fuck do you care?'

'Oh I care, ol' boy. I care a great deal.'

'I—I...firstly I didn't know you were involved, and secondly, kinda follows from that, I don't know anything that could drop you in the shit.'

'Oh yes you do. You know a great deal more than you realise right now. Tell you what, have a little think about a few things that didn't go your way during your career. Or think about a few things that *did*, when they shouldn't have.'

I look back. I think of the litany of dropped catches around me, the people who did things I knew to be sharply below their normal standards. Discordant errors that were blamed afterwards on tiredness, or the lights, or a fly, a seagull. I think of my accidental swipe in the Sydney game, and the charity gig that won me the sixty grand, the night I killed a perfectly innocent girl. He's still looking at me.

'Ever get the sense of a guiding hand in all that?'

'I thought you just hung around the team cos you were a loser.'

He snorts contemptuously. 'If I were you, I wouldn't taunt me. I hung around, *Daz*, so I could learn everything about you, your game, your team-mates, the pitch, the tactics. Injuries—the shit you guys talked about, all those boring, *boring* hours in the rooms, "Blah blah blah I'll need an op on the knee in six months." "I'm not doing the India tour cos Jacinta's rooting the pool boy..." Worth a fortune to various vested interests. I'd got at plenty of 'em, your so-called mates. I won't give you names, but as a rule you aim for the veterans who are carrying injuries, feeling a little shat off at the system. Rookies are so idealistic.

'But *if*—' he narrows his eyes—'if you can get your hands on a promising player really early on, compromise 'em before they have anything at stake...Well, that's the duck's nuts. A player who sells you their soul early on is an asset for life. See, if you manage 'em properly, they can *never get out.*'

He watches me for some time, assessing what I might think of this insight, then shrugs. 'Corrupting people, it's kinda fun but it's not where the money is. The money is in fuckwits like you. The ones with the information.'

His eyes have taken on a hooded quality, focused on a point somewhere beyond my left shoulder.

'Fuck me,' I grunt. 'You're a match-fixer?'

'Not really. You don't want to be the one with your arse on the line. I'm a broker. Just buy and sell information. About fuckwits like you.'

He wipes some imaginary lint off his front.

'Do you know I heard the Pope the other day going on about corruption in sport. The fucking *Pope*. Goes to show, doesn't it? Sport goes to the heart of everything. If you can reach inside it and fuck with its innards, *you're actually messing with society*, Daz. How 'bout that. Bigger than drugs. Bigger than hookers and porn, because people shy away, they can smell the desperation. But the same people will go on consuming sport long after they know it's rotten to the core. They're insatiable. And it levels people like me with people like you. Cos you can play it, see, or you could. But I can *play* it. And I can keep playing it long after your thumb takes you out of it, or some other guy's knee goes, or his back goes. It's a whole-of-life career for me.'

He shifts his bulk in the chair slightly.

'So what we need to do, Daz...' he reaches out a hand, palm upwards, and Babyface hands him an automatic, 'is make sure we have a clear idea of what you've been up to.'

He points the gun at me from his slouched position about six feet away. Sights me down the short barrel as though he's at a carnival booth. 'Have you made a statement?'

'No.'

'Got a subpoena?'

'Nope.'

There's a loud bang and it takes me a moment to work out what's happened. Smoke. Craigo withdrawing his extended arms. He's shot me. Fucking hell, he's shot me, and in the filaments of a blown second I can't work out where. I crumple downwards over my right leg and find it's through my knee, through the armchair. There's big fluffy wads of cotton around my foot like he's shot a stuffed toy, but the blood running down my shin confirms it's me, even before I register the pain.

The pain turns up now, oh yes. Great roaring waves of it. I imagine I'd clutch at the knee if I had free hands, but I don't. There's tears in my eyes, for God's sake. I look up at Craigo, and find him staring coolly back at me. The gun is resting on its side on his huge thigh, still pointed my way. A haze of smoke in the air between us.

'Now don't be a fucking idiot, Daz. I know you got served. I know your date. I know you've been to see a lawyer.'

I'm racking my brains, even as the knee threatens to rob me of the capacity for clear thought. This has never been a strength of mine, the ability to run inventory over my past conduct so I can be sure of a position. Craigo knows it. That's why he's pushing me. He's right about both things—I got served and I saw a solicitor. But I'm sure I didn't tell anyone.

'So I'll go back to the first question,' says Craigo. 'Have you been interviewed?'

I'm trying to compose a reply but Craigo gestures vaguely to Meth Man.

'Check his knee, will you?'

Meth Man approaches, standing squarely in his own puddle of piss, and grabs hold of my thigh. With his other hand he cups my shattered knee and finds the hole. Then he slides his grubby fucking finger into it and wiggles it around, leering at me as he does it. I can feel bone moving. A tendon pulls taut under the probing finger. I don't know if it hurts as much as he probably imagines, but the shock of it is enough to make me retch. The shock, and the notion that he might be finding this somehow sexual. He withdraws the finger after three or four hideous chemical breaths and wipes it casually on my thigh.

Craig hasn't moved. He's seen this, done this, before.

'Is there a statement, Daz?'

He picks up the gun again, points it at my other knee. Meth Man puts his fingers in his ears this time.

'Yes.'

He lowers the gun. Looks at me inquiringly.

'I met some people in an office, Docklands. Gave them a statement.'

'Did they give you a copy?'

They'd frisked me on the way out. They were very uptight about me not retaining anything that might identify them.

'No. Nothing went in or out of that room.'

'All right, so what did you tell them?'

So I start explaining to him about the statement, the things I'd thought were important to the Royal Commission, knowing now that I'd been miles off the mark. I'd told them the TV network often requested we string things out a bit towards the end of the short-format games; that we were positively encouraged to tamper with the ball provided we kept it discreet. I'd told them I was once asked by a player, since deceased, to get myself stumped at a particular stage of a particular game, and that I'd fucked it up and hit the ball out of the park. I'd told them that I'd got a much closer look at the culture once I moved into TV; that commentators would routinely check with the players in advance about tactics; that we'd report back to the network with batting orders and bowling changes so they could tailor their advertising to the appearances of the big names. I'd told them about the organised doctoring of pitches to suit particular bowlers, not as some sort of informal pact between a groundsman and a local official, but as an ongoing program that involved men in suits on Skype hook-ups, almost none of them cricketers.

I'd told them about the seminars in which the production team were encouraged to understand the game as a product, and not as a contest at all. The spruikers and management types who explained how the product could be 'optimised' with an eye to a thing they called 'maximal peak viewer penetration'. I'd admitted the whole thing is a reality show on grass. I'd told them about the time I watched a cowering franchise captain in a Twenty20 game being berated by an executive producer for instructing his most menacing fast bowler to bowl a conservative line on off-stump. The guy was trying to make legitimate cricket. The producer was making prime-time telly. I'd told them my own house was not entirely in order on things moral and legal, but that one thing I'd never done was throw a match.

At first Craigo's listening with interest. Then his eyebrows start to rise on his forehead. Then a smile appears at one corner of his mouth, spreads and pushes his hamster cheeks out towards his ears. Then he's laughing, slapping his thigh in a slightly alarming way with the hand that's holding the gun. The baby-faced guy's taken up another couch and a home interiors magazine, ignoring us completely. *I've just been shot, you big turd. At least feign some interest.*

'So you're saying you haven't mentioned me at all?' Craigo looks like a weight's been lifted.

'What was I going to say? I didn't know what the hell you'd been up to.'

He sighs elaborately as the laughter turns to reflection. 'Turns out we were both feeding on the same carcass. But I was making money, eh.'

He's fiddling with the gun, still smiling to himself. A well-fed man of forty-two, receding slightly at the temples, spreading at the waist. He'd have enough money lodged in betting accounts, fed through companies, to do whatever he wants. Dress better, for one. Buy a holiday pile among the finance barons at Portsea. He could swindle some poor grid girl or nightclub hostess into bearing him a

family, stand around with a takeaway coffee in his mitt watching his
fat kids trying to play soccer. He'd love that. He's got the charm to
pull it off and the wits to stay ahead of prosecution. So why is he
stuck in this perpetual man-child bullshit? The open-all-hours micro-
management that others could take care of. The suburbs are swarming
with aspirants to his role: the car rebirthers, pill wholesalers, standover
merchants and mixed martial artists, itching to graduate. As in any
industry, the rookies must have their time, and the journeymen must
evolve.

But not Craigo.

The only logical answer must be that he's trapped. Trapped like
me, stuck in a loop of denial about the dull decline of ageing. I've been
a performing parrot, a larrikin everyman. He's been a plywood cut-out
villain. Most of my income-producing activities have been approxi-
mately legal, but aside from that we're no different. His pleasures,
as mine, have been ephemeral. Nothing has lasted or accumulated,
other than the money. Nothing can be satisfying in reflection, because
there's no one to reflect with.

He's just put a round through my knee, but I pity the poor
schmuck.

Craigo finishes laughing and gives a nod. Meth Man appears
from my right with the pool cue, eyes wide with intent. He takes a
giant backswing as he lines up my head.

•

The next moments are like music from a scratched disc. Fragments,
passages, severed or blurred just as they promise to acquire meaning.
I know I've been carried by the two lackeys. I know I've been dropped
heavily. I'm aware I'm in a car boot, as I can smell the strong auto
rubber of a spare tyre.

Ah well. So. Doesn't matter.

But then the footage rectifies itself momentarily, comes good in terrible clarity. Craig is above me, one hand on the boot lid, looking down.

Could I plead with him? No, I could not. His face tells me I'm already dead as far as he's concerned. The others must be taking their seats in the car, because presently I feel the springs rock a little then hear the doors slam. He looks down again, lighting a smoke with his other hand. Drags on it, pulls it free. From a pocket he removes a roll of black gaffer tape. Roadie tape. Tears a length of it with his teeth and reaches down to press it over my mouth.

'You do know what happened to Hannah?'

His words are the first thing that's struck me with any force since the bullet. It's the framing of the sentence, as much as it being such a surprising thing to say. You *do* know. Not inquiring as to whether I might know, nor assuming that I actually do, but implying that I *should* know.

'Sydney. Your stupid lob when you were supposed to be stumped. Everyone did their dough on that deal, you know. *Everyone.*'

His face changes in a tiny way. Those eyes narrow a little and the eyeballs trace a vague circle around the inside of the boot as he brings the lid down.

Oh God.

I'm what happened to Hannah.

Release

I've been asleep at some point, dreaming my way through these things. The boot. The dark. The pain and the looming end.

We must be coming to the end. The physics have changed. We're going slower, and I'm being pressed from side to side: head against one mudguard, feet against the other. It's colder. There's very little discussion in the car—just occasional directions. *Left here. Don't take that exit.* Of course they wouldn't risk the sat nav. They've probably turned their phones off altogether. Craigo is no longer his ebullient self. Maybe he's reflective. *Isn't life funny. I'm off to bury my childhood bud Dazza.*

Just like when I was fiddling with the tail-light, I can feel half an instinct to have a go. Do something, anything, to disrupt the sad and inevitable progression of things. Another part of me is deep in fatalism. We're nearly there, and this part won't hurt as much as the previous part did. It's absurd: escaping would be nice, but I'm not really fussed.

At least one of them must be seated in the back, as there were three present for the kneecapping. I'm fairly sure Craig would be driving because it's his style to take charge. So it's one of the others I can hear snoring. For a ridiculous instant I'm tempted to thump the back of the seat to get him to shut up. In the midst of that idea I raise a fist and then remember with some surprise that it's free.

My hands.

I'd forgotten about them, must've fallen asleep right after I got them loose. Squibbly's a sticky mess, but of course he doesn't hurt. The rest of my left hand hurts. I flip it over and feel where it was lying. My fingers close around the big shard of the tail-light casing, like a prehistoric stone tool digging into the heel of my hand. My kingdom for someone to stab.

Then a tiny idea forms.

I rub the palm of one hand against the vertical surface of the back seat. It's lined with carpet and feels like it's backed with board of some kind. It doesn't take me long to trace my way to the edge of the board, where one section of the split-fold rear seat meets the other. I dig my fingertips into the fabric until I find the slim groove where it's been tucked over and stitched in. Then I take to it with the shard of plastic. At first, nothing happens, and I stop for fear that the scratching sound is audible. But the snoring continues and the rhythm of the car hasn't changed.

I slash downwards again, pulling at the edge of the covering with my other hand. This time it gives a little, and I can jam a fingertip into the opening I've made. I poke around and find there are staples, and I've pulled three of them out. I yank down harder and another three pop out. The sound of the tearing is slightly louder, so I have to wait again to see if I've been heard.

By rolling over and changing my angle, I can now get my flattened left hand inside the back of the seat. Fingers and palm dart about, painting me a picture: flat springs, padding. I can visualise the pattern of curving wires. Pinching with the good thumb and a forefinger, I can pluck out little scraps of the padding foam, and before long I've dug my way through the full thickness of the seat, about a foot up from the floor of the boot. I think about that height for a moment and I figure my tunnel would be located at roughly shoulder-blade height for a person sitting in the back seat. But I still don't know which side Back Seat Guy is sitting on, and there's only one way to find out. I press gently against the cloth at the back of the hole I've made. It feels firm. The snoring drones on. I poke hard and there's an abrupt snort.

'Bout time you clocked on, fuckhead.'

The voice is from the front seats, but it isn't Craig's. The reply comes from much closer to me, sleepy and gruff. I remember the voice. It's the skinny one, Meth Man.

'Fuck you. We there yet?'

'Ten minutes. Anything from the boot?'

'Nothin.'

Silence for a moment. Then Meth Man's voice again, whiny.

'When do we get fuckin paid?'

There's no answer at first.

'Huh?' he whines.

'You know how it goes,' responds Craigo. 'He's paid a deposit, and I'm holding that. Not *on* me, obviously. When the job's done, he hands over the balance, and you get paid. Got a problem with that?'

It seems Meth Man doesn't, but I do. If Craigo had his worries about the match fixing and needed to find out what I knew, then that's all covered off. He's done the work himself, and got the answer. So who's paying here? Who's *he*?

Within seconds, the snoring resumes. I start the process again on the other side of the divide between the seats. This is the passenger side, and it's wider than the other side where I made the first cavity. This time I can cut the covering fabric more cleanly and pull it away from the backing board, revealing the tops of the staples. By jamming the tip of the shard under each staple, I can wiggle them free one by one, until the whole right side of the seat backing comes free without a sound.

Once again, I start digging away at the padding, flicking the lumps behind me until I've made a fist-sized hole. When I reach the fabric on the cabin-side of the seat, I stop for a moment. It's clear there's no one sitting on this seat, but I need a little think. I could cut open the fabric and get a hand through into the interior of the car, but what would I do then? I have no way of knowing where the back seat recliner latches would be. And I can't very well feel around like Thing from *The Addams Family* until I accidentally pat Meth Man.

So I retreat for a moment and cradle the sticky, insensible form of Squibbly while I reconsider.

The latch that drops the back seat has to be connected to some sort of mechanism within the seat. So the answer is not to access the latch, but to find the mechanism. I start randomly picking at the foam, taking a pinch at a time, thinking all the while about those ten minutes and how fast they're ebbing away. I'm a hopeless, banged-up Houdini, unpicking padlocks while I slowly drown.

When I've emptied the near side of the seat without result, I start working towards the far edge. Almost all the way to the wheel arch, my fingers close around something unfamiliar: a plastic tube like electrical conduit, running vertically from top to bottom of the seat.

Pick, pick, pick.

At the top, the tube ends at a plastic box of some kind. I imagine the seat latch is contained within it.

More picking.

I've revealed the whole area around the tube and the box. Although the tube is one piece of plastic and is unlikely to be broken open without a lot of noise, the box is made of several pieces, clipped together somehow. The ends of my fingers are registering the fine

275

seams where the pieces join together. I crowd as many fingernails as I can along the seam and heave downwards.

Shit. Broken nail. And to no effect.

Taking the tube in both hands, I pull my weight over towards the corner. Crowded up against it, I can apply a little more weight to the task. And sure enough, leaning on a bunch of burning fingertips, I can feel the plastic start to give way. I release the pressure for fear it'll snap. Now I can slip the shard into the gap that's appeared, and pry away, the fingers of both hands now curled like whacked spiders' legs by cramp.

If I was briefly ambivalent about living and dying, that time has passed. Now I can feel it, the beginnings of a desire to solve the puzzle, shooting in synaptic pulses from my pounding chest all the way out to the fingernails that are currently responsible for my fate.

And it won't happen fast enough. I can't pull harder, can't risk the noise. And every time I get a good purchase on the tiny edge of the plastic, the car lurches from side to side, pressing me into the corner and then pulling me away. Left, right, left, right…it can mean only one thing.

They're in the hills.

In the end, physics does what I don't dare to try. Just as I've got a four-finger grip on the edge of the plastic, easing a little pressure into it, the car swings violently to the left and I'm ripped away from my work, sucked towards the driver's side with my fingers still jammed in the gap—inside the little plastic box, inside the back seat. The plastic gives way with a loud *snap*.

'Fuck was that?' I hear from somewhere in the car.

'Came from the boot,' is the reply, much nearer, from Meth Man in the back seat. Edge of concern in his voice.

'Just round the corner anyway. Fuck him.'

'I could pop him through the seat.'

'Don't be a fuckwit. You're not firing a gun in the car.'

Meth Man's got his ear pressed against the seat, listening for me. I can tell because I can feel the rounded lump of his head against the back of my hand. I feel like punching him hard in the scone. So tempting—the surprise, the stinging wonder of the one you don't see coming.

But no time for that.

Inside the box is what I expected to feel: the spiral steel wire that controls the seat release. It's guitar-string taut and hard to grip. The car lurches, and I flail hopelessly in the dark to grab onto something: I only succeed in jamming my right hand in the tail-light cavity again. Struggling for something to secure against, the hand closes around the electrical wires that led to the globe.

Answer.

I rip at them, caring little now about noise. They come free from their moorings, about a hand's length of wire. The car swings again, flopping me over onto my other side, conveniently facing my work again.

I want to live because I want to beat these morons. To my great surprise, I want to win.

I wrap the globe wires with their soft insulation around the steel of the seat wire, winding them tight until they grip the big wire firmly. Wrapping the rest of the wires around my hand, I start to heave upwards. Immediately, there's the sound of a spring twanging against a latch somewhere deep in the base of the seat.

No time to take stock now. Meth Man must be upright, because the car's last couple of lurches have brought me back to face the seat, and I can feel no pressure from the area where his head was. I rotate ninety degrees so I can crouch with both hands prepared against the seat back. The pain from the shot knee is like a volley of deafening, discordant music.

The car keeps swinging from side to side.

I have nothing left to do and no other chances. Just this chance. Right now.

I press the foot of the good leg against the metalwork near the tail-light and spring forward, crashing through the back seat and into the cabin of the car. I see the headlights on trees, the blips of colour from the dashboard display. Two large, dark blank shapes which are the backs of the two front seats. In my peripheral vision is Meth Man, just inches to my right, starting to move.

But I'm looking straight ahead, at one thing only.

The handbrake.

The forward momentum has carried me all the way to the handle, resting between the two front seats. Time compresses as I land on the flattened back seat, right hand outstretched. First stab at it misses by a mile but the second one doesn't.

There's shouts, exclamations, panic.

I rip the handle upwards with everything I've got left. I can hear the ratcheting sound of the handle coming up, the squeal of the tyres, and then Back Seat Guy is on me, with an elbow driven deep into the ribs of my back, right where they'd smashed me with a pool cue an eternity ago. The force of the blow has finished what my desperate dive started, pushing me deep into the narrow space between the front seats, wedging me in there with the handbrake handle, seconds ago the most important object in the universe, now stabbing painfully into my armpit.

Meth Man hasn't got a chance to get any more blows in, because Craigo, who is indeed at the wheel, is now fighting the car, over-correcting as it gyrates madly across the road. My only view of his world is out the driver's-side window, just past his gut, and he's way too preoccupied to give me a thought. The trees change plane, ripping towards the right edge of the window, then blurring towards the left.

The rest of my body is weightless now, floating above the seats and drifting left, as the car leaves the road and I'm watching tree trunks, not canopy, then canopy not trunks, then starry sky, and grass and sky and grass and trunks again.

There are thuds and cracks and bangs and small glassy tinkles and cusswords, silences and metal screeches, all of it closer together and closer still, telling me we're gaining speed not losing it and no one's minding anyone anymore, each enveloped in their own terror and my neck whips despite the confinement and my head bangs hard and my back bends in a way it shouldn't and I see Craigo's head smack blunt against the glass, so hard I can hear his brain slosh and that's it from him and I get one white hot jolt from the knee and then we're turning over and I can feel gravity taking me up towards the roof lining and there's a long, long silence like something's going to happen and then it happens.

The flat punctuation of impact, too giant to process. It's probably accompanied by a great cinematic *bang* but the force, not the sound, owns the instant.

I'm crushed against Craigo's left hip—climbing into the pocket of his jeans. He's come towards me, I've come towards him, and the dashboard has punched forward on both of us. There's takeaway food containers around our heads. The stereo has broken free of the plastic console and speared diagonally forwards like a half-brick on a building site, tearing into my scalp.

Then it's over. The world is still. The dimensions of the car are no longer what they were. A suffocating sort of reality, entrapment in multiple directions.

So I wait, and I listen. Ticking engine, leaking fluid somewhere. A wheel spinning above us, elliptical, bearings crushed and grinding. Breathing, short and crackled, from the back. No words, but a thin whistling sound. I've got no way of getting my head around to see what state he's in, but it doesn't sound good. I can't tell what's gone on in the passenger seat either.

Craigo I can see, in a way. He looms all around me, the wide bulk of his chest. Above an odour that could only be blood I can smell him, meaty man; no surprise given I'm lodged in his armpit now. His face bulges at me, caught in a grunting instant, eyes open and thoroughly dead. His head is looking where heads shouldn't, back over the rear of his shoulder, pressed there by the caved-in roof. No more Mister Nice Guy.

My feet are free. I can wave one foot in open air, though the other one, being dependent on the shot knee, won't co-operate. By tiny measures, I start to retrieve my arms from under my chest. My right hand is still clenched on the handbrake handle. My elbows are working fine, and so are both shoulders, but I can't get the arms free from their padded cell between the seats.

It's while I'm working in this problem that I see Craig's phone, wedged between his hip and the upside-down seat. It's not illuminated, and might be as dead as Craigo for all I know, but it's a finger-length away. I work it free and clutch it in my fist as I wriggle.

So I shrug my way backwards, grinding various exposed parts of my body over the jewellery box of shattered glass. None of it matters anymore. I've got my legs free now and one foot, out in the open air for the first time tonight, has found the stump of some small plant. I hook my toes under a branch and work the leverage it affords; hips then chest emerging through the shattered rear window until my main task is pushing the slumped bulk of Meth Man off myself. He's wet and heavy but offers no resistance.

As my shoulders come free, skin tearing on the window's ragged edge, I roll my eyes back to where I've come from. The mangled arse-end of Babyface is within reach, the pockets of his cargo pants. I slip my fingers in, rummage and retrieve my licence card. My head's left a slick of blood over the white roof lining, enough blood, I think, that I ought to be concerned. There's a stoned kind of fog descending over me and I'm sure the two things are related.

I'm out now and among the bush, the wet leaves and grasses in the darkness, an alien intruder in the forest. I want to rest here, cool and quiet, among the slugs and insects. Broken man beside a broken car. The towering spars of the eucalypts up there somewhere, stars above.

Stars above.

•

I don't know how long I've been unconscious. It's still dark, but the soundscape differs, the random percussion of the dying car a distant memory. I can sit up, woozy but stable.

The car's bent around the base of a great eucalypt, the trunk slicing into the bodywork right where Craigo's driver's door once was. The land climbs and falls sharply away from where the car is, and even in the dark I can see the trail of smashed undergrowth where we've crashed down from the road. I sit against a crumpled door, the shot knee crackling as the leg extends. The engine makes an occasional dying tick, and I can still hear Meth Man groaning faintly.

So I got my wish. I'm out and breathing the secret peppermint air of the night. But I don't know what someone like me does next. Do I ring the police? Do I find the yellow light from some fire-lit living room on the hillside and wander to the door, all smashed and gory? Just like it's always been, I'm whimpering for company. I want a light in the darkness, someone to come to me and resolve this. Set things right.

That someone would've been Mum, ordinarily. We're still children while we have parents. *Christ love, what on earth's happened here?* But it can't be her, so the next stop is obvious.

I fish Craigo's phone out of my pocket.

The screen lights up blue-white in the soft darkness of the bush. Everything around me becomes blacker. His home screen is a grainy shot of a stripper on a pole. Of course it is. I start entering the number, slowly, patiently, my fingers shaking at the ends of their jangled neurones. One after the other, the ten digits known only to a handful of people, the number every journalist in the land would once have killed for, still jealously guarded. The one that I am specially entitled to know, by reason only of my birth.

Wally. His name appears, and I feel the first visceral jolt as I read it on the screen. Such a carefully protected number, and yet it's saved into this phone.

What? *Why?*

They haven't spoken in years.

Craig's phone smells of his aftershave. The line rings once, rings again. Then a sterile click and Wally's voice, speaking before I get a chance to identify myself. He doesn't sound sleepy. He's alert; quiet, measured. A faraway human across the void. His voice is my voice in timbre and range, but with a different life overlaid. The boy I held and wrestled, betrayed, abused and idolised. And loved despite everything.

'You're late. Where is he?'

The words I'd meant to say catch in my throat and collapse into a choked, soundless cry. I jab at the phone, as if the possibility of undoing those words might depend on my reflex.

But the words are said now, and nothing can ever unsay them.

For a long, long time I sit there listening to the nocturnal bush, the distant high sound of the forest's moving canopy. The blood drying in my eyelids, sticking and cracking with each blink. The groans from the car fading and slowly disappearing. Dawn will be here soon and the world it illuminates will be nothing like the one that died last night.

There are two ways to understand what's just happened. Avenue One: this was to be revenge for Louise, with Craig as nothing more than external contractor. Bizarre, misguided, ugly; but more palatable than the alternative.

Which is that Wally was in it all along with Craig as his dirty and dispensable front man. Revenge for Louise, in that scenario, represents a bonus but not the main game. Or was it revenge for Hannah? Could it really go back that far? Could he be that bent, that he lost his fortune and then his daughter over a spot fix? A tepid day-nighter in Sydney, all those years ago; a wild swoosh in the flare of the lights and it would lead him to do these things?

Any explanation redefines my world. Nothing can remain the same, knowing how far he was willing to go. And any explanation leads to the same conclusion: that I was kept alive in order to be brought before him, to answer for my failings, or seek absolution at his feet. I see with terrible clarity how much he wanted to be the author of that moment.

After I've done enough thinking, I drag myself back to the driver's window and reach inside again. Ol' Craig would never be seen without a lighter, one of the many props he deployed to ingratiate, to weave his gangster aura. I fumble around between the splintered bark of the tree and his broken chest. My fingers trace over the sharkskin stubble of his cheek, cold now; down over his collar and across the bomber jacket, another signature of his. Round the metal press studs and hunting over the lining. Craig and his mortal ribs split like kindling under one side of my hand, the lining under the other.

A pocket. Hard metal in the pocket, a Zippo embossed with a Harley logo.

By the light of the buttery flame, I study the deep lacerations in Squibbly, my poor stupid shredded thumb. My desperate efforts to leave my DNA in the tail-light cavity have turned out to be not such a good idea after all. Best I was never here.

The flames are licking through the vehicle now, hungry for fuel.

They curl through its tight spaces in their search, pausing and taking grip where they meet sustenance. They've found the upholstery, the roof lining, the clothes and the bodies, and they roar lustily as they feast. They've found the tree at the centre of the wreck. A human head appears in silhouette against the eye-stinging core of the flames, charring and falling slightly aside under its own weight. Tendrils of new fire streak outwards from the dead car, over the leaf litter of the silently watching forest.

I shuffle as close to the blaze as I can bear, and carefully toss the phone into its heart. Turn my back on the warmth, dragging the bad leg through the twigs and leaves. I know you're coming. You'd never leave a task unfinished.

I start to search for a hiding place.

The Forest

Those headlights swinging now on the road above are bound to be you because who else would be out here at this hour?

I'm furled into a hollow under a fallen log, a place for wounded animals. Hidden from the light but close to its source: I've been transfixed while I was waiting by Craigo's hand protruding from the inferno, fat palm upturned, pleading; white as a marble Caesar.

The sound of a car door by the roadside up there. Heavy steps down the slope. Cracking twigs, the rustle of sprung branches from above and behind me. You'll be edging down the car's flattened track, drawn by the flames. Left foot forward, the stance that gave you balance.

You emerge into the irregular glow and now I can see you. Looking side to side into the darkness, a guilty man. Or a man calculating. City shoes, neat chinos. And I'm thinking: how can this play out? I hide from you now, wait for you to give up, then drag my useless leg out of the bush and we both live out our days with this night between us? Maybe the public scrutiny would keep me safe.

You'd have an awful lot to explain, for a man with a public cross-examination looming. Will the inquiry reveal what you are? For the first time in my life I realise I don't know who that person is.

Look at you now, shielding your eyes from the heat as you peer into the wreckage of the car at the char-grinning crims. Flinching at hot metal. Looking for me, hunting. Your body betraying the difference between checking if I survived and ensuring I didn't.

Your body, the way you move. All our wrestling, our gouging, our fanatical need to climb over each other and out into the world.

There will be no wrestling, no gouging this time.

I went back to that moment, Wally. While I was waiting for you I thought about that terrible day with the book, the one you got from Dad. Either given to you or just left, I never knew. Bradman's *Art of Cricket*, the grass-green cover with black-and-white pictures of the Don in high pants, executing a front-foot square cut and a straight drive so perfect it looks like the bow of a ship cutting the sea wide open. The great man's signature on the title page. I can still see you fanning the pages, looking for a detail here, a nuance of technique there. It lived on your desk at the end of the bunks, never moved by Mum, never touched by me, except on rare occasions and only with your grudging consent.

I knew what it meant to you. I knew how it lived inside you, how it guided you after he left. A light in the dark. Your lips murmuring the words silently in your bed, night after night.

That's why I went for it that day.

There had been a regulation fight over nothing much. Whatever it was, you'd exerted your dominion painfully and also, this time, humiliatingly, in front of some kid who'd come over after school. From memory there was blood streaming from my nose. With Mum away at work, there was no one to appeal to, no one to prevent the inevitable escalation. The kid stood there in shocked silence as I ran to our room, shamed and enraged. Took the book in my hands, the first thing I saw, and slammed it on the surface of the desk. Again. Again. Tore the glossy photographic plates from the spine one by one. Paused only to tear the pages I'd removed into even smaller pieces, to watch them fluttering around my feet.

You must have taken crucial seconds to work out where I'd gone, what I was doing, because I'd ripped my way through the Don's carefully ordered chapters—*Batting, Bowling, Fielding, Keeping, Captaincy*—and the book was all but destroyed by the time you found me.

And I can still see your face as you stood in the doorway of our room. I'd prepared myself for more violence and I knew it would hurt. You, applying every ounce of your will to vengeance. I was fine with that, I suppose. But what I saw—your slack mouth, your horrified eyes, your *grief*—was something I hadn't anticipated.

You rushed forward, ignoring me completely. Took the shreds of paper in your cupped hands, swept them up and stared at the pile. Fretting, reaching for the smaller scraps further out, then weeping, tiny wounded sounds issuing from deep within you. Flipping the broken book open to place the pages back where they should be, tears falling on the creased-up photographs. The Don and his plain timber bat. And I had no idea where to look, what to do, and so in my hopeless way I walked out of the room and cried as well, somewhere else.

Unthinking me, destroying something precious.

The last time I saw you cry.

And now I finally understand it was the beginning. The beginning of my clumsy habit. Of your refusal ever to care again.

I'm standing now, sort of. It's taken a while. I must have grunted with the effort of getting up because you turn to the sound. Your hands are by your sides; you're unarmed, of course. I don't imagine you're acquainted with the shop-floor grubbiness of hands-on violence at your level of management. Unless it's the only option left.

After a long look that assesses the state of me, the busted, feeble state of me, your eyes are searching the ground between us and they've found what they were looking for. A branch, thick as a human arm and about the length of a bat. Slight bulge at one end where a knot has kinked the timber into a heavy club, split fibres spiking out at the break and, Wal, doesn't the splintering remind you of our apricot stump?

You're holding that timber low and relaxed and I can't outrun you, can't even walk, and more than anything, more than the fear, I'm curious. Are you the man who'd use that lump of wood, or the man I've believed in all these years?

Your eyes never leave me but they're not seeking a connection and the answer's delivered swiftly, swung from low to high, right handed, catching me under the ear.

Massive, so big I can't even call it pain. So big that I know I'll never get up once I fall. And I'm crumpling, collapsing: knees and hip and face no hands and tiny curls of bracken in my eyes and the warm glow of the fire turning towards me now but my belly's cold and I'm seeing it all askew, a camera tilted sideways.

The second one, you lean forward to deliver it flat, grunting with the effort, and there's a sound inside my skull like something large coming apart. Pain ebbing, sound changing and past me go your feet, business shoes on twigs. Always with the business, Wal, never time to talk; off to see Craigo, throw the branch onto his pyre and out into the dark, away up the hill without a look back. Busy man, Wal. Busy busy.

Eyes unfocusing turn the firelight to summer sun on your shoulders, twelve years old and the centre of my world. Ashes swirl in the heated air landing soft around me snowflake shreds of Bradman. I'm so sorry, Wal.

Acknowledgments

Darren Keefe's various troubles will, unfortunately, be familiar to anyone who takes a close interest in professional sport. His temptations and failures are not unique to cricketers, although I looked to cricket to build a world around him as a character. I knew the game from playing it as a kid and from watching it as an adult, and fortunately it is a sport that has built up around itself a wealth of great journalism and literature. Among the books I read as I developed this story were Christian Ryan's wonderful biography of Kim Hughes, *Golden Boy*, and two detailed examinations of corruption in sport— Ed Hawkins' *Bookie, Gambler, Fixer, Spy*, and Declan Hill's *The Fix*. On cricket itself and the mysterious hold it has over so many of us, I read Buzo and Grant's essay collection *The Longest Game*, and C. L. R. James's classic *Beyond a Boundary*.

I would like to thank the three former players who gave me insights into the game through interviews: Mick Lewis, Michael Holding and Dean Jones, the last of whom explained to me the exquisite horrors of the Rolando's fracture. My gratitude also to the friends and family who read the manuscript and provided much-needed feedback: Tim Baker, Nick Batzias, Dom Serong, Chris McDonald and my wife Lilly. Thanks also to my *Great Ocean Quarterly* comrades Mick Sowry and Mark Willett for their understanding when I went missing at times to work on this tale.

I'm especially grateful to have worked once again with the talented team at Text, and particularly to be edited by Mandy Brett. If this book has pace and bounce—and that's a judgment for others to make—it was Mandy's doing.

The characters in this book are not meant to be real people in disguise. They are all products of impressions and half-forgotten memories, with a couple of exceptions: Hope Sweeney, who was a much-revered figure in Victorian cricket, and Amy Harris, who it turns out shares a name with a real journalist based in Sydney. It goes without saying that the real Ms Harris has never investigated Pitbull Freer, nor interviewed the Keefes.

I only ever had one mentor in cricket and that was my father Julian: patient, ever-available and a deadly exponent of swing bowling. Lastly, because someone's bound to ask, yes I played backyard cricket against my brothers. Thousands of hours of it. We did microwave the ball and most of the rules herein are rules we used. It got pretty willing at times and the dog was struck once or twice, but no-one was ever seriously injured and we all remain the best of friends.